Bruce

Murder at the Wake

A detective novel

LUCiUS

Text copyright 2016 Bruce Beckham

All rights reserved. Bruce Beckham asserts his right always to be identified as the author of this work. No part may be copied or transmitted without written permission from the publisher.

This is a work of fiction. Names, characters, places and incidents either are the product of the author's imagination or are used fictitiously. Any resemblance to actual persons, living or dead, events and locales is entirely coincidental.

Kindle edition first published by Lucius 2016

Paperback edition first published by Lucius 2016

For more details and Rights enquiries contact:
Lucius-ebooks@live.com

EDITOR'S NOTE

Murder at the Wake is a stand-alone crime mystery, the seventh in the series 'Detective Inspector Skelgill Investigates'. It is set largely in the English Lake District, a National Park of 885 square miles that lies in the rugged northern county of Cumbria, and in particular in the north western area of the Vale of Lorton, home to the deceptively tranquil twin ribbon lakes of Buttermere and Crummock Water, and source of the winding River Cocker.

BY THE SAME AUTHOR

Murder in Adland
Murder in School
Murder on the Edge
Murder on the Lake
Murder by Magic
Murder in the Mind
Murder at the Wake
Murder in the Woods
Murder at the Flood

(Above: Detective Inspector Skelgill Investigates)

Murder, Mystery Collection
The Dune
The Sexopaths

1. GRASMOOR – Sunday 2.50pm

'Guv – we've got a problem.'

'Leyton – hold your horses – I can't hear you.'

Skelgill jams his mobile phone inside his fur-lined trapper hat and presses the flap against his ear.

'Come again, Leyton?'

Skelgill is shouting over substantial background noise – wind and engine combined – and the sergeant now raises his voice accordingly.

'Cor blimey, Guv – that's some racket!'

'I'm in the chopper – distress call from a hillwalker.'

DS Leyton hesitates – if his superior is in the midst of a live mountain rescue the last thing he needs is the news that he bears.

'Spit it out, Leyton.'

'What it is, Guv – you've heard of Crummock Hall?'

'Aye – just flown over it.'

'We've had a report of a suspicious death.'

Now Skelgill pauses.

'How suspicious?'

'Blow to the back of the head, Guv – sounds like it could be deliberate.'

'Sounds like, Leyton?'

'Guv – we can't get anyone within three miles – the lanes are completely blocked by the snow. There's eight-foot drifts in places.'

There is a silence – at least as far as conversation goes. Skelgill, eyes narrowed, teeth bared against the gale, grimaces at the landscape that drifts a thousand feet below, the lower slopes of Grasmoor, a pure white blanket besmirched only by the odd yellowing stain where sheep have gathered to feed at a hay bale, and creased by the occasional snow-capped dry stone wall. His mute deliberation prompts his sergeant to speak.

'What do you reckon, Guv?'

'Leave it with me, Leyton.'

*

Crummock Hall. Only two days before, and somewhat under duress, Skelgill had attended the funeral of its erstwhile proprietor, Sir Sean Willoughby O'More KBE. As a longstanding Lakeland landowner – a manor comprising some four thousand acres east of Crummock Water – his was a name that Skelgill had revered since boyhood. The gnarled gamekeeper in his employ was notoriously trigger-happy; a trait that extended beyond his loose definition of vermin to include pesky local urchins caught scavenging within his ambit. Thus it was with mixed feelings that Skelgill had obeyed his superior's whip to represent the Cumbria constabulary. However, if pushed, he would confess to being less troubled by the prospect of confronting repressed traumas of peppering by buckshot, and rather more irked by the inconvenience of having to relieve one of his two presentable neckties of its duty suspending fishing rods in his garage.

The ceremony had taken place on what was a bitterly cold December Friday morning, at the little stone chapel of St James above Buttermere, a site of worship that dates back to 1507. The location was an additional, if incidental reason that Skelgill might have received the assignment, for this was his old stamping ground. Close by, his mother, a cantankerous septuagenarian still resides in the modest family cottage, whence she cycles daily over the Honister Pass to char in Borrowdale. Before the service Skelgill had kicked his heels in the cramped churchyard, debating the weather with a coterie of tenant farmers and outdoorsmen, glowering shepherds scanning the ominous skies. He was well known to them in his various capacities – police officer, mountain rescue team member, fell-runner (of note in his youth), fisherman and, not least, one of their own. Advantaged by a detailed forecast fed through his emergency services connections, Skelgill had pontificated – and they had listened grim faced.

Not that Skelgill's gloomy prognosis was one difficult to reach. Northern Britain had been in the grip of a prolonged cold spell, a Soviet anticyclone that had extended its chill fingers across Western Europe. The ground was solid and the lakes had begun to ice over at their fringes. Such uncomfortable conditions, however, were manageable in their constancy. Lanes, once gritted, were untroubled by run-off that becomes treacherous black ice; hill flocks were easily reached by a surefooted combination of quad and dog. Country folk could get about their business. But storm *Arabella* was coming. Shaking her broad hips to the calypso beat, barrelling across the Atlantic, she was all set to breach the cold iron curtain that for a fortnight had cloaked Cumbria. And when moist Caribbean air meets a frozen mountainous seaboard there is only one outcome: snow. Big snow. Inadequately clad in their unfamiliar funeral wear, it was the first such flurries that finally obliged Skelgill and his cronies to seek sanctuary.

As a consequence, even within the thick walls the weather remained the pre-eminent subject of conversation, albeit in more reverent tones and with the vernacular substantially edited. In due course something of a resigned hush had descended, rather as if the flakes that fell past the long windows had a palliative effect upon the uneasy congregation. And the serenity of the surroundings surely contributed; indeed, as William Wordsworth wrote, *"A man must be very unsensible who would not be touched at the sight of the chapel of Buttermere."*

Skelgill, for his part, had stared pensively through an adjacent window, where a stone tablet in the sill commemorates Alfred Wainwright, and the outlook is of Haystacks, site of dispersal of the legendary Lakeland biographer's ashes. This unlikely literary conjunction – Wordsworth and Wainwright – happens to reveal something of Skelgill's true colours as regards matters spiritual. For the latter authority has many times led him to spectacular places, whereupon occasionally he has uttered in awe words penned by the former. That said, during the service he was observed to sing along respectfully if tunelessly with *The Lord is My Shepherd* and bow his head and state *Amen* at the required junctures.

The family party were late to enter the church. They had earlier swept by in a small fleet of glossy black limousines, preferring to bide their time in a private room at the local inn, where stiffeners were surely imbibed. Upon their entrance to take the front pew, there was an expectant ripple as the congregation strove surreptitiously to get a better view. And no wonder – for here was a cortege that might have graced Ascot's Royal Enclosure. Fine bespoke outfits, regal bearing, they filed in as if accustomed to the red carpet. Skelgill had experienced a small frisson: a sudden recalibration of his own place in society; for these were people he once knew. These were the Regulus-O'Mores.

Educated without regard to cost at boarding schools in the south of England, ascending thence to Oxbridge or whatever Parisian finishing schools were deemed most apt, they had spent their childhood vacations at Crummock Hall. Of an age with Skelgill, for a few years their gilt-edged path had crossed with that of the gauche and gawky country boy who illicitly shared their ancestral domain. Come their teens, however, and visits to Cumbria gradually dwindled. But likewise had Skelgill's own interest in trespassing diminished – or at least it became transferred to the fairer sex among his contemporaries. It was over twenty years since he had set eyes upon any of this well-heeled family.

But he was also reminded of something else: for these thirty-something adults were the five *grandchildren* of Sir Sean Willoughby O'More. Catastrophe had caused the dynasty to skip a generation. Their parents were dead, drowned in Crummock Water, a boating accident when the eldest child was no more than ten.

Their mother, Shauna O'More, had become a stage actress of some renown, her husband, Edward Regulus, a merchant banker in a long-established family firm. Such untimely deaths had sent shockwaves through both the City of London and its neighbouring West End. The tragic couple's metropolitan funeral had been an altogether grander affair, the venue being St Paul's Cathedral, no less.

In St James's, Buttermere, however, the little procession had included someone of a former generation. Supported on the left by the arm of an elderly retainer and on the right by a walking stick rather too short to be effective, the congregation was afforded a sight as unusual as it was a contrast to the magnificent young family: the venerable personage of Declan Thomas O'More. Here was a rare public appearance of the reclusive twin of the late Sir Sean. According to local hearsay, this younger brother had spent his entire ninety-three years within the confines of the estate of Crummock Hall, give or take the odd such visit to church, or hospital. A tall, though now crooked figure, he wore an ill-fitting double-breasted suit – in pre-war style, with broad angular lapels – and shuffled unsteadily to take a seat, his lined countenance pallid, his watery eyes lacking expression.

There had been one other notable member of the funeral party, a small, dapper man in his mid-fifties whom Skelgill did not recognise. It was he alone of the group that appeared more outwardly focused, exchanging words with the Vicar, and acknowledging in a general way with a series of polite nods the inquiring gaze of those persons seated most close by. The remainder of the incoming contingent, half a dozen surly domestic and estate workers, mostly elderly and again unknown to Skelgill, had followed him. The household 'lived in', and did not much mingle with the local community.

*

Taken together, it was a mixed bag that Skelgill had watched enter the church. The experience had aroused both his curiosity and his sense of vocation. This notion of destiny is now recalled as he gazes down from a heavenly perspective – having pulled rank in order temporarily to divert the rescue helicopter from its original purpose. As Crummock Hall enlarges beneath his dangling feet, he ponders who among its company has fallen victim – and, indeed perhaps more pertinently, who might be the perpetrator?

2. CRUMMOCK HALL – Sunday 3pm

On his knees, Skelgill shrugs off his harness and signals the all clear to the winch-man. Another squall is arriving and the coastguard pilot wastes no time, he dips the nose of the Sikorsky S-92 and beats away to the south, the winch rope trailing like an umbilical cord that has served its purpose. Skelgill reorganises his outerwear, which has become disarranged during his descent. The mountain rescue is an organisation funded by donations, and its budgets do not stretch to suitable uniform for its team members; they must clothe themselves. Skelgill sports a typically uncoordinated ensemble of navy blue boots, maroon ski trousers, fluorescent orange cagoule, and the aforementioned fur-lined trapper hat – tartan – a recent acquisition in an after-hours pub bet over who could win a left-handed arm wrestle (Skelgill's opponent being either unaware, or too inebriated to remember that Skelgill is in fact left-handed).

He rights himself in the midst of the circular snow-covered lawn, and casts about. The ground behind him rises quickly through ornamental conifers, a bank of midnight-green foliage laden with snow; ahead stands Crummock Hall. Believed to be one of the oldest houses in the Lake District, it has something of an ecclesiastical appearance, almost Normanesque. Grey harled walls topped by bluish slate roofs are tinged with yellowing moss and silvery lichen; many of the transoms are arched, and there is a squat, square tower with crenellations; from this centrepiece various halls and wings extend like the nave and transept of a church, and connect with other similar buildings added down the centuries. Skelgill becomes conscious of faces, vague shadows like pale ghosts beyond the diamond-paned leaded lights of the long windows; it looks the sort of place that might be haunted.

He has made something of a snow angel in his ungainly landing, and now he seems reluctant to carve a path through the perfect surface that lies before him, knee-deep and crisp and even. But fresh flakes are falling and, caught and thrown by a swirling wind into his face, prompt him to end his deliberations;

he strikes a beeline for a low tiled porch that might be the principal rear entrance.

Although it is not yet dusk, at his approach a bulb comes on over the heavy oak door, and from within there is the scraping of a key in the old mortise. Skelgill can hear a male voice, its owner evidently cursing his inability to get the door open. And although the lock is turned, it seems the door is now jammed. There are more profanities and a faint tremor that suggests it is being tugged from the inside. At this point Skelgill loses patience and gives a helping hand – or, rather, foot – and slams the sole of his left boot just below the blackened cast-iron knocker. It does the trick – at least as far as the door is concerned, although it does not entirely endear him to the surprised occupant.

'Good lord!'

The man, of about his own height and age, and attired in the casual county outfit of blue tattersall check shirt, cream corduroys and polished chestnut brogues, has recoiled against the inner door. Presumably intending to admit Skelgill as a welcome arrival – hearing the roar of the helicopter and observing Skelgill's descent – now his expression is filled with doubt, as though he fears some kind of special forces raid is in progress. Skelgill appears oblivious to the man's concern and, dispensing with pleasantries – or anything resembling an apology – thrusts out his warrant card.

'DI Skelgill, Cumbria police.'

*

If the tale is true that Declan Thomas O'More lived all of his life within the bounds of Crummock Hall, then Skelgill must reflect that its final chapter brings a certain concluding symmetry – for there can be no doubt that this is the aged man he saw taking tentative steps to his pew; indeed, the gaunt features are little altered in death. He sighs and steps back; the inert form lies on the carpeted floor of a wood-panelled study, a dark stain extending from the back of its skull. DS Leyton was right, suspicious it is.

Skelgill knows he must take care not to compromise any evidence that may come to light upon detailed forensic examination. But instinct tells him that now is equally important for what his own senses might divine. And in any event the scene is not uncontaminated: the butler – Thwaites – discovered the body; several of the family responded to his cries of distress. Some time elapsed before they heeded DS Leyton's advice, conveyed by telephone, to vacate and lock the room.

A police photographer will record the scene in its minutiae, but certain details strike him as salient (if not yet significant). The study is of a generous size, a good fifteen feet by twenty. On the same wall as the door through which he has entered hangs a pendulum clock of considerable age. Its casement is made of light oak, and its hinged front is wide open. He squints at the silvery face; it is pitted, and scored with circular markings that might reflect decades of adjustment of the hands, which read two o'clock. However, there is no tick and Skelgill realises the pendulum is missing. He glances about and sees it is lying in the nearest corner of the room, protruding from beneath an antique wainscot chair. Further scrutiny reveals a brass winder key, generally tarnished but shiny like a new penny on one wing, cast upon the rug a yard from the corpse. Was he attending to the clock when he was struck?

Slowly Skelgill scans around, his gaze moving left from the stilled timepiece. There is the chair in the first corner, the pendulum beneath; the adjacent wall is mainly taken up by two arched windows glazed with leaded glass and towards the next corner an external oak door with a square porthole; beyond, in the descending gloom, Skelgill can see only a narrow expanse of snow-covered lawn, hedged by the dark trunks of conifers. The third wall is lined floor to ceiling with bookcases, and in front of these stands a writing desk, its chair backing on to the shelves and facing into the room across the desk. There is an antique library step with three rungs and a turned hand pole. The final wall houses the fireplace, a substantial stone affair with the date

1666 carved into the mantel. Wood ash smoulders in the grate and infuses the air with a sweet fragrant residue. A pair of old-style leather walking boots rest splayed upon the hearth and a tweed shooting-coat hangs on a hook to one side. Beneath this is a capacious walnut coffer with its hinged lid open, almost full of hewn timber. Skelgill finds himself staring into the gilded mirror above the mantelpiece – he sees a vision of himself, alarmed – it can only be his unexpectedly unruly appearance, his hair matted and spiky, his jowls sporting a weekend's worth of stubble, his red-rimmed eyes hooded by anxious brows. No wonder the family had regarded him with apprehension.

He pulls himself away and glares at the external door. He wants to try it but knows he should not touch the handle. There is a key, turned at an angle, which suggests it might be locked. He squats down and squints into the crack between the door and the jamb: sure enough, the dead bolt is engaged. He checks the windows; they each have panels that open, but these are clearly fastened with lever latches. With the jab of an elbow he disengages one such catch; then he reaches up and with the screwdriver blade of his penknife prises open the panel until he can lean right out. The dusk is well advanced and now he produces a small but powerful tactical torch. The snow beneath the windows is unblemished, but between the door and the belt of conifers there is a line of disturbance. However, these tracks are not fresh – at least, that is to say they have already been covered by new snow, and more is falling as Skelgill watches. He pulls in his head and closes the window, reversing his no-touch method.

Now he turns to consider the room. Immediately he notices that a tumbler – a rocks glass of the type that would be used for whisky – is lying tipped on the floor halfway between the desk and the door. Beside the glass is a damp patch on the rug – and more clear droplets on the wooden tiled surround near the door. Skelgill decides to leave the glass where it is, and moves on to the desk itself. It is of the kind known as a partners' desk, expansively designed for use by two persons, one working at either side. Only shaded wall-lights and a cowled table lamp illuminate the study, and in the last vestiges of daylight the atmosphere is becoming positively Dickensian. Skelgill rounds to the chair and takes a seat. There is no trace of a computer or laptop, or indeed any electronic device or connections, and the telephone is of the old candlestick variety with a corded receiver; it has no dial and seems merely to be an extension to which calls may be put through, or requested via a switchboard. There is a stack of matching textbooks with pale worn dustcovers – *The Handbook of British Birds, Volumes 1-5* – and beside these a pair of binoculars in brown leatherette and black enamelled brass that must date from an era when they would be called field glasses. Before him on a framed blotting pad lies a bound manuscript jotter embossed with the initials, *D.T.O'M.* Beside it there is a traditional fountain pen. Skelgill opens the cover. In compact handwritten script on the flyleaf are the words, *Ornithological Log, Crummock Hall.*

He begins to examine the pages. The first entry dates back almost thirty-five years, and Skelgill for a moment is transfixed – for here are scenes in which he may have figured, a long lost newsreel vignette of the locale, a small boy an unobtrusive extra poking about in the far distance. It takes an effort for him to shrug off the thought – he frowns and flips to the end of the journal and thumbs back until he finds the most recent entry. Now again he stiffens, but for a different reason: it is dated today. He slides the book a little closer to the desk lamp and reads:

Barnacle Goose c. 20 – small skein N from Buttermere. Raven 8 – unkindness W from Grasmoor End, high to Mellbreak. Fieldfare c. 30 – mutation taking haws at Lanthwaite Beck. Brambling 13 – charm amongst beech mast in copse below Cinderdale Crag.

Skelgill immediately recognises the topographical aspects of the account; as for the birds, however – he is familiar with their names (if not the traditional collective nouns), and could identify them at a push, although maybe not Brambling. The entry comprises two paragraphs, and now he peruses the second:

"Mainly overcast; frequent snow showers; wind force 4-5, NNW; temperature 35F; pressure 982mb, rising slowly; 1155 – 1335 hrs."

Skelgill stares pensively at the page. His eyes are glazed and it is a good fifteen seconds before he breaks out of his reverie and begins, rather cursorily, to leaf through the journal. It is crammed with entries of an identical format: two paragraphs, one to record the birds, the other the weather and time; and written in black ink in the same neat slanted hand. Although there is not a record for every day, it seems that most weeks there was a sighting worthy of mention. Finally Skelgill returns to today's entry and reads it once again. Then he takes out his mobile phone and captures his own snapshot of the morning's events.

Now he rises and inspects the impressive library that backs the desk. Most of the books are of an antiquarian appearance, frequently in sets. He notes, *Familiar Wild Flowers* (8 volumes), *The Birds of the British Isles* (3 volumes), and *Cassell's Natural History* (5 volumes). There appears to be a complete collection of Warne's pre-1960s *Observer's* series – and then Skelgill spots something that makes his heart take a little leap: a set of first edition Wainwrights. Dating from between 1955 and 1966, the seven dwarf tomes capture a labour of love that is without parallel, and one that – via their wonderfully intuitive maps, diagrams and drawings – once memorably and explosively illuminated the hitherto alien world of books for a young Daniel Skelgill and his particular brand of dyslexia.

Skelgill selects Book Six, *The North Western Fells*. He locates the section on Grasmoor – 2791 feet in this book, he knows it off by heart – and flicks to the page that best features Crummock Hall. Drawn up to one side of the desk is a rosewood harpist's chair, set on casters for manoeuvrability, and Skelgill sinks down upon it. He ponders over the map for some time, and then traces with an index finger the lines of a paragraph of text. Now he taps the page and looks about, rather aimlessly, it must be said – until his gaze falls upon a polished silver cloche on a tray at the corner of the desk. He reaches forward and with a napkin raises the dome: beneath is a rectangular china plate holding a neat array of sandwiches, white bread with crusts removed, cut into little triangles. He ponders for a moment, and then replaces the silver cover. He returns his attention to the book. After about a minute, still perusing the page, absently he lifts the cloche and eats one of the sandwiches.

*

'Sir?' There comes a faltering knock upon the door of the study; the voice is rasping. 'Excuse me – sir?'

Skelgill starts, rather in the manner of one who has been woken from an unplanned catnap. He stares with some surprise at the book in his right hand, and the half-eaten sandwich in his other. He jams the latter into his mouth, and rises and replaces the Wainwright in its position between *The Northern Fells* and *The Western Fells*. Then he carefully lowers the cloche over what is left on the plate – a truncated pyramid of about one-third its original length.

He stalks across the room, carefully rounding the body on the carpet, and – pausing to swallow and wipe his mouth on his sleeve – unlocks the door. Thwaites, the manservant, takes half a step backwards.

'There is a telephone call for you, sir – Detective Sergeant Leyton.' He bows subserviently, his uneasy gaze hovering somewhere about Skelgill's chest. 'I didn't like to put it through on Mr Declan's line, sir – in case you couldn't touch it due to smudging fingerprints.'

'You've been watching too many detective programmes, Thwaites.'

'We don't have television, sir – neither Sir Sean nor Mr Declan approved of it.'

Skelgill narrows his eyes – for a moment he looks like he might not concur – however, more likely the man's ready adoption of the past tense is the source of his reaction.

'That's fine by me.'

Thwaites interprets Skelgill's remark as consent to the redirecting of the telephone call, rather than agreement to the outmoded dogma.

'You could take it in my butler's pantry, sir – at the end of the hall here.' Arthritically, as though his neck is fused to his shoulders, he makes a slow quarter turn of his upper body and vaguely extends his left arm behind him. But he seems to detect some discontent on Skelgill's part and proffers an alternative suggestion. 'Or there's the smoking room in the east wing – just along this corridor, sir.' Now he ratchets in the other direction and indicates with a raised little finger of his right hand.

'That sounds more like it, Thwaites – I'll need privacy for interviews.'

Thwaites dips his head in what for him must be an enthusiastic gesture. 'It should be ideal, sir – I'll show you in and set a fire.'

Pedestrian progress now enables Skelgill to take in his surroundings. The walls are mostly panelled in the same dark oak as the study, and adorned with antique guns and swords and armour, and display cases that contain stuffed birds or mammals or fish. He pauses to read the faded inscription on the exhibit of a sea trout, "Mort, 7lbs 13oz – Crummock Water, 22nd July 1934."

'Caught by Mr Declan when he was a young boy, sir.' The butler has turned to observe Skelgill's interest. Now he slowly wheels around and continues on his way, speaking over his shoulder. 'Of course, sir – all angling was stopped after The Accident.'

Skelgill would like to dwell upon the fish – it interests him that it has been described by its local name, *mort* – and not least because Crummock Water is a devil of a place to tempt even a brownie out of, never mind a specimen sea trout. But the manservant's intonation, capitalising the generic expression 'The Accident' as though it were a proper noun obliges him to respond.

'Aye – that were in the eighties, though.'

'That's correct, sir.'

'You worked here then?'

'Since 1959, sir.'

Skelgill expels a small puff of wonder.

'No thoughts of retiring?'

Skelgill's quip is glib and when old man stops and crabs about to face him, there is an expression of pathos that causes him some regret.

'I don't know what I shall do now, sir – now that both Sir Sean and Mr Declan are gone.'

Skelgill manufactures an unconvincing grin.

'Surely they'll keep you on, Thwaites?'

'I doubt they'll keep the *place* on, sir.'

But now the old man seems to pull himself together, and sets off as purposefully as he can muster, as if he realises he has spoken out of turn.

'Better get you to the telephone, sir – it was a mobile your sergeant was using and the signal didn't seem very regular.'

'Aye.'

He leads Skelgill through a door on the left side of the passage, into what is a relatively small, narrow room with a fireplace at the far end and a multiple lancet window with a deep sill along much of the external wall. The remainder of the interior is papered in a heavy flock of a fleur-de-lis pattern, in deep blood red. Like the study the lighting is subdued – just three shaded wall lamps – and outside it is now almost dark. Skelgill pauses to stare out into the gloom; he checks his watch: sunset falls at around 3:45 this time of year and he must reflect that the helicopter team will have done well to locate the stray walker.

'If you would care to take the call there, sir – I could get the fire started.'

The butler refers to a writing bureau, its lid opened out and another old-fashioned telephone on the surface. Skelgill glances about. There are various items of antique furniture, and ranged before the hearth two winged chairs upholstered in dark leather, each with a small side table. He notes there are no ashtrays – nor the lingering smell of stale tobacco; perhaps the designation of smoking room is one that has been brought forward from a bygone era.

'Don't bother with the fire, Thwaites.' The old man immediately looks a little crestfallen, which prompts Skelgill to add a poorly considered rider. 'Tell you what – I could murder a cuppa – wash down those sandwiches.'

This unfortunate turn of phrase – not to mention the revelation that Skelgill has plundered the comestibles – might ordinarily draw a disapproving response, but Thwaites is evidently long schooled in discretion, and indeed visibly perks up at the prospect of providing some domestic service. He bows once more and shambles away, leaving Skelgill to wrestle with the technology of the 1920s.

'Leyton?'

'Ah – Guv – I was beginning to think you were lost – I've been trying your mobile for the past half hour.'

'No signal, Leyton – this place sits below two thousand foot of rock.'

'I'm well on my way, Guv – we've got a snowplough – the Chief managed to swing it. Roads boys have taken the right old petrol pump.'

Skelgill allows himself a wry grin at his sergeant's imaginative use of Cockney slang. Then unseen by his colleague he shrugs indifferently, as if he considers in any event his need is greater.

'You're not driving it, I hope, Leyton.'

'Nah, Guv – I'm with a couple of the SOCOs and Dr Herdwick – in his Defender. We're following the gritter. Seems there's some farmer with a backhoe loader who's clearing the worst drift about a mile ahead.'

Skelgill nods.

'Aye – that'll be George Robinson.'

'That's it, Guv.'

'I'll see you when I see you, Leyton.'

'One other thing, Guv.'

'Aye?'

'I rang the mountain rescue – when I was trying to get you. They told me they'd dropped you off okay – but they never found the woman – the coastguard had to return to base.'

'Aye – but we'll still have a team out on foot.'

'That's what they said, Guv.' DS Leyton now makes an exclamation of alarm, as if the vehicle in which he is travelling has narrowly avoided some danger. But he continues without explanation. 'Thing is, Guv – I don't know if you realised – I ran a name check on her – Rowena Devlin, she's called – she's a writer, quite well known by all accounts – but that's not her real name – she's actually Perdita Regulus-O'More – staying at Crummock Hall.'

*

By the time Thwaites returns to the smoking room bearing a tray of refreshments Skelgill has a fire crackling in the grate, and with the toe of a boot is adjusting a sizeable log to catch the flames. The old retainer is somewhat perturbed; a condition exacerbated as Skelgill barges in to pour his own tea and toss a handful of sugar lumps into his cup.

'Get one yourself, Thwaites – and have a seat.'

'Sir – Master Martius was saying he would see you first – now that he is the head of the household.'

Skelgill has moved the chairs so that they are angled towards one another, and settles down with his hot drink and a generous helping of biscuits. He dunks a shortbread finger and despatches it, nodding approvingly. He glances at Thwaites and affects surprise that the butler is hovering indecisively.

'I'll talk to *you*, Thwaites.'

That Skelgill is riding roughshod over his orders is plainly disconcerting for a man who has spent his entire working life in service. He edges a little closer to the empty seat but still is reluctant to comply.

'I shan't have tea just now, sir, if it's all the same – it's not my regular break time.'

'As you like.'

Skelgill regards him with calm indifference. He can't remember if the old man has on the same suit that he wore to the funeral – certainly the black tie, which may now be retained as an extended mark of respect. The outfit is the traditional butler's morning coat with a grey vest and wing-collared shirt beneath, grey striped trousers and white cotton gloves. It could not, however, be said to be in prime condition. Finally, beneath Skelgill's unrelenting gaze, the man yields and gingerly lowers himself into the chair – but preferring to perch on the edge of the seat with his hands playing nervously upon his lap.

'Tell me what happened when you found him.'

Paradoxically, the elderly butler is prepared for this question – he looks relieved at being set a straightforward task. He clears his throat with a chesty wheeze.

'I knew right away he was dead, sir – what with the eyes staring and him not breathing. I must have called out – because it wasn't long before Master Martius and Miss Cassandra came rushing in, and then Master Edgar. I believe it was Master Edgar that ran and dialled 999. And Miss Cassandra took me along to the drawing room – she insisted I drank a brandy.' He glances apprehensively at Skelgill. 'I'm usually teetotal, sir.'

'What time was it – that you found the body?'

'2:15, sir – I went to collect Mr Declan's lunch things.'

'When did you take them in?'

'12:15, sir.'

'But he didn't eat.'

Skelgill's statement – when it might be expected to be a question – seems to cause a shudder to run through the old man's bent frame.

'He was bird-watching, sir – he went out almost every day.'

Again there is the past tense.

'At the same time?'

'It would depend on the weather, sir – and how Mr Declan was feeling. It must have been later today. Ordinarily he would be back for his lunch at 12:30.'

'When did you last see him?'

'That would have been about 8:45, sir – when I collected his breakfast tray.'

'From his study?'

'Yes, sir – he would spend his waking hours there, sir.'

'And how was he?'

'Just as normal, I should say, sir.'

Skelgill dips another biscuit into his tea and casually stirs it around.

'What happened to the clock on the wall?'

'The clock, sir?'

Skelgill stops what he is doing and raises a quizzical eyebrow.

'The front is open and the pendulum and key are lying on the carpet.'

The old man looks troubled.

'I can't say as I noticed that, sir.' He wipes his brow on the back of a gloved hand – it could be the heat from the fire, which is beginning to roar, compounded by his layers of formal clothing. 'I imagine I was quite upset by the sight of Mr Declan.'

Skelgill nods. The soggy end of his biscuit crumbles into his cup, but he ignores it and nibbles pensively at the residual stump. His silence prompts an aside from Thwaites.

'It's an eight-day clock, sir.'

He evidently expects Skelgill to know what this means. Skelgill dips his head in such a way as to convey that he doesn't.

'It was Mr Declan's custom to wind it on a Sunday – today, sir – that way the clock never needs to stop. I believe it's never stopped since his mother Lady Elizabeth passed it on to him as a 21st birthday gift, sir.'

Skelgill appears only marginally interested in this rather extravagant claim. He yawns and takes a sip of his tea. He has removed his outer jacket and now he pats a breast pocket of his shirt.

'This key – it's usually left in the door of the study?'

'That's correct, sir. Mr Declan would lock it at night when he went up to bed.'

'What about during the day – when he was in the study?'

'It was generally unlocked, sir. Of course I would always knock when I brought a meal and if he didn't answer I would know he was out bird-watching.'

'What about the door that leads outside?'

'I believe he usually locked it whenever he went out that way, sir. I couldn't say for sure what he did about it when he came back.'

'It's locked at the moment.'

The butler's countenance undergoes something of a change. He appears to be wrestling with the possible implications of this fact: his master attacked and it might not have been by an intruder? He seems to will otherwise.

'Perhaps someone could have slipped in while he was out, sir?'

'But where would he hide, Thwaites?' Skelgill's tone is unduly scornful.

The man is forced to concede, there is nowhere in the room that would conceal a person. He nods sadly and does not offer a suggestion.

'Was anything of value stored in the study?'

'Not to speak of, sir. We don't keep more than petty cash in the house – Hindscarth of Cockermouth delivers all the groceries on account. I've once or twice overheard Mr Declan say he'd put all his capital into his books, and warn the maid to go easy with her duster. And neither Sir Sean nor Mr Declan was one for having showy wristwatches and suchlike.'

Skelgill nods. He doesn't doubt the literature would make a tidy sum – he couldn't buy that set of Wainwrights for a month's wages – but it is not the currency of the common-or-garden thief, who seeks pocketable items. And clearly the study bears none of the usual hallmarks of a burglary, when every drawer and shelf is ransacked.

'What were you doing in the hour before you discovered the body?'

Thwaites looks alarmed.

'I, sir?' His voice is rasping and hoarse, but then his words come without hesitation and there is a ring of authenticity about them. 'It was my own lunch hour between one and two o'clock, sir. I went back to the staff quarters and heated up some soup and took it to my room. I listened to the wireless – there was *The World This Weekend* and after that *Gardener's Question Time*. Just after two o'clock I came back along to my butler's pantry and polished up the crystal glasses for tonight's dinner.'

'So you were back on duty for what – ten minutes – before you went to collect the lunch tray?'

'That's correct, sir.'

'And you didn't hear or see anything – any disturbance – anyone entering or leaving the study?'

'No, sir – nothing at all, sir.'

Though Skelgill's question is narrow in its scope, he poses it in the knowledge of the bird-watching log, which has Declan O'More returning at 13:35. Then there was time taken to remove his outdoor gear and write up his field notes. Only forty minutes later he was found dead by the butler. Furthermore there is the clue of the stilled eight-day clock.

'What about this morning – did anybody visit Declan?'

Thwaites shakes his head.

'Not that I can say, sir. It's the maid's day off – I believe she stayed in the staff quarters – I saw her making some lunch. And as for the family, sir – they weren't really in the habit of coming to this end of the house. All of the main public rooms and the guest bedrooms are on the north side of the tower.'

'What interaction would they normally have with Declan?'

The butler appears surprised by this question.

'Oh – none at all, sir. Bear in mind they are uncommon visitors. And of course Mr Declan was a very shy person, you might say, sir.'

Skelgill takes it that *shy* is probably not what the butler means – but that the corollary is the same, whether or not this is a euphemism for a less amenable adjective.

'Are you aware of anyone having more than passing contact with him – since the funeral on Friday, say?'

Thwaites again shakes his head but then he raises an index finger to indicate a thought has struck him.

'Well, no, sir – except for Mr Mullarkey, of course.'

'Mullarkey?'

'The O'More family lawyer, sir – he's across from Dublin for the funeral. He was due to travel back yesterday – but of course he's become snowed in and unable to return.'

Skelgill nods as he makes the connection with the middle-aged man whom he observed in conversation with the Vicar before and after the service.

'You saw him and Declan together?'

'Mr Mullarkey came to the study on Saturday afternoon, sir. Mr Declan rang for tea at about a quarter to three. Then I noticed Mr Mullarkey leaving the study about three-quarters of an hour later.'

Skelgill is silent for a few moments. But if this account troubles him, it is something he can easily follow up, given the lawyer is stranded like the rest at Crummock Hall.

'How did Declan react to the death of his brother?'

'It was a long time coming, sir – if you get my meaning? Sir Sean had been ill for over a year and hadn't been expected to live beyond the summer.'

Skelgill nods grimly.

'So it was business as usual for Declan – is that what you're saying, Thwaites?'

The manservant looks uncomfortable on his late employer's behalf.

'He wasn't a sentimental person, sir – kept his feelings to himself.'

'Was there a disagreement, a dispute – between him and anyone else – a member of the family or the staff?'

Thwaites is slowly shaking his head.

'Nothing that I can call to mind, sir.'

'What about you, Thwaites?'

Skelgill leaves the question hanging, open to interpretation. The butler's features take on a cornered expression, that this policeman might suddenly be suspecting him, since he has failed to cast suspicion upon anyone else. He clears his throat with a stuttering cough and speaks, rather more disjointedly now.

'I'm sure Sir Sean – and Mr Declan – both – have been happy with my work, sir – else I don't know that they would have kept me on all this time.'

It is a somewhat oblique rejoinder, but the man has a point – his tenure spans seven decades. Skelgill relents and leans forwards, resting his elbows on his knees, his body language altogether more convivial.

'Thwaites, how did you come to Crummock Hall?'

'My mother worked here, sir – she was a local girl, Mary Ann Thwaites of Lorton – went into service when she were just fifteen.' Now a haunted expression suffuses his features. He stares into the fire and his brown eyes appear to smoulder as they reflect the flames. 'Got herself into trouble, sir, in a manner of speaking.' He pauses, though he does not glance at Skelgill to check that he has understood. 'But the war had begun and the family took pity upon her. The master of Crummock Hall back then was Mr Padraig – and his Lady Elizabeth – she hailed from a titled Cumberland family.'

'You were born here.'

Skelgill has correctly divined the nature of the maid's little difficulty.

'There's a little cottage near the gates to the estate, sir – very generous they were, to let her stay there. As a small child I didn't have cause myself to come up to the big house. I remember Mr Padraig calling by occasionally – but he died of a sudden when I was aged ten and the estate passed to Sir Sean.'

'And what about you?'

'I went off to do my National Service – Cumberland Rifles, sir. Afterwards I signed up as a Regular – but I was wounded in action – you'll perhaps have heard of the Mau Mau Uprising?'

Skelgill nods grimly – his impression of this rather frail old man is perhaps undergoing some conversion. He waits for Thwaites to continue.

'My mother fell ill around about the same time, sir. I was able to come back and Sir Sean was good enough to find me a position. It meant I could look after her at the cottage. When she passed away after a long illness they kept me on – and shortly after that Sir Sean gave me the promotion to butler, sir.'

'Had you known them – Sean and Declan – when you were growing up?'

'Only in passing, sir. They would be seventeen years older than me, sir – so you can imagine, folk of their station, they didn't ordinarily pay any great attention to a poor lad off the estate.'

Skelgill narrows his eyes as he regards the faithful old retainer. Perhaps there is something in this sentiment with which he empathises. Whatever the feeling it evokes, it points him to a particular line of questioning.

'What age are you, Thwaites?'

'Seventy-six, sir.'

'Did you go to the village school in Lorton?'

'I did, sir – the church school.'

'Do you remember a girl called Minnie Graham?'

'I do that, sir – quite a character if I recall.'

Skelgill is plainly uncertain of what he should say next. The Grahams are an ancient Borders clan of considerable notoriety – known down the centuries for their reiving of cattle, thieving of possessions, looting of properties and worse. Also aged seventy-six, also schooled at Lorton C of E, and also still referred to by some under her maiden name Minnie Graham, is Skelgill's mother.

3. INHERITANCE – Sunday 5pm

'She's just walked in, Guv!'

'Who, Leyton?'

'The missing woman – the novelist.'

DS Leyton – having initially reported to his superior on arrival – has now returned rather breathlessly to the smoking room bearing this news. Skelgill puts down what must be a third or fourth cup of tea and rises from his chair by the fire. He strides to the long window and rests his elbows upon the deep sill. All that is visible are falling flakes of snow, illuminated by the weak light cast from within; beyond a foot or so they dissolve into total blackness. He stares broodingly into the hypnotic scene; it is like a tank filled with a great swirling shoal of tiny pale fish. That the woman has found her way back is no mean feat – through snowstorms and darkness, descending two miles of mountainous terrain from the location of her last distress call – when it appeared that her mobile phone's battery died. Skelgill swings about, arms akimbo, gunslinger fashion, his features stern.

'Has anyone notified the team?'

'Done it, Guv – got through to your mate, Woody. They've stood down. He said to tell you they'll be in the pub at Buttermere later, if you fancy a pint.'

Skelgill scowls at this suggestion. He stalks over to the bureau where Thwaites has deposited his tray and selects a shortbread finger from the now somewhat depleted plate of biscuits. DS Leyton watches a little hungrily, but Skelgill offers no invitation for him to partake.

'How is she?'

The sergeant notes that Skelgill's first thoughts rested with the mountain rescue team that has been combing the fell in such treacherous conditions.

'Dr Herdwick's checking her over. Seems like she's in one piece, Guv – mild hypothermia – but they've had to tell her about the death – I don't think she's taken it too well.'

Skelgill is munching and seems in no hurry to reply, so DS Leyton continues.

'Do you want to see her, Guv?'

'What time did she set out?'

'They'd had a buffet lunch in the dining room from noon onwards. She left after that – one of the brothers reckoned about 12:30.'

Skelgill purses his lips.

'She did well to get so far.' He finishes the last of his biscuit and begins to fiddle with the teapot, a large antique affair in much polished silver with an ebony handle. 'We're going to be asking people where they were in the hour before the body was found, Leyton. I think we know her answer – she'll keep until tomorrow – no point speaking to her if she's in shock.'

DS Leyton nods. His boss is being uncharacteristically sympathetic.

'What next, Guv?'

'Has Herdwick finished in the study?'

'Reckons as much as he can, Guv. He says he'll need to run tests and do a proper job back at the path lab – but he's found a substantial blunt trauma injury to the base of the skull – a rounded impact – couldn't be the edge of that desk or the hearth. Someone whacked him good and proper, Guv.'

Skelgill is upending the eighteenth century teapot in a manner that would surely bring on palpitations in Thwaites were he watching.

'Leyton – I want you to check around the whole place – all the doors and windows – any signs of a break in – anything unlocked or easy to open – and check the snow for tracks, so we know which entrances have been used recently. Make a list.'

'Righto, Guv.' DS Leyton turns towards the door, but then he hesitates. 'The posh geezer called Martius – the eldest brother – he's been bending my ear, Guv – champing at the bit he is to talk to the senior officer, as he put it.'

Skelgill grimaces – though it could be the stewed tea as much as the idea that someone is trying to set his agenda.

'Leyton, you talk to him and the other three siblings – just get the top line on their movements. Send Mullarkey along here, will you.' This is an instruction rather than a request. He bangs down the teapot unceremoniously. 'And tell Thwaites to bring a refill for this lot.'

*

Skelgill glances cursorily at the business card that precedes Fergal Mullarkey LLB LLM AITI(CTA) TEP; it seems he is something of a man of letters, literally at least. Lacking any such crutch himself Skelgill settles for an extra hard squeeze of the offered hand – not that handshakes, either, are an exchange in which he customarily indulges with interviewees yet to be cleared of involvement in a murder. In his mid fifties, the lawyer is of medium height and trim figure, a pale complexion, freckled, a largely bald head, formerly ginger, with remnants above the ears, deep blue eyes. Yet rather fleshy pink lips and prominent round ears add a clownish effect, contributing to an overall impression that is at once friendly and slightly sinister. However, it is plain from the family solicitor's manner that he considers himself on the side of the law, and not by any stretch of the imagination a suspect. Indeed, he seizes the initiative with an opening question that reveals his lawyer's mind has been at work.

'I take it you're treating this whole thing as suspicious, Inspector?'

Skelgill indicates the seat opposite his. It goes against the grain to be informed what he might be thinking – never mind to reveal to a civilian his perspective in such a circumstance – but there is some endearing quality about the unaffected Irish pronunciation – 'd' for the soft 'th' of this, and 't' for the strong 'th' of thing. He raises his shoulders in a noncommittal shrug.

'We received a call that there had been a murder, sir.'

'But I understand there's no witness – and certainly no one confessing.' The lawyer seems to have a twinkle in his eye – that he understands Skelgill's obligation to be taciturn.

'Aye.' Skelgill grins ruefully. 'We shall have to wait for our pathologist's report.'

The man nods understandingly.

'The family is sticking together.'

Skelgill shoots a sharp glance at the lawyer.

'What I mean to say, Inspector, is that they've gathered for safety in the drawing room. They are concerned there might be an intruder at large.'

This clarification seems to disappoint Skelgill.

'My sergeant is checking the place over. We've got two uniformed officers on the way. They'll have a scout round outside – make sure no one's hiding in a storeroom or stable.'

'I don't suppose there'll be tracks you can follow?'

The suggestion is made with the same unassuming enunciation as his opening question. Skelgill glances doubtfully at the window.

'What there are – they're fast disappearing – if you could even follow them in these conditions. We might get something in the morning. These snow showers are due to die out overnight.'

'That's assuming it *was* an intruder, of course, Inspector.'

Skelgill is staring into the fire. Unhurriedly he picks up a cast iron poker and gives the nearest log what seems to be an unnecessary prod.

'Do you have reason to believe otherwise, sir?'

'If this were a detective novel I most certainly would.' The man chuckles at his own joke. 'I'm no criminal lawyer, Inspector – inheritance and taxes are my bag – but I know enough that you'll need to eliminate everyone, myself included – provided of course it turns out to be foul play and not just an accident.'

Skelgill cranes around inquiringly.

'Did you see the body, sir?'

'I did not.' The man shakes his head, closing his eyes as he does so. 'As a matter of fact I was in my room. By the time Martius came knocking to tell me what had happened they'd already telephoned your good selves. It seemed sensible to follow the officer's instruction to keep out of Declan's study.'

Skelgill nods and Fergal Mullarkey deems this is an opportune moment to provide his alibi without being pressed.

'There are some complex issues – where English tax law differs from the Irish – I was working on these from after breakfast until noon, when I came down to the buffet in the dining room – after a short while I took a cold platter back up to my room and stayed there until the alarm was raised, as I said.'

'Did you see Perdita – at lunchtime?'

The lawyer nods.

'She looked all set to go out – at least that's one small crumb of comfort – that she's home safe. Two deaths in a week are enough for any family to take, estranged or not.'

Skelgill furrows his brow.

'So how come you handle their affairs – from a foreign country?'

Skelgill's blunt diplomacy brings a rueful smile to the Irishman's lips.

'I suppose you could say we were all part of the same country when my firm first represented the family – at least we had shares in King Charles.'

Skelgill stares rather blankly at his Celtic cousin; it is evident that this genealogical marker does little to enlighten him. He opts for silence.

'Naturally we have offices in the UK – Glasgow, Liverpool, Bristol – places with strong historical Irish connections. There was a time when we even had a branch in Whitehaven. So I can call upon expert assistance on local law when I require it.' He makes a gesture with his hands to indicate his immediate surroundings. 'But as far as the family goes, old habits die hard. They say a man's more likely to change his wife than his lawyer, Inspector.'

Skelgill narrows his eyes.

'If the lawyer's any good a man might find himself changing them both.'

Fergal Mullarkey gives Skelgill a knowing look; it sounds like a pearl of wisdom that stems from bitter experience. However, Skelgill's hardened countenance deters him from further inquiry; instead he elucidates as far as his own clients are concerned.

'We've served the O'Mores since the seventeenth century; they were successful merchants from Dublin. Among other British ports they traded through Whitehaven, and bought Crummock Hall in 1720. A branch of the family has lived here ever since. These young folk are the twelfth generation.'

'So what happens next?'

'As regards inheritance, Inspector?'

'Thwaites mentioned Martius is now head of the household.'

The lawyer visibly baulks at this suggestion.

'Ah, Inspector – it is not so simple as that – this is not a titled estate – we're not talking Downton Abbey.'

'That's not in Cumbria.'

'Yorkshire, I understand, Inspector?'

Skelgill scowls.

'Never heard of it.'

Again the man grins, though he is clearly unsure if Skelgill is being flippant.

'No matter, Inspector – my point is that ordinary rules of inheritance apply – not primogeniture. There is no such requirement or right under English law – or Irish, come to that. Indeed in Ireland there was a time when it was positively prohibited if you were a Catholic family – though I digress. Suffice to say Sir Sean was at liberty to leave his property to whomsoever he wished.'

'So who did he leave it to?'

At this juncture there is a tentative knock on the door, and a familiar clearing of the throat: Thwaites. If he were hovering, eavesdropping even, then he has declined the opportunity to loiter longer and learn something he presumably does not know. Instead he enters bearing a large silver tray and fresh supplies. Fergal Mullarkey hops briskly to his aid; there is only room on the bureau for one tray at a time – he removes the original and waits and hands it to Thwaites, who bows several times as he backs away. Skelgill espies sandwiches and swiftly makes himself acquainted with their fillings while the lawyer pours tea. Armed according to their wants they resume their seats.

'You were saying, sir – about the will?'

In fact the lawyer has not used the word, and a flicker of doubt crosses his eyes.

'To answer your question, Inspector, I should perhaps take a moment to explain the family tree?'

Skelgill indicates his agreement.

'Padraig Willoughby O'More died shortly after the second war, 1949 if I recall correctly. He bequeathed the estate to his son, Sir Sean. I don't know the reasoning, but he was the elder twin. Declan received an index-linked income. In turn Sir Sean's linear successor was his daughter Shauna O'More. Sadly she died together with her husband Edward Regulus in a boating accident when their own five children were very young.'

Skelgill is nodding, but he refrains from revealing his extreme local provenance. The lawyer continues.

'Sir Sean's last will and testament decreed that the estate should continue intact while his brother survived – to be held in trust until Declan's demise. This has of course come to pass – so soon as to obviate the need for a trust to be established. The succeeding provision is that the family are to decide – the five grandchildren are each allocated one vote. They can chose to maintain the estate, to appoint one person as nominal head – or even to cede the estate to that person and their descendants. Or they can sell it – and the proceeds are to be split into five equal parts. Their decision must be in a simple majority, at least three votes to two.'

Skelgill hesitates as he digests this information.

'What would it be worth – a fifth?'

The Irishman turns out his bottom lip; now he looks like a sad clown.

'I shouldn't imagine a person would need to work again, Inspector. The equivalent of a generous lottery win.'

Skelgill sighs, perhaps thinking of his own bad luck as far as raffles and sweepstakes go.

'When did the family find out about this arrangement?'

'On Friday evening – after the funeral. I convened a meeting – it was the secondary purpose of my trip, Inspector. The primary being to pay my respects on behalf of the firm.'

Skelgill nods amenably.

'Could they – or any of them – have known about the will beforehand?'

'Of course, Inspector, it is possible that Sir Sean – or indeed Declan if he knew – told one or more of them, but –'

The man shakes his head, gainsaying his words with his actions.

'Aye?'

'I have read a good number of wills to expectant families, Inspector – and I would say that Friday's reading was no different. Universally the reaction was one of innocent surprise. If someone knew, they concealed their feelings.' He brushes a palm over his shiny crown. 'And, in any event, it is not as though Sir Sean's last wishes were contentious – unusual, perhaps – but certainly not controversial. They provide for a fair allocation of the inheritance.'

'Is that how Declan saw it?'

'He seemed quite content in that respect. After all, he leaves no heirs.'

Skelgill takes a bite of a sandwich followed rather too swiftly by a swallow of tea.

'You went to see him in his study on Saturday afternoon – what was that about?'

The lawyer momentarily looks like he feels Skelgill has done the dirty on him – going easy, but now suddenly throwing in a curved ball. He takes a measured drink of his tea, perhaps to buy a little time in order to compose his rejoinder.

'He wished to be reassured that his own position would be unaffected during the remainder of his lifetime.' And now Fergal Mullarkey sends one back to Skelgill. 'He also wanted to make a will.'

Perhaps intentionally, Skelgill looks unimpressed.

'There can't be much in that, sir?'

'There is no heritable property, of course, Inspector – no real estate – but his moveable property has a value that is more than inconsequential.'

'His books.'

The lawyer is nodding.

'A lifetime's work – a collection that he did not wish to see dispersed.'

Skelgill is frowning.

'That sounds more like sentimental value. What about a museum, a library, a university?'

Fergal Mullarkey shifts in his seat; perhaps he is wondering if he should discuss this confidential matter.

'I made a similar suggestion – and in fact there is what you might call a back-stop provision in place, if I may use such a crude term.'

Skelgill now grins.

'A back-stop to me is what you need when you've got a dodgy wicketkeeper. If you don't want to embarrass him you call it fine leg.'

This is a cricketing analogy, and though Fergal Mullarkey is Irish, where the game has no great tradition, he probably has the proper schooling.

'Quite, Inspector. In this case we have a comparably ancient library in our Dublin offices – mainly books of law, of course – some years ago Declan entrusted us via a legal instrument with guardianship during any emergency, or period of abeyance or deadlock over the fate of the collection.'

'What's it worth?'

'It is nothing on the scale of the entire Crummock Hall estate – but certainly a small fortune – and I say that literally, Inspector. There must be several thousand books – some of them are worth over a hundred pounds apiece – let alone the complete sets. We're certainly talking six figures.'

Skelgill raises an eyebrow; perhaps he considers this a conservative estimate.

'What did he decide?'

The lawyer puts down his cup and saucer and turns to look at Skelgill.

'He said he would make a draft and hand it to me. I have received no such draft.' He spreads his palms in an imploring gesture. 'You may know better than I if there is such a thing, Inspector.'

Skelgill shrugs.

'We haven't searched the study with that in mind, sir.'

The lawyer nods.

'He may not have got around to it – he may not even have reached a decision.'

'What else was he considering – who else?'

'The family, naturally – his great nephews and nieces.'

'Did he have one of them in mind?'

'He confessed to knowing them little. Their lives were led in London and abroad. It is more than twenty years since they last spent their summer holidays here. And then – he was something of a recluse. He asked my opinion.'

'What did you say, sir?'

The Irishman inhales and lets out the breath in a sigh.

'I find myself equally in the dark, Inspector. Until now, during my working life – my entire lifetime – the estate has been under the stewardship of Sir Sean Willoughby O'More. I have had no cause to deal with any of the younger generation.'

Skelgill remains pensive. If he suspects the lawyer of being economical in his answer he chooses not to press the matter.

'What about their parents – did you know them, sir?'

Fergal Mullarkey shakes his head.

'I was little more than a trainee at the time of the accident. My uncle – one of our partners – the O'Mores were his client at that time.'

Skelgill glares into the fire, as if he is dissatisfied with some aspect of its combustion.

'If Declan did write a draft – would that be legal, sir?'

The man nods with a modicum of enthusiasm.

'It is quite possible – provided it were signed by two witnesses.' He regards Skelgill closely, as if he is trying to read his reaction. 'Of course, Inspector, a witness cannot benefit from a will.'

This statement appears to provide some food for thought for Skelgill, and it is half a minute before he raises another question.

'What will happen to Thwaites – and the other members of staff?'

The lawyer relaxes into the high wingback chair; perhaps he was expecting a more challenging line of enquiry.

'If the estate is maintained as a going concern then their positions may be unaffected – even were it to be sold to a third party. If it became a hotel, for example, there would be many more jobs created. However, there is a provision for Thwaites to have use of the gatehouse, a *liferent* as the Scots aptly call it – a continuing legacy from the will of Padraig Willoughby O'More. And I believe Thwaites has a war pension along with his state entitlement and therefore could live comfortably whether he works or not.'

Skelgill's features are cast with a degree of scepticism – but he rouses himself and stands up, flexing his spine and yawning simultaneously; it seems the interview is drawing to a close.

'And what about you, sir – your travel plans?'

The lawyer seems in no hurry to leave.

'I have a hire car which I must return to John Lennon.' He refers to Liverpool airport, but chuckles. 'Now there's an Irish name if ever there were one. I imagine I shall need my secretary to reschedule my flight – heaven knows when I'll get safely through the snowdrifts.'

'It isn't hard to do, sir – we'll be keeping the back lanes clear through to the A66 – you'll be fine in the morning.'

The lawyer grins.

'So we shan't have the pleasure of you for dinner, Inspector? Having dropped in as you did, I thought you might be staying the night.'

Skelgill affects a degree of dutiful modesty.

'I shall be heading down to Buttermere – there's an old lady I need to check on.'

4. HEADQUARTERS – Monday 9.15am

'Shanks's pony, Guv – all the way to Buttermere?'
'Aye, why not?'
'How far was that?'
'Couple of miles, Leyton – stroll in the park.'
'The park in the dark, Guv – never mind the snow. How did you find your way?'

Skelgill takes a gulp of his tea and pulls a disapproving face.

'Safe enough on the road – I wasn't going to get run over, was I?'

DS Leyton shrugs resignedly. His superior has arrived late looking distinctly hung over, unshaven and wearing the same outdoor clothes as last night. That he had abruptly disappeared from Crummock Hall, passing an ambiguous message via Thwaites inferring a visit to his elderly mother, had not entirely convinced the sergeant. The knowledge that Skelgill's mountain rescue cronies were likely bunking down for the night at the inn in Buttermere suggested an alternative scenario. It had all the makings of the classic lock-in: impassable country roads and the police joining the party. Skelgill now claims to have obtained a lift back to Penrith in the team's Defender, tailgating a snowplough over the Newlands Pass. But DS Leyton knows better than to question the mysterious movements of his boss.

'DS Jones should be up with the lab report and photographs any minute, Guv. She's briefed on what we know. I've printed out the statements, so I can run through them if you like?'

He leans over from his regular seat beside Skelgill's token filing cabinet and slides a single sheet of paper across his superior's desk. Skelgill glances somewhat disparagingly at the item, and sinks back against his headrest and folds his arms.

'Give it a minute, Leyton. Wait for Jones – no point wasting time if Herdwick's come up with some innocent explanation.'

'Don't seem very likely, Guv – going by what he reckoned last night.'

But Skelgill already has his eyes closed, and does not reply. A silence descends. DS Leyton watches his boss with growing consternation – or it might be exasperation, for eventually he begins to pull faces of simulated annoyance – and is caught in the act by the arrival of the soft-soled DS Jones. She can't help herself from breaking out into a giggle – and this rouses Skelgill from whatever trancelike state he had entered. He jerks forward in a rather ungainly fashion.

'Jones – what've you got?'

'Morning, Guv.'

She beams endearingly, unperturbed by his dishevelled appearance and abrupt reception. She bears a tray with fresh drinks from the canteen, and deposits this upon his desk. Skelgill greedily lurches for the nearest mug. DS Jones lifts up a manila folder and settles in her seat beside the window. Skelgill takes a couple of slurps, inhaling loudly over the piping hot liquid. His attention is restored.

'Well?'

She glances at her papers.

'There's no doubt he was attacked, Guv – a severe blow from behind at a rising angle of about 30 degrees – some sort of club with a rounded end – possibly a baseball bat.'

Skelgill scowls over the rim of his mug.

'That lot wouldn't know a baseball bat if it smacked them between the eyes. Croquet mallet, aye.'

His sergeants simper amenably. With a kick of one boot Skelgill rotates his chair away from them in order to scrutinise the map of the Lake District pinned upon the wall behind his desk. DS Jones glances at DS Leyton, who grins encouragingly; she continues.

'The provisional tests suggest a time of death around twelve noon – but with the falling temperature of the room and the considerable age of the victim, there could be an hour's margin of error either side. However, the midpoint does correspond to the time that the clock stopped – so he could have been struck from behind while he was winding it.'

Skelgill is silent – but it is apparent that his posture has markedly stiffened. After a moment, still facing the map, he speaks in a strained voice.

'What do you mean – the time the clock stopped?'

Again DS Jones glances at her fellow sergeant – though now with heightened apprehension. Having not attended the scene, she is less sure of her ground, and she detects some discontinuity is afoot. DS Leyton, longer-serving by a decade, is more inured to Skelgill's capriciousness. He extends an arm and signals with a flicking of his fingers that she should pass him the file.

'There's a bunch of photos taken by SOCO – one of them shows the clock face stopped at twelve.' He leafs through the papers. 'Here we go, Guv.'

Skelgill spins around. He takes the proffered colour copy and stares at it, alarmed. His features grow increasingly severe, as though a storm is brewing behind his troubled brow. There is only so much to see – the rectangular casement clock on the wood-panelled wall, its front open, the pendulum missing, the hands neatly aligned, pointing to twelve – but Skelgill takes a good half-minute before he returns the picture to DS Leyton.

'The study's secured, right?'

'Both doors, Guv – I've got the key for the internal door and SOCO still have the external one for prints – I said we'd drop down for it before we go back over. Plus we've taped off the hallway and PC Dodd's on duty. According to the butler there's only one key for each door in the whole place.'

Skelgill glowers unreasonably.

'Happen the horse has already bolted, Leyton.'

Both DS Leyton and DS Jones wait in anticipation – but in characteristic Skelgill fashion, it appears he is not about to divulge the source of his contradiction, and to what metaphorical equine he refers. Of course, the informed fly on the wall would see the paradox: the facts of the photograph tell him twelve noon, while his senses, his memory – albeit dulled by little sleep and no little beer – scream out that twelve noon cannot be right. It is an impasse compounded by the nature of Skelgill, a man who does not like to admit he is wrong, or – worse – to look a fool.

'We'll get over to Crummock Hall as soon as we've finished here.' He fixes DS Jones with a stare. 'What else from Herdwick and his crew?'

She gazes rather helplessly at the file held by DS Leyton. She seems unnerved by Skelgill's erratic manner.

'That was really all from the lab at the moment, Guv.' But then she gathers her wits as she recalls a point. 'Oh – they did say there's no evident blood spatter from the primary blow. The bloodstain on the carpet came from a secondary wound – probably when he toppled back and hit his head – he would have already been unconscious. Death occurred within two or three minutes as a result of massive internal haemorrhaging.'

Skelgill turns to DS Leyton.

'Run me through what you know. Start with security.'

DS Leyton nods. He glances at DS Jones to indicate he includes her in his address.

'I found no signs of a forced entry, Guv – the place is a rabbit warren – but all the ground-floor doors were locked – except the main one at the front – but of course we came in there.'

'Who let you in?'

'It was the butler, Guv - Thwaites.'

'What did he say about it?'

'Said he couldn't remember, Guv – he was upset by what had happened – but he reckons it's not normally locked during the daytime – and especially with some of the guests having their motors parked out there.'

'What about tracks?'

'Crikey, Guv – there were plenty at the front – some of them were ours though – but all mixed up – it was as much as I could see in the dark, and what with more snow falling. We might find something leading away if we have a proper butcher's in the daylight.'

43

'Other doors?'

'There's about a dozen, counting French windows. I checked outside them all – mostly no disturbance. You know about the study. The kitchen door leads onto a yard with storerooms round about it. There were footprints there – but the cook said she and the maid had been out for supplies every so often. Plus the gamekeeper and gardener who've got cottages in the grounds use that as the tradesmen's entrance – seems they'd both been in for their breakfasts. Then there's a cellar where they keep fuel – that's got a door up some steps leading to the woodsheds. Quite a lot of tracks there – Thwaites said that would be him as they've been getting through stacks of logs.' Skelgill is looking unimpressed, and DS Leyton's features become increasingly strained. However, it seems he has saved his most promising item until last. 'But there's this, Guv – at the back of the main part of the house there's a kind of porch, like a church. There was a single line of tracks coming from across the lawn out of the darkness – definitely some geezer with big feet walking right up to the door.'

Skelgill pulls a sour face.

'That was me, Leyton, you donnat.'

DS Leyton looks somewhat crestfallen – but he is naturally thick-skinned (a necessary qualification for working with Skelgill) and doubly protected by his limited understanding of the Cumbrian dialect.

'Oh, righto, Guv.'

Skelgill clicks his fingers.

'The family.'

Now DS Leyton wavers.

'I know you said to concentrate on the hour before the finding of the body, Guv – but I asked what they each did from the time they got up in the morning.'

He is clearly expecting a rebuke – but the photograph of the clock has dislocated Skelgill's picture of events, and none is forthcoming. DS Leyton gestures to the untouched notes on Skelgill's desk. He slips another copy from his file and passes it to DS Jones. He glances hopefully at Skelgill, but his superior resolutely ignores the paper.

'Chop chop, Leyton.'

DS Leyton realises he must orate. He is about to begin when it strikes him that DS Jones will not be fully informed. He tilts his notes towards her.

'These are the grandchildren of Sir Sean Willoughby O'More, who died a week ago of natural causes. Declan – full name Declan Thomas O'More – was his twin, and their great uncle. They were orphaned when their parents died in the eighties. There's five of them.' Now he closes a fist and sticks out a thumb and successive fingers as he begins to count. 'An older brother – next a sister. Then twin brothers. And then the youngest sister – the writer who was missing in the hills. She got back safely, but I didn't speak to her.'

DS Jones nods in appreciation.

'Twins run in families – expressed through the females.'

DS Leyton widens his eyes. Skelgill appears disinterested.

'How do you know that, girl?'

'Remember I was on a forensics course at the University of York in October? There was a module on identical twins – there are historical cases where offenders have escaped justice because there was insufficient proof of which twin committed the crime. There are new developments in DNA profiling that can overcome that.'

'Cor blimey. How come –' But DS Leyton must suddenly sense Skelgill's disapproval. He lifts up his paper and mutters under his breath. 'Well – let's hope it were the butler and not one of the twins.'

'They'll *all* be escaping scot-free if you don't get on with it, Leyton.'

DS Leyton squints dutifully at his notes.

'Martius Regulus-O'More first then, Guv. Age 39. Resident of Royal Tunbridge Wells, Kent. Married. Two children at private school. Occupation merchant banker. Arrived on his Jack Jones by car on Thursday for the funeral on

Friday. Had intended to travel home on Saturday. On Sunday went down for breakfast as soon as it was called at 8am. Saw his brother Edgar and the younger sister Perdita. Returned to his room and worked there on documents he'd brought with him until lunch at 12 noon. At lunch he saw Mr Mullarkey – the family solicitor,' (he adds this qualification for the benefit of DS Jones) 'as well as Cassandra, Edgar and Perdita – the missing one being the other twin, Brutus.'

He pauses now, and looks from one to the other of his colleagues. His expression is rather belligerent – as if he expects to be accused of making up these extravagant names. Certainly they are idiosyncratic, traditionally Irish among the older generations, more latterly classical. DS Jones, however, seems to appreciate his disquiet.

'It sounds like a Shakespearean tragedy.'

Now Skelgill intervenes tersely.

'Their mother was an actress.'

Compliantly they nod – let this be the explanation.

'Martius went back to his room after lunch and continued to work there. At about 2:15pm his sister Cassandra came hammering on his door and that's when they rushed to the study. Moving on to her, Cassandra – next eldest, age 37. Resident of Knightsbridge, London. Divorced, no children. Occupation party planner.'

DS Leyton now pauses, as though he anticipates an objection from Skelgill – however it is restricted to a doubting glower, to which the sergeant responds accordingly.

'I asked her twice, Guv – and she insisted. I thought it was the gin talking – but give the lady her due she seemed most affected by the death, and what with seeing the body and all – so I just got on with finding out what her movements were. Claimed she never made it to breakfast and couldn't remember for certain being at lunch – despite Martius saying he saw her. She was complaining that one day merged into the next, what with them being trapped indoors by the snow since Friday afternoon.'

'But she raised the alarm, Leyton.' Skelgill's retort is thick with indignation.

'I pointed that out, Guv. She heard Thwaites calling – she said she might have been in the drawing room. I notice that's where they keep a drinks trolley.'

Now he shrugs and exhales rather wheezily. The actions serve to punctuate entries on his report.

'Edgar. Eldest of the two twins. Age 35. Resident of Hampstead, London. Occupation chartered accountant. Single. Quietly spoken – polite – a bit stiff, know what I mean?' DS Leyton's intonation suggests that such humility is not a trait shared by the entire family. 'He was at breakfast and lunch, and who he saw there corresponds to the others' statements. He'd brought work with him, too – said he'd set up a makeshift office in a room at the top of the tower – reckoned he could get a weak signal every so often to do his emails. Said he'd worked there either side of breakfast and lunch – heard the commotion just after 2:15pm and ran down to see what it was all about. Martius and Cassandra were already in the study with Thwaites. It was Edgar that called 999 – and a bit later I had a phone conversation with him about locking up until we could get there. We've got those calls recorded, Guv. He sounded quite unemotional.'

'You said it yourself, Leyton – he's an accountant.'

DS Leyton nods in deference to Skelgill's omniscience.

'Finally, his twin brother – Brutus.' DS Leyton stares at his notes and makes a sudden gurning expression, as though he is reminded of some unpleasant experience. 'Chalk and cheese, considering they're twins. Resident of Covent Garden, London – although if you ask me, Charing Cross Road is Soho. Arrived by train and taxi with Cassandra and Edgar on Thursday evening. Occupation actor. Didn't recognise him, myself – Brutus Regulus-O'More – you think you'd remember that one if you heard it.' Now he gives a small introspective shake of the head. 'Anyway – he's another one who slept in – missed breakfast *and* lunch – said he wandered down to the drawing room in his dressing gown about 2:30pm – claimed that was the first he knew of it.'

47

DS Leyton looks up to find Skelgill is glaring at him.

'There's someone missing, Leyton.'

'But, Guv – I thought you said we'd interview the youngest sister this morning?'

'I'm not talking about her, Leyton – what about Declan? Who saw him, and when?'

DS Leyton rocks back and flaps his sheet of paper.

'Ah, Guv – no, I mean, yes – I was saving that to the end.' Now he brings the page forward and jabs at it with a sturdy forefinger. 'All four gave me the same answer on that one. No one saw Declan on Sunday or went anywhere near his study before the alarm was raised. The only person who admits to any contact with him is Thwaites.'

Skelgill springs up and retrieves his jacket, earlier discarded in a corner.

'Leyton – get a pool car – a 4x4 – go ahead of me and interview the other staff – same thing – their movements – who saw Declan – who saw anyone near his study – anything unusual – anyone seen walking in the grounds. And get Thwaites to have a good look around the study – stay with him – see if he can identify anything that's missing.'

'Righto, Guv.'

DS Leyton rises more circumspectly; he nods to DS Jones and departs the office. Skelgill meanwhile is punching a fist into his jacket.

'Get your coat, Jones. I need a driver.'

5. PERDITA – Monday 10.30am

'Aye, best part of thirty years ago it happened.'

DS Jones shakes her head sadly. She is holding a framed photograph that she has lifted from the lid of a grand piano in the bright drawing room. Although it is printed in colour, it is faded almost to sepia and this effect, combined with the traditional dress of its subjects, could give the impression of a 1920s *Pimm's* party. Raising their glasses at the centre of a laughing coterie are the late couple, Edward Regulus and Shauna O'More; milling in the background are wearers of striped blazers and boaters, and bearers of tennis racquets and whites, and beyond a rising skyline that Skelgill recognises as Mellbreak, and – more ominously – a horizontal sliver of bluish grey that is Crummock Water.

'I've never heard of the accident, Guv. Do you remember it?'

Skelgill's brow is furrowed. Slowly he shakes his head.

'I were just a kid – folk seemed to drown in the Lakes every year back then. I reckon it made a bit of a splash in the London press.'

DS Jones glances sharply at him, but he appears to have used the metaphor in all innocence, since he continues without seeking her approbation for his wit as he might habitually do.

'I knew this lot, though.'

Now he points to a photograph of the children, of a comparable vintage. They are lined up in descending age order, left to right, in wellingtons, waving fishing nets and proudly dangling jam jars crammed with tadpoles. Martius, the eldest has a face of noble triumph. Cassandra, blonde and pouting, is the tallest – a girl's growth spurt, perhaps. The twins Edgar and Brutus with their crewcuts are very near identical – except that one is serious, while the other sticks out his tongue and makes a two-fingered hand gesture. Perdita, just a toddler, grasps the shorts of the joker and looks up to him with laughing admiration.

'What do you mean, Guv – when you say you knew them?'

Skelgill shrugs.

'I used to knock about here – birds' nesting, fishing, exploring.' He grins. 'Trespassing, in their gamekeeper's book. They used to come for their summer holidays.'

'Even after their parents died?'

'Aye, well after.'

DS Jones remains thoughtful for a moment.

'Do they recognise you?'

Skelgill throws back his head scornfully.

'A peasant like me – what do you think?'

He digs his hands into his trouser pockets and saunters rather aimlessly over to the windows that give on to the Christmas cake lawn of his landing yesterday. His mood of urgency seems to have dissipated since their arrival at Crummock Hall, and now he calmly surveys the south-facing scene. There is a clear blue sky, though the winter sun is screened by the bulk of Grasmoor, which towers like a great white pyramid above the shelterbelt of conifers. He squints as he tries to determine the topography, but the flat light defies his efforts to spy familiar crags and gullies, and the blanket snow conceals the natural contour bands of first bracken, then heather, and finally rocky scree. His gaze falls closer to home as a movement in a shrub border catches his eye. He realises a flock of birds is busily plundering berries of guelder rose. He watches as they compete to gobble the glistening ruby globules, almost too big to be a beak-full; yet they vanish in the way that a magician folds a foam ball into a palm. Though he is no ornithologist, he has a vague idea that these are waxwings – surely a sighting to have pleased Declan, who would no doubt know their collective noun.

'So sorry to keep you waiting, officers – nobody told me you had arrived, now.'

Simultaneously the detectives swing around – the soft Irish accent might almost emanate from hidden speakers.

'Good morning to you – I'm Perdita.'

The young woman has slipped unobtrusively into the carpeted drawing room; now she stops a couple of yards short of them. She links her hands behind her back and makes the tiniest bending movement at the knees, like a maidservant presenting herself for inspection. She is of below medium height and slight of frame and she wears a fitted short-sleeved dress in viridian that accentuates her narrow waist. She has a pale complexion and long strawberry blonde hair, parted rather mischievously to reveal fine upcurving brows; equally striking are high cheekbones and full pink lips, elegantly sculpted and set within a diamond face. And where green Irish eyes might be expected, dark brown irises merge with black pupils to produce an expression of dilated awe.

Skelgill is plainly swayed by her striking presence – though he might be thinking she is not the hearty hillwalker he anticipated. She detects his dubiety and smiles quizzically. Rather awkwardly he gestures that they should be seated – a matching pair of large country sofas are arranged perpendicular to the hearth, a low table between them, and they take opposing sides, DS Jones (who exchanges polite nods but whom Skelgill fails to introduce) settling undemonstratively beside her superior.

'We were looking for a Rowena Devlin.'

'I'm sorry, Inspector?'

'Yesterday – out on the fell.'

Skelgill's contrary opening gambit seems designed to shift his disharmony back upon her. Perdita takes an anxious breath, her pale skin flushing at the cheeks. She raises finely boned hands in an apologetic gesture.

'I had no idea my call would bring out the mountain rescue team – let alone a helicopter.' She regards him from behind long fluttering lashes, and bites her lower lip in a signal of self-reproach. 'And then I understand you abseiled into Crummock Hall. You're something of a *Local Hero.*'

Though she likens him to the multi-tasking protagonist of the eponymous movie, a clichéd figure of fun in rural parts (and apposite given his dual role as rescuer and policeman), Skelgill's ego chooses to interpret the allusion as a direct compliment. Now he must play down his greatness.

'It wasn't exactly an abseil – and you wouldn't normally have got a helicopter.' He shrugs casually. 'We'd just stretchered a climber off Scafell Pike and taken him to Carlisle. On another day the chopper could have been two hundred miles away.'

'I was really just hoping for advice with a bearing – but then my battery died.'

'Did you have a compass?'

'I'm afraid I was trusting to the app on my phone – but the data signal was intermittent and I got all sorts of wonky readings.'

Skelgill is wearing a thermal base layer beneath his shirt, and now he hooks a finger into the turtle neck and draws out a grubby length of nylon cord to which is tied a small rectangle of transparent plastic – a field compass – and an alloy mountain whistle.

'Essential kit – as important as your boots – no battery needed.'

She bows in deference to his expertise.

'Inspector – anywhere else I should have gone prepared – I even have avalanche reflectors built into my jacket – but, in spite of my accent, I first climbed Grasmoor when I was knee-high to a grasshopper – I thought I couldn't go wrong.'

There is a degree of consternation in Skelgill's expression. Her explanation is reasonable, if not entirely an excuse; however it also contains a piece of information – the implication that she does not recall him from her childhood. His features harden.

'You still could have walked off Dove Crags – then we'd have been bringing you down on a stretcher, if you were lucky.'

She lowers her eyes and again bites her lip in contrition – it is a ploy that causes Skelgill to relent.

'How *did* thee get down, lass?'

She glances up in surprise: that he has suddenly lapsed into the vernacular.

'I waited at the summit – I squatted in the lee of the stone shelter – I thought another walker might appear. But after a while I got a faint glimpse of the sun – I guessed it was about 2pm – I knew if I went carefully due north I could descend into

Gasgale Gill – and then follow Liza Beck to our packhorse bridge.'

Skelgill raises an eyebrow – but it is a grudging recognition of her competence – and at least she had ventured out adequately clothed – albeit she hardly looks strong enough to have battled through deepening drifts and swirling squalls.

She may detect that such matters of practicality sidetrack him – for now she seizes the initiative and brings the exchange full circle.

'So you see, Inspector – I said I was Rowena Devlin without really thinking about it. I suppose it's a lot easier to shout out in the midst of a blizzard – and to be honest, for work purposes I mainly go by it these days – it's quite a relief after being saddled for thirty-odd years with a real name like mine, I can tell you.'

Skelgill regards her broodingly – she has a point, at least. And now she takes advantage of this little hiatus to address her own concerns. She looks imploringly to Skelgill and then to DS Jones and back.

'Is my great uncle's death really a murder?'

That the family came straight to their own conclusions has not yet received any corroboration from the police – but now Skelgill breaks the embargo.

'It's hard to see it any other way, madam.' This abrupt switch to formality – to *madam* – plainly discomforts him, but there is the matter of professional distance. 'The autopsy has confirmed he was struck before he fell.'

The woman is silent for a moment. She is not outwardly distressed, but her demeanour is one of helplessness – that something has been taken from her.

'He was alive and kicking when I last saw him.' She shakes her head ruefully. 'At his cantankerous best.'

'When was that, madam?'

'Just before lunch – it must have been 11:40, thereabouts.'

'And where were you?'

'In his study – I went to see him.'

53

'What for?'

She smiles in a considered way.

'You might say I received the imperial summons, Inspector.'

She hesitates; Skelgill is impatient.

'What did he want?'

Now she shakes her head – perhaps a demonstration that she herself is still a little bemused.

'To give me a dressing down, it would seem.'

'What about?'

'My books, Inspector.' She grins self-consciously. 'I'm a writer?'

Skelgill makes a faint inclination of his head to confirm that he knows this. He looks pointedly at DS Jones – for the first time properly acknowledging her participation – and now only for the purposes of passing the buck, so to speak – for plainly he expects her to be informed on the subject of Rowena Devlin's literary output, should the need arise. DS Jones folds her arms. Skelgill turns back to Perdita, who is observing this little exchange with some interest.

'What's wrong with them?'

'It seems I am in danger of invoking the family curse – he said I am my mother's daughter – even if I don't know it – he called me a witch.' Now she folds her hands upon her bare knees and leans forwards in a conspiratorial fashion. 'On reflection I think he meant it as a statement of fact rather than an insult.'

That the course of the conversation has taken an unexpected, even surreal turn, robs Skelgill of any familiar landmark to guide his next question. He glances expectantly at DS Jones, but she seems determined to withhold her reaction. However, Perdita begins to elaborate of her own volition.

'I don't imagine you have read any of my novels, Inspector,' (she does not wait for confirmation) 'but I write romantic historical fiction – I write about the plantations and slaves and their masters and mistresses in the eighteenth and nineteenth centuries.'

Skelgill is seated with his forearms resting upon his thighs, and now he regards his fingers as they entwine. He might be reflecting that there are sufficient digits to count the novels he has read – or, at least, started.

'Inspector, if Great Uncle Declan were to be believed then back in the mists of time the O'Mores had a hand in such events – and that one of our more ruthless forbears double-crossed an African slave trader – who in turn enlisted his tribal witch doctor to lay a curse upon the family.'

Now her accented eyes narrow in a decidedly feline manner.

'Great Uncle Declan claimed the curse strikes among every generation – that my mother was the most recent victim.' Her eyes suddenly widen and she opens her palms as though she is appealing to the detectives that they should believe her. 'I have researched plantation society in the British and Irish colonies – but I have never come across anything in the family history that suggests such a connection.'

Skelgill grins somewhat inanely.

'Happen there's your next plot.'

She regards him pensively.

'To be truthful, Inspector – I was thinking just that. Until –'

'Until what?'

'Until – a couple of hours later – I became disoriented on a mountain I ought to know like the back of my hand.'

'Even the shepherds struggle when they can't see which way's up.'

'And then Great Uncle Declan dies?' She looks imploringly from one detective to the other.

But Skelgill is unwilling to entertain this line of speculation. His face is the mask of a man who suspects he is being sold a tin of snake oil, albeit a by a salesperson whom he finds far from objectionable. He sits upright and folds his arms, and manifestly composes his features.

'I believe his collection of books is valuable.'

Perdita is quick to react to this change of tack; and her tone is cooperative.

'I'm sure it is, Inspector. It's a life's work.'

'Did he say anything about it?'

There is just the smallest hesitation while she brushes a strand of hair from her cheek.

'Now you mention it... not directly – but he did ask if I still have my Bible.'

'What's the significance of that?'

'Well – I don't remember this, of course – but when I was Christened he gave it as a present – he did so for each of my siblings – a valuable illuminated antique edition.'

'And do you still have it?'

She nods – now she smiles sadly.

'It has pride of place beside my bed.'

'And what did he say about it?'

'That was all, really – that was when he started to lecture me about my writing – he began to get agitated and shouted at me.'

'How did you respond?'

'I'm afraid I swore at him and stormed out. I told him he was a feckin dinosaur.' Now she combs the fingers of both hands through her hair, revealing small delicately pointed ears that contribute further to her elfin appearance. 'I've got a bit of a temper, now. It was with good reason that the others used to call me *Paddy* and not Perdy when I was a wee girl.'

Skelgill looks rather blank.

'I thought feckin wasn't considered as swearing.'

'Well, to be sure – in Ireland it's a regular minced oath – but it was the best compromise I could come up with at the time.'

Skelgill inhales pensively.

'Did you like him?'

'Great Uncle Declan? To be honest, Inspector – ridiculous as it might sound I didn't really know him – I've only met him on a handful of occasions since my childhood – and then barely to have a conversation. I was only three when my parents died – after that it was always Grandpa Sean who hosted us when we came for the holidays. Great Uncle Declan kept to himself, and you might not see him for days – except perhaps at a distance, out in the grounds with his binoculars.'

Skelgill seems more comfortable with this line of interrogation.

'So you left him, what time was that?'

'I was only at his study for a few minutes, Inspector – I should say, 11:50.'

'Did you see Thwaites?'

Now she appears puzzled.

'I don't believe I did – though you never know when he's secreted himself in that butler's pantry of his – Grandpa Sean used to tease us that there were spyholes and secret passageways – so the adults always knew what mischief you were up to.'

Skelgill follows her gaze as she turns to look at an oil painting hung to one side of the chimney breast. It is a full length rendering of a youngish man dressed in the manner of a country squire, with tweeds and a shotgun and a dog at his heel, a backdrop of forested fells that Skelgill does not recognise. The legend, hand painted on a brass nameplate, states 'Padraig Willoughby O'More, 1878-1949'. It is Perdita's great grandfather, a figure to whom she bears no great resemblance – except perhaps the dark eyes, which Skelgill scrutinises as if he half expects them to blink as a silent watcher lurks behind the wainscot.

'So, how come you're Irish?'

His question suggests his musings have been clambering about in the family tree.

'I'm one of those people for whom nationality is more difficult to define. My parents were English, naturally. Indeed, on the O'More side I don't think our branch has been born Irish for ten or more generations.' Now she grins rather impishly. 'But my mother contrived to be staying in Dublin with a distant cousin when I put in an unscheduled appearance. So I dropped a little anchor there. To be sure, much of my childhood was in

London – but at eighteen I returned to Ireland to read English literature at Trinity. I've lived in Dublin ever since – fifteen years altogether now, Inspector.'

It would be like Skelgill to be mulling over the respective merits of Britain and Ireland, and indeed his rejoinder confirms such.

'What do you reckon to it over here?'

His question, however, is ambiguous, for he could refer to the entire island of Great Britain, or to the more finite estate of Crummock Hall, or to anything on a sliding scale in between – England, Cumbria, The Lake District, the Vale of Lorton – but Perdita chooses to interpret his meaning as their present locus.

'I shudder to think of the upkeep, Inspector – but it's a house that holds a deep attraction for me – in spite of everything.'

Skelgill nods – as if he appreciates the rider. His manner becomes sympathetic.

'What will happen to the place now?'

'In what respect, Inspector?'

Skelgill pauses as he chooses his words.

'Your family solicitor told me about Sir Sean's will.'

'Oh – I see.' She meets his inquiring gaze with convincing inscrutability. 'I don't know what will happen, I'm afraid.'

'Don't you have to decide, as a family?'

Now she nods compliantly.

'On Saturday at dinner there was a lively debate, Inspector. Rather too lively – we agreed to postpone proceedings until Sunday night – but then of course there was Great Uncle Declan's death. Martius has proposed we each think about it and reconvene – in order to reach a consensus.'

'What's your vote?'

Skelgill's question is to the point. Accordingly there is something guarded about the way she allows her hair to fall across her face, forming a partial veil. Her tone becomes somewhat detached.

'It would be a shame to see the old hall go out of the family after three hundred years.'

'What about the others?'

Now she shrugs and inhales slowly, and lets out a small sigh.

'It's a matter of practicality, Inspector – they've forged their careers, made their lives – they're tied to London and its environs – nor has any of us been groomed, "to the manor born" – as the saying goes. It has always felt like Grandpa Sean and Great Uncle Declan would go on forever.'

Skelgill might be expected to press for her siblings' stated preferences – but there are times when he is obstinate if it means revealing something of his hand – and perhaps for this reason he changes tack.

'What are your plans?'

She glances at DS Jones – and for a moment her eyes linger upon the younger woman's athletic form – and then she turns her gaze back upon Skelgill.

'Well, to be sure, now – I was going to ask your advice, Inspector.'

'Aye?'

'You see, I've driven from Dublin – I came by car ferry to Liverpool. We're assuming there will be a funeral for Great Uncle Declan at the end of the week. I'd no sooner get home than I'd need to come back – so I was thinking I might as well stay.' She presses her palms together in the manner of prayer, and regards him with a supplicating stare. 'If you feel it is safe?'

Skelgill's posture stiffens just perceptibly. Her coyness aside, it is a challenging question: should he advise her to remain alone in this great rambling mansion where a murder has just been committed and no suspect identified?

'You might find it more agreeable down at the inn at Buttermere – I could have a quiet word with the landlord if they're busy with bookings – or I know folk hereabouts who'd open their B&B for you.'

Perdita responds with a gracious smile and a flicker of her lashes. It would appear to be an acceptance of his offer.

'I should like to do something for you, Inspector.' She sees uncertainty cloud Skelgill's eyes and qualifies her statement. 'For the mountain rescue – if you would recommend what would be an adequate donation for the trouble I caused – perhaps I could give you a cheque – if I could see you for a few moments before you depart?'

Skelgill is conscious of DS Jones's gaze upon him. He sweeps back his hair with the fingers of his left and then tugs at the knees of his trousers as he rises. It seems he is ready to conclude the interview.

'The team's funded by the generosity of the public – they'd have my guts for garters if I don't take your hand off.'

'Inspector, then I shall trust your bite is not as sharp as your bark.'

6. MARTIUS – Monday 10.45am

'Reckon I was hard on her, Jones?'

DS Jones breaks away from her examination of the clock in the late Declan Thomas O'More's study. Such soul-searching is not a sentiment she would normally associate with Skelgill, however minor. He has his back to her as he peruses the bookshelves that line the opposite wall.

'Perdita? Not really, Guv – I would have said the opposite – especially considering what she said about the argument – and her temper – and that she's the only person other than the butler who admits to seeing Declan yesterday.'

Skelgill appears reluctant to turn face about. He continues to stare at the rows of books, and folds his arms. He and DS Jones have ducked under the police tape in the hallway and entered with the key obtained from the safekeeping of DS Leyton. It seems that Skelgill wanted to inspect the clock before enlightening his colleague. Now she is apprised of his conundrum: that despite the forensic photographer's unequivocal image of the old timepiece stopped at 12 noon, when Skelgill arrived the hands (he swears) were pointing to 2 o'clock. If only he had photographed it as well as the logbook. Slowly and deliberately he places a finger on the spine of a Wainwright, as though by touching it he makes some psychic connection.

'Fact is, Jones – we've got her distress call logged at 1:45 – plus we'd used a search and rescue app to get her grid reference – so the pilot knew where to drop us. If 2 o'clock is the real time of the murder, she was the best part of an hour's yomp away – and that's on a summer's day.'

DS Jones regards her boss uneasily.

'Are you certain, Guv? I mean – 2 o'clock could easily look like ten past twelve – or even just twelve at a glance.'

Now Skelgill spins on his heel. There is a wild cast in his eyes and though he glares in the direction of his colleague he seems to see straight through her.

'Come here, Jones.'

He gestures with a cursory flick of his fingers, and then he drags the chair away from the desk and opens the journal that still lies upon the blotter. He locates the most recent entry, and taps the page. DS Jones joins him at his side, and obediently reads.

'What is it, Guv?'

'It's Declan's bird log.' He stands back. 'Look at the times.'

DS Jones pores over Sunday's entry. Then she starts as the implications strike home.

'He went bird-watching between 11.55am and 1.35pm?'

'And he had time to write up his notes.'

DS Jones begins to leaf back through the pages.

'This *is* genuine, Guv?'

'Jones – keep going and you'll find the birds he spotted on your birthday – and I mean *birth* day. It's genuine, aye.'

She looks up at her superior.

'So Declan couldn't have been killed at noon?'

Skelgill's features are a grim mask. He need not reply.

'Guv – do you think someone changed the clock – turned it back two hours?'

'I *know* someone changed the clock.'

DS Jones pushes off from the desk, rounds it and takes a few steps across the room. The carpet has been removed for forensic examination, and her heels rap on the polished wooden boards. She places her hands on her hips and considers again the clock, head tilted to one side. She is wearing a crop-cut leather jacket and matching pointed ankle boots, and stretch black jeans – an ensemble that accentuates her figure and makes her look rather less of a sensible detective sergeant and more like a sexy biker chick. Skelgill's eyes narrow as he follows her movements.

'Why would they do that, Guv?'

Her question breaks his reverie, though he blinks several times before he can fashion a reply. And, true to type, he immediately rows back from the premise she might wish to propound.

'Playing silly buggers.'

DS Jones spins on her heel, drawing a squeal of protest from the floorboard beneath. She is frowning – but prudently she resists the urge to gainsay him. Instead she moves on to what is the next logical question.

'When could it have been done, Guv?'

Skelgill inhales deeply, in the manner of a reformed smoker, and pulls his gaze away from his colleague. He closes the logbook and gently pats its worn leather binding.

'Take charge of this.'

'Will do.' But she waits unmoving for Skelgill's reply.

After a moment he looks up, his features a little strained. 'I arrived at three. I reckon I was in here for fifteen minutes. The garden door was fastened, the key blocking the lock – so there was no way in from the outside. I locked the hall door and took the key. I gave it to Leyton when the crew arrived about an hour later.'

'So – between 3:15 and 4:15?'

'Aye.'

'And there's no spare key?'

Skelgill grimaces.

'Not according to Thwaites.'

DS Jones turns up the palms of her hands.

'It seems unlikely, Guv.'

But Skelgill continues to scowl. He may be playing devil's advocate – though he shows no inclination to inspect the panelled walls or the bookcases for some mysterious secret door. Now DS Jones folds her arms, her brow becoming furrowed.

'The times in the logbook, Guv – they also mean Dr Herdwick's assessment is wrong.'

Skelgill emits a scornful exclamation.

'Wouldn't be the first time he's skimped on a Sunday. He likes his pint in The Queen's Arms.'

'Doesn't he go to Evensong – I heard he was in the church choir?'

'Aye – you and his missus.'

DS Jones raises her eyebrows – but her tone is forgiving.

'I suppose he did say there were variables that made it difficult to be accurate – the age of the victim and the room temperature falling significantly after the fire burned down.'

Skelgill glances cursorily at the hearth; cold grey ash is all that remains of what might have been a sizeable blaze – it is something he ought to confirm with Thwaites.

'Jones – if the murder took place at 2 p.m. Perdita is in the clear.'

DS Jones nods pensively. She inhales to speak but then she checks herself.

'Aye?'

She half turns away and slides her hands into her midriff pockets, her elbows angular.

'I've read most of her books, Guv.'

'And?'

'She's a good writer.' DS Jones looks down and reflectively kicks one sharp toe of a boot against the other. 'The plots are a bit clichéd – beautiful downtrodden mistress of the house falls for hunk of a manservant – but they kind of draw you in and you feel like you're there – amidst the sweat and the fear of the slaves.'

'Sounds like our HQ.'

DS Jones chuckles.

'She calls the setting the Venusian Islands – an archipelago in the Caribbean. Fictitious I suppose.'

Skelgill is swiftly losing interest. But now DS Jones seems to want to make the point that she had hesitated over, and he reads sufficient of her body language to offer a prompt.

'What, Jones?'

'It's just that –' She casts a tentative sideways look, as if she anticipates his disapproval. 'You would think to meet Perdita she's not got a bad bone in her body.'

'Aye?'

'But as Rowena Devlin – I'd say she's pretty ruthless, Guv.'

Her unintended oxymoron seems to captivate Skelgill – his gaze now drifts away, to the view through the nearest of the two windows. There is little to see but snow and conifers, though he stares unblinking – until his musings are interrupted by an impatient rap upon the door. Without invitation it opens and – to Skelgill's evident dismay – a man peremptorily enters and marches towards him. Skelgill shoots out a palm at arm's length, like a traffic policeman warning a renegade motorist to halt.

'Hey up, pal – this is a crime scene!'

The interloper stops dead in his tracks, but his obvious agitation only becomes compounded. He thrusts his hands onto his hips and tilts forwards at the waist. It is Martius Regulus-O'More, the man who had first admitted him to Crummock Hall yesterday.

'Inspector – this is my... my *home*!'

Skelgill for a second seems to waver – a rekindled sense, perhaps, of his destiny to serve. His reply is stilted.

'I shall have to ask you to leave the room.'

But it is plain that Martius is determined to stand his ground.

'Look here, Inspector – this is becoming intolerable – I can't just wait while you and your colleagues sit around drinking tea – I have an important dinner at Guildhall this evening.'

Indeed, he is wearing a camel polo coat and a pinstripe suit beneath, as though he might be due at his City of London office any minute. His unseasonal suntan apart, his features are rather nondescript, and bear little similitude with striking younger sister Perdita. His fairish hair is combed back from a receding hairline, and held by a slick of cream. Close set mid-blue eyes, rosebud mouth, small nose and weak chin – they cluster in Churchillian surroundings. It is not a face built to strike fear into an opponent – a stark contrast to Skelgill's rugged countenance. But his inner seething boils over as a froth of spittle at the corners of his mouth.

Skelgill does not immediately reply, and in this hiatus Martius notices DS Jones, who stands a couple of yards apart. He regards her with equal hostility, but cannot conceal a sly hunger in his eyes, and his gaze lingers excessively. It sparks Skelgill's intervention.

'Aye – tea's a thought. Jones – see if you can rustle up Thwaites while I have a word with Mr Regulus-O'More. Get him to take it to the drawing room. I'll lock up here – for what it's worth.'

Martius bridles as DS Jones nods obediently and slips quickly past them. That this uncouth officer, who barefacedly requisitions Crummock Hall's services, exposes his covetousness serves only to stoke his ire. He appraises Skelgill's outfit disparagingly, and his polished tone ascends to a new level of outrage.

'Didn't I see you at the funeral?'

His delivery might have been more fitting had he accused Skelgill of urinating into a potted plant. Skelgill's reply is forced between gritted teeth.

'I was representing Cumbria Constabulary – Sir Sean O'More was a supporter of our charity, Care of Police Survivors.'

Martius's reaction is one of indifference. Skelgill has wondered if he would be recognised – not merely from the funeral, but from times long past. As the eldest of the family – in fact two years his senior – Martius would be most likely to remember him. But if he does, he shows no inclination to renew what was a tenuous acquaintance, Skelgill a mere irritant, some unwashed juvenile itinerant who had the cheek to sneak about their property and entertain his more gullible siblings with lizards and newts and birds' eggs, or whatever else he had in his grubby pocket that particular day.

'This is preposterous. We need to know when our great uncle can be buried. I shall complain to the relevant authority.'

His demeanour does not soften. But then neither does Skelgill's.

'You were the first to come into the study, sir?'

By means of the ostensibly deferential title 'sir' – employed for the first time – Skelgill contrives to create the impression that Martius is being questioned under caution. The man might be on home turf, but Skelgill has authority on his side. And Martius shows himself to be uneasy.

'Yes – well, no – not before Thwaites – he found the body. And then Cassandra alerted me – look, I have already provided this information to some overweight buffoon of a sergeant.'

The fingers of Skelgill's left hand, hanging slack at his side, twitch. And perhaps his eyes measure the distance to the chin of Martius Regulus-O'More. If so, the latter cannot appreciate quite how close he is to an impromptu nap. When Perdita confessed to possessing a combustible temper, Skelgill's ears were surely burning. In an ideal world he would offer a withering verbal riposte – but this is not his forte. Never mind that he is no match for a man for whom debating in some august hall came as part and parcel of his expensive education. By comparison, such scholarly disagreements as Skelgill experienced were settled behind rusting cycle sheds with a rather less urbane exchange of oaths and fists. Yet perhaps some inkling of this inequality is conveyed across the class divide, for Martius breaks the silence.

'I'd jolly well like to know what you're doing to catch this intruder – hadn't you better unleash your bloodhounds – or whatever the heck you get up to in the sticks?'

Despite the incremental slur, Skelgill suppresses a small smirk of satisfaction.

'There's no evidence to suggest it was an intruder, sir.'

For a moment Martius appears confounded. Now a hint of alarm, a hunted look, even, narrows his eyes.

'Don't be ridiculous, man – who else could it have been? There is clearly a lunatic at large.'

Skelgill is implacable.

'Did you move the body at all, sir?'

'Of course not – it was plain he was stone cold dead.'

Despite his tone – which remains at once insulting and tinged with dissent – that he has answered tells he understands that cooperation is the prudent exit strategy.

'What about ornaments, furniture – did you disturb anything?'

'I had neither desire nor opportunity – Cassandra was half... half hysterical,' (*hysterical* is evidently not the word that first came to mind), 'And Edgar appeared looking like he'd seen a ghost – I shepherded her out and sent Edgar to phone 999.'

Skelgill gestures casually towards the garden door.

'What about that door, sir – was it locked?'

Martius turns and glares in the direction indicated.

'What? Yes – no – I don't know – I locked it.'

'You don't sound sure, sir.'

With a scowl Martius wipes perspiration from his upper lip.

'I can't remember – it might already have been locked – I checked it and I know it was locked when we left the room – when Edgar returned from the lobby I told him to go round the whole place and make sure all the entrances were secured.'

'Then what did you do?'

'I took a shotgun and we gathered in the drawing room. It wasn't so long after that you made your dramatic entrance. Lucky for you I didn't have it to hand when you kicked in the door.'

Skelgill does not respond to this latest slight.

'Thwaites tells us there are no spare keys – in particular for this study.'

'I wouldn't have the faintest idea – thankfully I only visit the damned place once in a blue moon.'

Now Skelgill affects surprise.

'I'd have thought you'd be looking to take over, sir – as the eldest of the family.'

Martius recoils, his expression instantly belittling.

'Don't make me laugh, Inspector – have you the first idea about estate management? Crummock Hall barely washes its face – the electricity bill alone probably exceeds your salary.'

There is another twitch from Skelgill's left hand and his eyelids momentarily droop. Perhaps he sees in his mind's eye a little fantasy – if so, it seems to placate him sufficiently to terminate the encounter, surely for the benefit of them both. He moves across to the study door and opens it, standing aside to indicate that the man should depart.

'Be good enough to keep us informed if you intend to leave the country – that will be all for now, Mr Regulus-O'More.'

'It's just Regulus, I'll have you know – Martius Regulus.'

7. CASSANDRA – Monday 11am

'You okay, Guv?'

'Aye.'

But Skelgill is sullen; DS Jones hesitates.

'You just look a bit... peaky.'

Uncharitably, he shrugs off her concern.

'I could murder a cuppa.'

'It's on the table by the fire, Guv.'

Skelgill inclines his head in acknowledgement but makes no move in that direction. Instead he saunters across to the grand piano where the family photographs are arrayed. He selects another group portrait; the children are older in this, ranging from an imperious Martius at perhaps sixteen down to impish Perdita at ten. It would likely have been the final year that they came. The photographer has induced cheesy grins, but there is a certain strain in their eyes; only young Perdita seems truly at ease, and Edgar does not even smile.

'Memory lane, Daniel?'

Skelgill swings round. Rosy blotches begin to break out at his cheekbones. Enter Cassandra.

Although it is yet mid-morning she carries a half drunk aperitif in her left hand and a cigarette trailing smoke in her right. Before Skelgill can speak she has accosted him – he still holds the framed picture, two-handed, defensively – but she is long-limbed for a woman, almost his height, and before he can react she leans in and plants an air-kiss on either cheek, while he stands stiffly to attention, as though immobilised by her fragrance. DS Jones, who has correctly interpreted Skelgill's implied command to pour his tea, gazes with some amazement – such that Cassandra throws her a line of explanation.

'One never forgets one's first crush, darling.'

DS Jones instinctively returns the woman's amiable grin – but she becomes aware of a glowering Skelgill and ducks back into her duties. Skelgill mutters under his breath, a rejoinder intended for Cassandra's ears only.

'I shouldn't like to have overstepped the mark.'

'Oh yes you would, Daniel!' Now Cassandra lets loose a peal of liquid laughter. 'But I shall spare your blushes – I can see your colleague already has ample ammunition to embarrass you back at your headquarters.'

She understands that she should be seated opposite DS Jones, and she floats across the carpet marooning Skelgill like a tardy cockle picker consumed by the flood tide, uncertain which direction offers a sure footing. She flicks her cigarette into the fire and declines graciously as DS Jones motions the offer of tea. Of an age with Skelgill she has worn well, as the saying goes, and sports the smooth sun-kissed skin and glossy hair that speak of a privileged lifestyle. In her features there is a marked likeness to brother Martius, though she lacks his incipient corpulence, and in consequence her proportions seem more regular and appealing. Her hair is shoulder length, blonde streaked with gold and bronze highlights, natural enough looking, but exposed as an expensive coiffure by the photograph, which reveals her at fourteen to be a brunette. She settles back into the familiar curves of the sofa, seemingly unconcerned that her cocktail dress rides up to reveal more of her tawny thighs.

There could now be some cause and effect at play, for Skelgill wrenches himself free of his inertia. Rather uncharacteristically he seems self-conscious about his attire – his faded ski trousers and creased lumberjack shirt of his rescue mission yesterday – and he wades ponderously to sit beside DS Jones. But Cassandra pays no heed to such trivia, and engages him expectantly, her lips parted to signal her anticipation. He lifts his cup without the saucer and takes a couple of big gulps. Then he wipes his mouth on his cuff. He seems lost for somewhere to begin. DS Jones is looking at him – also willing him, it seems, to make the first move. At last he appears to realise he is still clinging to the photograph. Now he raises it rather absently.

'I believe it's some time since you were in these parts.'

That he omits his customary 'Madam' – but also refrains from using her name – is a further indication of his discomfited state.

'A good decade – I last visited Crummock Hall with my first husband, the late Freddy Remington-Smythe.' She takes a decorous sip of her drink. 'He was trampled by his horse, poor fellow.'

Skelgill looks none the wiser. DS Jones has placed the notes from DS Leyton's initial interviews on the table between them, and now he leans to squint at the top sheet.

'We have you down as Cassandra Goodchild – I take it that's from your second marriage?'

Now she regards him rather coyly.

'Third, actually.' She tips her head briefly to one side – it is a gesture of *mea culpa* – and raises her glass in a 'cheers' motion. 'I don't mind admitting – in town it's a name that opens doors – and comes with an account at *Harrods* – so I've hung onto this one – if not the husband.' She winks ostentatiously, and the detectives would be forgiven for thinking the cocktail is not her first of the morning.

'You're more at home in London.'

Skelgill's remark is bland, but she looks puzzled – as if she has never seriously considered the idea.

'Oh, I don't know – when I think back to our salad days. Nanny read us *Swallows and Amazons* and we believed it was about us.' She turns earnestly to DS Jones – politely acknowledging that she is the newcomer to the situation. 'Until the accident: a rather unpalatable dose of reality. And such bad luck – Daddy came so rarely.'

There is a silence, until Skelgill finds a few words of commiseration.

'Can't have been easy – for children to understand.'

She tosses her hair and simultaneously closes her eyes, as if the action will dislodge a long-filed memory.

'In some respects it was not so difficult. I was only seven and had already been despatched to prep school. Up until then I saw more of Nanny than my parents – what with Mummy treading the boards so successfully, she was often working away. And Daddy was home even less so – he had an apartment near his office and a regular seat on *Concorde*.'

Skelgill is gnawing pensively at a thumbnail.

'What happened after – the accident?'

'In spite of this place the O'Mores were forever on their uppers – while the Regulus clan had oodles of cash. So we were nominally brought up in London under the eye of a maiden aunt – though a good part of the year was spent at boarding school. We still came here for summer – but there arrives the day when the lure of London society trumps the joy of squelching about in soggy wellingtons – notwithstanding the local attractions.'

Now she casts a conspiratorial glance at DS Jones, who in turn looks at Skelgill – but he is pretending to read the notes, and indeed rather disjointedly he jumps to matters of the present.

'Your great uncle was definitely attacked. Can you think of any reason why someone might have done that?'

'Miss Scarlett with a candlestick in the study.'

Her glib retort catches him off guard. He looks up with a jolt, but Cassandra is already sipping demurely at her drink, a mischievous glint in her eye.

'Come again?'

'Well – the study is correct, at least – but, seriously, *Inspector*,' (she puts emphasis upon his title) 'I haven't a clue – aren't you the expert in these parts? Surely you have a suitable village idiot you can scapegoat?'

Skelgill deposits the photograph and notes on the coffee table and sits back rather woodenly.

'Happen we haven't ruled that out.' He darts a sideways look at DS Jones, as if he seeks corroboration. 'But there's no evidence it was an intruder, I'm afraid.'

'Then I suggest you look among the domestics – Thwaites has always been a shifty character.' But she makes a doubting click of her tongue. 'Though he hardly has the strength to mix a gin and tonic – so he might be eliminated. However, I don't imagine the prospect of Great Uncle Declan as master of the hall filled the staff with glee, no matter how short lived his tenure was to be.'

Her somewhat blasé acceptance of the idea that the crime is an 'inside job' is in marked contrast to her elder

73

brother's indignation, and seems to contribute further to Skelgill's unusually tense manner.

'What will become of the place now?'

She appears surprised that he asks this, and regards him more closely, as though she suspects some disingenuousness on his part.

'Oh – we have to decide – don't you know? Stick or twist.'

He looks rather pained.

'And what's your inclination?'

'Oh, I'm not the gambler in the family.' She chuckles mysteriously. 'But it doesn't matter what I think, Inspector – I'm sure Martius will have his way – whatever that turns out to be.'

Skelgill nods. He already has a good idea of what Martius Regulus-O'More thinks of the financial viability of Crummock Hall. Meanwhile Cassandra drains the last of her cocktail, and then slides the glass onto the table, a slow, deliberate movement that draws his eye. In bending forwards she exposes sufficient of her cleavage to suggest that her bra – if she even wears one – is of a decidedly low cut variety. Somewhat languidly she stretches and reclines into the sofa, like a cat that has determined to make itself comfortable beside the hearth. There is a healthy blaze burning in the grate and, while the room is cool, the radiated heat warms them. Skelgill is overdressed – although it may not be the sole cause of his flushed complexion.

Indeed, now he rises and restores the photograph to its place on the grand piano by the window. He turns and rather formally addresses Cassandra.

'I think that will be all for now.'

Again he drops 'Madam' or 'Miss' or some version of her name, and she seems amused by this omission. With a degree of reluctance she rises and straightens her hem. She nods politely to DS Jones, and begins to move away from the settee, leaving her empty glass upon the table. She stops at the point of equidistance between the exit and Skelgill.

'I shouldn't imagine you have finished with me yet, Inspector.'

Her tone hints at disappointment – and there is a certain regal insistence that she expects him to take her statement as a command. Skelgill clears his throat.

'What are your travel plans?'

She shrugs casually.

'Oh, I expect Edgar has arranged the train up to London – though of course we shall need to return for the second funeral.'

Skelgill nods – he seems a little relieved that she provides this get-out.

'We'll keep that in mind, then.'

She smiles with satisfaction and gives a little bow of her head, maintaining eye contact as she slowly turns and drifts towards the door. She begins to hum a tune, and then – just before the click of the latch cuts her off – she breaks into song, a pleasant voice, clear, almost angelic – and there comes the line, *"Or when the valley's hushed and white with snow."*

DS Jones glances at Skelgill; she catches his expression – at once sheepish and remorseful.

'What is it, Guv?'

Now he glowers and turns to stare out of the window.

'Danny Boy.'

8. THE TWINS – Monday 11.15am

Skelgill's first impression of Brutus is coloured by DS Jones's reaction, which it is plain she tries to suppress. Shock and awe overtakes her features and she sinks onto the settee – whereupon she scrabbles for their papers and buries her head in an exaggerated pursuit of some point. Skelgill becomes immediately suspicious. Certainly the fellow is handsome, despite bearing something of the family resemblance – however, in contrast to his elder brother and sister his physiognomy is altogether more sculpted; beneath dark wavy hair worn boyishly, angled brows, high cheekbones and an aquiline nose combine with tanned skin and a carefully cultivated five-o'clock shadow to create a Mediterranean appearance. Yet it is a look strikingly offset by piercing powder-blue eyes that seem to penetrate the thoughts of those upon whom they settle. His physique is trim, his musculature revealed by informal but expensive attire, a skin-tight black merino pullover, and snug stressed skinny jeans that do not leave a great deal to the imagination. Despite heeled boots he is probably an inch or two below average height – but it is no impediment to his self-confidence, and he carries himself with a certain swaggering narcissism.

Indeed, his natural expression is pre-set at the hint of a smirk, and it is thus that he regards DS Jones, while paying lip service to Skelgill's introduction. Once seated, his gaze unashamedly wanders to appraise her, apparently intrigued that she could be a police officer. He is further amused when she wriggles out of her leather jacket and twists her slender waist to lay the garment over the back of the sofa. She fans herself with the sheaf of notes, and casts a resigned glance towards the hearth.

It is possible, of course, that Skelgill's antennae have become over-sensitised: engaging in quick succession with Perdita, Martius and then Cassandra he has ridden a testing rollercoaster – and first impressions of Brutus offer little prospect of respite. However, he seems more than content to follow the undulating pattern and dispense with any niceties as far as Brutus is concerned.

'You gave Sergeant Leyton an account of your movements yesterday – basically that you were in bed until you went to the drawing room at 2.30pm.'

Skelgill's tone is loaded with doubt – but Brutus merely yawns, as if theatrically to illustrate his response.

'I'm in the *Guinness Book of Records* for late afternoon lies, Inspector.' He flashes an insouciant glance at DS Jones. 'I imagine the lack of company eventually drove me downstairs.'

Skelgill declines to acknowledge the lascivious insinuation.

'So you're not in a position to corroborate the movements of other members of the household – prior to the discovery of your great uncle's body?'

Brutus's smirk extends upwards from the corners of his mouth.

'Surely you wouldn't expect me to snitch on one of my siblings?'

'I'd expect you to tell me the truth, sir – it's an offence to obstruct an investigation, as I'm sure you're aware.'

'I am being facetious, Inspector – I don't for a moment believe my family had anything to do with Great Uncle Declan's death.'

He leans forwards and regards Skelgill with a certain curiosity – as if he is assimilating the details of his character for a future role – a rather slow-witted country detective, blind to the shortcomings of his parochial existence.

Skelgill obligingly conforms to this stereotype.

'Who might you suggest then, sir?'

Again there is a conspiratorial glance from Brutus at DS Jones – an invitation to join a game of bluff for their mutual entertainment. He flexes his biceps, and tilts backwards, hands behind his head, leaning against the threadbare silk antimacassar in order to contemplate the ornate ceiling – though its gilt paintwork is in need of restoration. Then he jerks upright, articulating at the waist, demonstrating impressive abdominal control. His features are quite transformed – perhaps it is the actor's practised malleability – for now he presents a most forthcoming countenance, a little excited even.

'What about old Gilhooley? I saw him and that hideous wife of his gloating from their pew at Grandpa Sean's funeral – perhaps he thought he'd sneak in and finish the job. Wasn't there a family feud – generations back?'

Skelgill looks irked – and perhaps it can be deduced that here is a fragment of local knowledge of which he ought to be in possession (but is not). Indeed, his next question, couched with casual indifference, could be a crafty attempt to appear better informed.

'What do you know about it?'

Brutus gives a flick of his hair and grins at DS Jones; she responds with an encouraging nod.

'As youngsters we were warned not to stray onto their land – up through the oak woods. The story rang like something out of Brothers Grimm – the old crone was barren and on the lookout for a child to misappropriate.'

Skelgill shakes his head dismissively.

'More likely you were told that because there's a dangerous pit up there – Lanthwaite zinc mine. To scare you away.'

Brutus shrugs nonchalantly.

'Well, I rather liked the notion of a gingerbread house – so the threat was counterproductive as far as I was concerned – much to Gerbil's dismay.'

At this unexplained reference – to *Gerbil* – Skelgill seems to register some recognition; however he declines to become sidetracked.

'And if it's not the Gilhooleys?'

Now Brutus reiterates what is emerging as the family line.

'I buy into Mart's random intruder theory – what other explanation could there be? Aggravated burglary, you call it, I believe?'

'There's no indication of anything being taken.'

'Perhaps the fellow panicked before he could bag the O'More silver plate.'

'The evidence points to your great uncle as the target.'

Brutus tosses his head rather indifferently.

'He was a reclusive old stick – it's hard to imagine why anyone would want to bump him off.'

'What did you do yesterday afternoon?'

Brutus unhurriedly settles back into the sofa and folds his hands upon his stomach. It is the demeanour of a diner, replete having consumed a sumptuous meal.

'Of course – you arrived in some style not long after I had joined the others.' He squints at Skelgill with affected admiration. 'We decided we no longer needed the protection of Mart and his gun – so I hopped into bed with Cassie.'

A flicker of disapproval creases Skelgill's features, which seems further to please Brutus.

'To keep warm, naturally.' He winks at DS Jones. 'This old place gives one the shivers at the best of times – and Cassie has commandeered the only electric blanket. Not to mention the brandy. A conjunction of kindred spirits, one might say.'

Skelgill regards him obdurately.

'I believe you're travelling back to London by train with your elder sister and twin brother?'

'Oh, I don't doubt Gerbil has it all arranged – seating plan and all.' He pouts, as though he is bored by this idea. 'But I am considering otherwise.'

'Why is that, sir?'

Languorously Brutus stretches out his legs before him, admiring his own form – then he glances sharply at DS Jones and catches her watching him. She averts her eyes and he smirks with satisfaction.

'Oh – I'm resting until late January – London's one big party in the run-up to Christmas – I might give the old liver a break and stick around for a while.' He looks pointedly at DS Jones. 'See what I've been missing all these years.'

Skelgill's expression has been progressively darkening, but now he is distracted by a tentative knock on the door, followed by the appearance around its edge of the anxious-looking face of DS Leyton.

'Sorry, Guv – word in your shell-like?'

Skelgill hesitates. Then he begins to rise, and glares at DS Jones. Without excusing himself he stalks across the room and exits, keeping hold of the handle and pulling the door not quite to behind him. DS Leyton hovers close by.

'What is it?'

'Thought I should let you know, Guv.' DS Leyton clears his throat and inhales rather wheezily, as though he has come along at a lick and has yet to recover his breath.

'I've had Thwaites looking around in the study – like you said.'

'Aye?'

'Nothing gone what you'd call valuable – not that he'll admit to – but there is one thing.'

Skelgill is agitated and not properly concentrating. He cocks an ear to the crack in the door, for voices now emanate from within.

'Get to the point, Leyton.'

DS Leyton wipes his brow but it is more of a nervous tic.

'Seems old Declan kept a favourite walking stick beside the garden door of his study.' DS Leyton has his notebook in one hand and now he refers briefly to it. 'Antique – made from the root of sandalwood. Thwaites reckons he called it his *shillelagh* – Irish, know what I mean? Just the ticket for bashing someone's brains in. And it ain't there, Guv.'

Skelgill, still trying to eavesdrop, is forced to pay full attention to DS Leyton.

'What about Forensics?'

His question might seem oblique, but he refers to a small arsenal of ancient weapons removed from the walls of Crummock Hall for testing, should they reveal fingerprints or traces of blood and DNA. The act was perhaps optimistic – it seems improbable that a murderer might have returned his weapon to its display.

'I just called 'em – they've drawn a blank on the gear they took. Odds on it's the shillelagh, Guv?'

Skelgill grimaces.

'We're talking needle and haystack until this snow melts.'

DS Leyton nods glumly.

'Even worse if it's sunk in the lake, Guv.'

'Leyton –'

A burst of laughter from the drawing room diverts Skelgill from an unjust (and perhaps misinformed) rebuke of his sergeant for his stupidity concerning the relative densities of sandalwood and water. Instead he begins to push open the door and back away.

'You know what we're looking for, Leyton.'

'Righto, Guv – what shall I tell –'

But Skelgill turns and re-enters the drawing room. His alarm intensifies – for DS Jones is standing alongside Brutus before the hearth, and the pair step apart for all the world as though they have just taken a selfie, and that DS Jones is surreptitiously slipping her mobile phone into her back pocket. Her cheeks seem to colour, but Brutus shows no such discomfiture, and indeed saunters to intercept Skelgill.

'I was just telling your colleague,' he bows and makes something of an ostentatious sweep of the hand in the direction of DS Jones, '*Emma* – that should you ever be in town and wish to get tickets for the West End, I have some exceptionally reliable connections – all above board, naturally – and tables at the top restaurants.'

While he beams widely, Skelgill cannot conceal his displeasure – that Brutus has induced DS Jones to introduce herself – but before he can fashion some appropriate complaint the man melodramatically launches into a suggestion.

'One can't help drawing the parallel between our situation and *The Mousetrap*.'

'What?'

'I refer not to the anti-rodent device – but to the Christie play, of course. A gathering entombed by the snow in a great country house – the dramatic arrival on skis of the local police detective.'

Skelgill senses he is being filibustered – but before he can muster a response Brutus makes a telling quip.

'And we all know who did that one, don't we?'

This draws a compliant chuckle from DS Jones, and Brutus glances at her rather proprietorially. Skelgill, for his part, simply bristles – and, if he has any more questions, puts them into abeyance. He folds his arms and draws himself up to his full height, as if to emphasise his advantage in this minor respect.

'An important piece of information has just reached us.' He inclines his head in the direction of the door. 'I shall need to discuss this with Detective Sergeant Jones.' His enunciation of her title carries extra stress.

Brutus understands he is being dismissed. However, he nods gracefully at Skelgill, as though acknowledging the officer's profound thanks for his assistance – and bows again to DS Jones, who stands a little unbalanced, cross-legged and with her hands behind her back. To Skelgill's eye she appears to respond with a flutter of her lashes.

As soon as Brutus has left the room and closed the door behind him, Skelgill rounds to face his colleague. He thrusts his hands into his pockets and glares at her as though he expects her to wilt beneath his gaze. But though she is certainly red-faced there is some stronger urge that gets the better of her.

'Guv – you know who that *is?*'

'Aye. Brutus Regulus-O'More. Smarmy little git.'

But DS Jones is undeterred by Skelgill's antagonism.

'You must have heard of Owain Jagger?'

'I've heard of owing money.'

It is plain he is being uncooperative, and DS Jones smiles patiently.

'He plays the heartthrob in the new TV adaptation of *Empty Hollow* – he's been on all the chat-shows – he's all over the media – the magazines – and the newspapers.'

Skelgill glowers disparagingly.

'Not the *Angling Times*, he's not.'

If Edgar Regulus-O'More is not actually smaller than his identical twin Brutus, then here is a phenomenon that would fascinate the psychologists: that persona alone can manifest itself in physical impression. Where Brutus exudes a powerful aura of suave self-confidence, projecting his presence upon those around him, Edgar is but a pale shadow of his photogenic brother, a sterile doppelganger stripped of make-up, wig and costume. Thus, while Skelgill is no great student of character – preferring to judge people on what they *do*, rather than what they pretend – the stereotypes of actor and accountant must seem apposite.

The man wears a grey business suit that is a tad too roomy – off-the-peg when he could surely afford bespoke? – and wire-framed NHS-style spectacles with circular lenses. His features certainly match those of his twin, but his complexion is wan and his countenance lifeless, his eyes less piercing. But the most striking contrast is that he ignores the presence of DS Jones entirely.

He perches upon the edge of the settee in a way that makes the onlooker feel uncomfortable – like a person who keeps on a coat indoors. He chooses the position directly opposite Skelgill, and a silence descends upon the trio. Edgar stares, unblinking. His only movement is the twitching of his fingers – nails bitten short – upon his knees. It would not at this moment seem untoward if he were suddenly to blurt out, "I did it – *I* murdered my great uncle."

Into this stand off, Skelgill rolls a little hand grenade.

'Why do they call you *Gerbil?*'

Edgar's features are now revealed to be capable of hidden depths of expression, contorting as though he literally swallows some bitter pill. For a fleeting moment there is a much closer likeness to his twin. His fingers pinch into the cloth of his trousers.

'It is not *they*, Inspector – it is Brutus – the others let it drop twenty-five years ago.'

Skelgill leans forwards with interest, and this action is sufficient to encourage Edgar to continue.

'It was when we were at prep school in Surrey. I was aged about seven. Despite our academic differences they always placed us in the same form.' He sniffs dismissively, his gaze fixed on the table between them. 'One day Brutus and I were given permission to play with the class pet. Two pupils, and one... gerbil.' He swallows, his mouth suddenly dry. 'The equation doesn't resolve – small mammals being indivisible, unlike whole numbers.' He removes his spectacles and rubs an eye with the heel of one hand. 'We lifted the lid of the cage and simultaneously made a grab for the creature as it darted from its lair. Brutus has always been damned careless. I got the body. Brutus got the tail. Except he wouldn't let go.'

At this juncture DS Jones – perhaps still star-struck, and thus not fully in command of her faculties – is unable to suppress an involuntary giggle. Edgar affects not to notice. Skelgill, meanwhile, is more interested in the outcome of the tug-of-war.

'So what – the tail came off?'

Edgar nods helplessly.

'I don't mean the entire structure – the bone – but the sheath of skin and fur was stripped clean away – in a split second.'

'Aye – it would be a natural defence against predators.'

Edgar regards Skelgill with what is a look of gratitude.

'Precisely, Inspector – in time it grew back – but can you believe we were *both* caned for that? *I* – caned for my brother's selfishness.'

His resentment is plain for all to see – but his story does not end here. There is the legacy.

'The caning lasted five minutes and my buttocks were raw for a week. However, Brutus contrived to tar me with the brush of his misdeed – and the epithet *Gerbil*. It was a nickname that quickly gained traction and he made sure it stuck. I had to carry it all through my school years – and to this day he resurrects it whenever he can.'

Skelgill creases his brow in sympathy, and spreads his palms in a way to suggest there is a silver lining – but it is his hunter's instinct at play.

'At least you did catch the actual gerbil, sir.'

For a moment Edgar appears annoyed – that Skelgill has missed the overarching point and prefers to champion a pyrrhic victory. But, as DS Leyton has noted, Edgar is the least combative among the Regulus-O'More clan, and after a little consideration he nods ruefully. Skelgill, meanwhile, stares blankly at him (which must be disconcerting) – but in fact he replays distant memories: of Lakeland summer days, the long school vacation, when he would observe from some heathery hidey hole or treetop vantage point as the children played a game of tag or rounders or unruly clacking croquet, calling one another's names aloud – diminutives as they have been employing during these interviews: Mart or Marty, Cass or Cassie, Perdy, and Teddy for Edgar – but, yes, there was the occasional shrill, *"Gerbil you're pathetic!"* yelled out in a boy's treble. Brutus.

'You were first to find the body, sir.'

It is a statement rather than a question – but Edgar jolts and seems to shrink into himself. His rejoinder is hasty.

'No – no, Inspector – the others were before me. Martius and Cassandra were there with Thwaites.'

Skelgill looks baffled and gathers up the notes and glances cursorily at the top page, affecting to read.

'Aye – my mistake – that's right – that fits in with what the others said. Did they call you directly?'

Edgar shakes his head.

'I heard raised voices – I have set up office in the attic room of the tower – I went down to investigate.'

'And what did you see – what were they doing?'

Edgar has replaced his glasses and now he pushes them back onto the bridge of his nose with a forefinger.

'It looked just like a scene from a murder mystery play – the three of them froze as I entered – Cassandra was clinging on to Martius – Thwaites was holding onto the edge of the desk as if he were disoriented. I saw Great Uncle Declan lying spread-eagled – I said I would telephone for an ambulance and turned away – you can't ring out from the extensions in the rooms. Martius shouted after me – to make it the police – that he was dead.'

'You didn't check, sir?'

Edgar is not expecting this suggestion.

'I took Martius's word for it.' A looks of alarm grips his features. 'He *was* dead?'

From deep in his repertoire Skelgill pulls another of his bewildering facial expressions.

'The autopsy puts the time of death at around noon.'

'Noon?' Edgar is further confused. 'But – I thought –'

Skelgill waits but Edgar is not forthcoming. DS Jones recognises that Skelgill is playing some sort of game – but she finds the silence disconcerting and begins to scribble methodically. Edgar at last pays her some attention and glances worriedly in her direction, but she holds the notebook upright and he cannot see that she is merely doodling, florally embellishing the words *'Empty Hollow'*. Eventually Skelgill breaks the impasse.

'You thought what, sir?'

Edgar looks again at Skelgill; for a second he seems startled to find himself being interviewed.

'Well – I assumed – that it had just happened – that he must have cried out – for help.'

'Thinking back, to earlier on – you didn't hear anything unusual, sir?'

Edgar folds his arms and concentrates his thoughts; once more he focuses upon the table before him.

'It's three flights up to the attic in the tower. My door was closed – and I have been employing a rather noisy electric fan heater. If the study door were also closed – the sound would have a good distance to travel – the hall, the staircase, and a thick oak door at either end.'

'And you went to lunch at – what – 12 noon?'

Edgar still has his eyes downcast. He looks like he wishes there were an alternative to this inauspicious time of day.

'I knew the buffet would be laid out from midday – I had intended to take a plate back upstairs – but I got into conversation with Fergal Mullarkey.'

Skelgill casts a cursory glance over DS Leyton's briefing notes – they have this information, of course, although Edgar does not protest the repetition, unlike elder brother Martius.

'What about after you rang 999? What did you do then?'

'Your Sergeant Leyton called back. He advised that we lock the study and gather together. It seemed to be sensible advice. We all went to the drawing room. We had known since morning that we were cut off by the snow – there had been a message from the gamekeeper that the lane was impassable. But you came within minutes – we weren't expecting that.'

'So then what happened?'

Now Edgar glances up. He must wonder that Skelgill is asking him about the period when he was himself present. But, of course, having ascertained there was no imminent danger Skelgill had promptly made for the study.

'Everyone began to drift away. Martius said he had work to do – and Fergal Mullarkey the same – so I felt it was reasonable to return to my own administration.'

Skelgill regards him evenly. While Edgar looks to a small degree apologetic, his emotional reaction equates roughly to that of a person coming upon a road accident: a certain human empathy, but no great vested interest. Mysteriously, he seems to divine Skelgill's perspective, and offers an excuse.

'It wasn't as though any of us really knew the man – Great Uncle Declan – and once you arrived we realised the attacker must be gone – that we were safe to return to our own devices.'

He looks at Skelgill in a rather submissive manner – as one might regard a more competent elder brother. Skelgill, however, is unmoved by this minor adulation.

'What made you think he was attacked?'

Behind the lenses Edgar's eyes widen.

'But he *was*, surely?'

'Aye – but how could you tell? It's not uncommon for someone keel over and die from the impact injury.'

'But – did I say attacked?'

'When you called for assistance, you told the operator he'd been hit on the head.'

Edgar looks confused – now he stares at Skelgill with a rather pained expression. Skelgill might imagine him as a seven-year-old stuttering before a stern schoolmaster, tucked behind his back an incomplete gerbil that gasps and kicks in his tight little fist, while Brutus (with Edgar's 'alibi') is nowhere to be seen.

'Perhaps I said *hit his head?* Martius must have –' He checks himself. 'When Martius shouted to call the police they all began yelling – Cassandra and Thwaites – one of them may have given me the idea – Thwaites, I expect – he found the body. I probably put two and two together – I panicked and bolted for the telephone.'

Skelgill holds fire for a few moments. His tone, if businesslike, has been neither aggressive nor accusatory.

'When was the last time you saw Declan alive?'

Edgar seems more comfortable with this line of inquiry.

'As I told Sergeant Leyton – to the best of my recall, it was at the reading of the will – on Friday evening after the funeral.'

'How was he then – how did he react?'

'Well –' Edgar seems perturbed – that he doesn't know the answer to this. 'I can't honestly say that I noticed, Inspector. I mean – I took it for granted that he already knew – that my grandfather would have discussed it with him. It seemed the logical arrangement, since Great Uncle Declan had no heirs to confuse the situation.'

'And what advice did you give him?'

Edgar looks bemused.

'I'm sorry – I'm not with you, Inspector.'

'You being an accountant – didn't he want your opinion?'

'Oh – I see.' The tension in his shoulders diminishes. 'There is a firm of land agents – based in Cockermouth – I assume they handle the estate management and the accounts.'

'That'll be Foulsyke & Dodd.'

Edgar does not reply. Skelgill looks pensive.

'And what do you expect to become of the place?'

Edgar understands he refers to the terms of the will.

'I think it's too early to say, Inspector.'

'I gather you had a discussion on Saturday night.'

Edgar is about to answer, and then he hesitates and makes a face of distaste. Now he chooses his words with evident care.

'It was not constructive – and I felt disrespectful to Great Uncle Declan to be debating the future of the hall while he was still alive...'

He tails off – for of course a change in the status quo quickly came to pass. However, Skelgill remains silent and in due course Edgar continues, his tone gaining an edge of bitterness.

'But someone will always play devil's advocate – just for the sheer hell of it.'

Skelgill regards Edgar patiently. But it seems he has no more to add.

'So who's the troublemaker?'

Edgar now backtracks.

'Oh, it was a bit of a free-for-all – I couldn't really say – on reflection there was probably too much wine consumed for it to be taken seriously.'

'You must have a sense of which way the wind is blowing, sir? How about yourself, for instance?'

Edgar looks patently uncomfortable.

'I had not given it proper consideration – and now it has been overtaken by the death of Great Uncle Declan.'

This would appear a reasonable get-out – but Skelgill is gently persistent.

'Would you not fancy being the country squire?'

Edgar glances with alarm at the papers that Skelgill casually brandishes, and then at DS Jones's notebook – as if he suspects they have compiled some secret dossier on him.

'I have a thriving practice in Hampstead, Inspector.'

Skelgill nods accommodatingly, but he must register that the reply skirts his question. He consults his wristwatch – the time is getting on – and perhaps he wonders if very shortly Thwaites will bang the gong, or whatever he does to signal that luncheon is served. A man must eat, and Skelgill more often than most. Additionally, he has plans that will be better served by some mode of refuelling. As he rises, a little stiffly, Edgar is watchful, and takes this cue that the interview is concluding. He mirrors Skelgill's action and gets to his feet, and eagerly offers a palm. Skelgill grudgingly accepts, but now it his turn to be disconcerted, for Edgar prolongs a rather limp handshake. In prematurely detaching himself, Skelgill perhaps feels obliged to offer a parting crumb.

'Happen the coroner will release the body today – so you can tell the others – and make plans for the funeral.'

Edgar looks pleased – indeed pleased with himself: that he has been chosen to bear the news. For the first time he smiles, revealing two rows of uneven teeth – a further contrast to his beautified twin.

9. HISTORY LESSON – Monday 1pm

Of the five hundred-odd recognised fells in the Lake District, Grasmoor is arguably the single biggest solid lump of rock. Designated by Wainwright as a *"monstrous monolith"* its looming presence darkens the southern reaches of Lorton Vale, its western slopes sliding precipitously into the depths of Crummock Water. In one variation of a little game Skelgill sometimes plays, in which the mountains are animals and Blencathra a maned lion and Skiddaw a horned rhino, Grasmoor is a great brooding bull elephant. In fact its name – on the face of it a touch oxymoronic, that 'grass' and 'moor' can be juxtaposed – tells a tale of another creature altogether, since the prefix 'gras' (correctly spelled with a single 's') is merely a derivative of the Old Norse word 'grise', which means *wild boar*.

Munching pensively on his packed lunch – smoked ham sandwiches as it happens – Skelgill gazes down upon the place of its origin, a smudge of grey slate rooftops ringed by shadowy conifers, fine columns of wood-smoke rising from chimney stacks: Crummock Hall. It is a remarkable day, blue and white and crystal clear, and he must reflect on his good fortune to combine occupation with the love of his locality. However, at such times there is always a feeling of the 'busman's holiday' – or, at least, a peculiar inverse of it – for he ought only tread such paths as prescribed by his need, and not roam entirely at will. He has inspected the cairn shelters – where there are walkers' tracks aplenty in the fresh snow, though nothing to excite his curiosity – and has moved a little north, off the broad plateau-like summit *("rather dull"*, according to Wainwright) to obtain his current perspective.

Right now he ponders Perdita's reported route of descent – not the most direct, nor the safest, but certainly one that provided her with tangible clues to her intended course, cleverly making use of the immediate topography to hold a bearing. Had she drifted east from the summit – the kindest gradient on the broadest slope – she might soon have found herself lost in the centre of the massif, the featureless wilderness beneath Wandope (where, down the years, Skelgill has put right many little groups of disoriented hillwalkers – sending them on their way, bemused, with the phrase "two-dopes" or "three-dopes" ringing in their ears). Perdita, however, like a dog thought to be irrevocably lost, had turned to an innate homing ability, and arrived bright-eyed if not bushy-tailed: her exploits revealing resourceful grit to complement her elfin allure.

Before his departure from Crummock Hall Skelgill had convened his lieutenants. His announcement that he was setting out on foot had barely raised an eyebrow – they are all too familiar with his idiosyncrasies in this regard. (The only surprise might have been that he had not taken down a fishing rod from one of the walls.) Conversely, their reactions to his parting instructions were more mixed.

DS Leyton was delegated to reprise with each member of the household their movements and observations, between the time of rising and the arrival of the forensic team at 4:15 yesterday afternoon. Although a straightforward job (other than having to reach Martius via his mobile telephone), its nature rarely elicits a positive response – people tend to conclude that the police do not believe their original account. Of course, there is some truth underpinning this sentiment, for any discrepancies may be pounced upon with a Holmes-sized magnifying glass. Therefore the investigating officer can expect a prickly reception. DS Leyton, however, had maintained a stiff upper lip, and stoically acquiesced to his superior's command.

DS Jones grew agitated as this task was handed down; and soon enough Skelgill outlined something further afield as far as she was concerned. Firstly she was to track down the allegedly disreputable Gilhooleys, and establish their whereabouts on Sunday; secondly to visit the land agents – Foulsyke & Dodd of Cockermouth – whereupon to gain an understanding of the financial position and management process of Crummock Hall estate. It was to her undisguised consternation that Skelgill had effectively chaperoned her off the premises, on the grounds he had left his trapper hat in the 4x4 she had requisitioned from the car pool, and that they could leave together. To compound her discontent, he had issued a typically vague instruction that he would be making his way to Keswick and she should rendezvous with him at a particular café (located on upper floor of a well-known outdoor gear emporium). Skelgill had loitered beside the vehicle until she set off grim faced, staring ahead of her. Such petulance is out of character.

Before climbing the fell, Skelgill had doubled back around Crummock Hall. He made a complete circuit of the perimeter walls, finishing up outside the garden door of Declan's study. His findings had been much as he had anticipated. The fresh snow that had fallen yesterday afternoon and overnight had smothered all fine detail. Any new tracks were of the four-legged kind, fox, badger, roe deer, and red squirrel. Certainly there was the line of disturbance he had previously noted, leading from Declan's door into the conifers – but this could be explained by the old man's daily bird-watching expedition, to and fro perhaps Friday, Saturday and Sunday. Skelgill guessed that beneath the snow lies a regular path. He had followed this to the edge of the shelterbelt, to a boundary wall with a stone stile of sharply protruding rocks. Immediately beyond, the snow at the foot of the wall was even more disturbed – and now there were also sheep prints and flattened patches; quite likely one or more creatures passed in search of food or suitable shelter. The marks of human trudging hugged the wall away to Skelgill's right – presumably Declan's usual route. He had eschewed this, opting instead for a smooth ascent of the mountainside, a curving course visible as a rim of shadow, suggestive of a well-defined path beneath the crust of white, highlighted by the low angled sunlight. In due course, panting and perspiring, he had attained his goal.

Now he finishes his sandwich and folds the greaseproof wrapper into a pocket of his jacket. He rises and turns his attention away from Crummock Hall. Keswick is seven miles due east; en route he intends to call at the hamlet of Braithwaite. It is with a glint in his eye that he sets off, for the early part of this journey takes in some rewarding landmarks. First he must cross above the deceptively named Dove Crags, and pass beneath the rocky buttress of Eel Crag to reach the watershed of Coledale Hause. Immediately there is a steep descent beside Force Crag, where the waterfall of Low Force spills down past the abandoned workings of Force Crag Mine, the last remnants of half a millennium of man's labours on the site. Thence the character of the route changes altogether, for an arrow-straight mining track follows the contour line above Coledale Beck and guides the walker beneath the impressive slopes of Grisedale Pike (or 'peak above the valley of the wild boar', to translate from the Old Norse).

As Skelgill drinks in the splendid scenery and notes with appreciation the *mew* of a circling buzzard or the *brok* of a passing raven, the casual onlooker would be hard pressed to guess he is a policeman at work. Certainly he throttles back on his regular pace. Indeed it would seem a reasonable charge that, given an inch, he has taken a mile (or several) in order to admire the fells and dales, doubly spectacular in their rare coat of ermine. But he is hunting a killer – and it seems unlikely the culprit will turn himself in. Forensics may yet play their part, but Skelgill cannot afford to lean on such a cheap crutch. He must be prepared to solve the case by detective work – and perhaps already has the wherewithal to do so. Thus, if he were challenged that he wastes valuable time, his retort would come without hesitation: "How am I supposed to *think* in an office?"

*

'Daniel, is that you beneath that preposterous hat?'
'It's bloody effective.'
'In that case, maybe I should get one.'
Skelgill stamps snow from his boots, pulls off his trapper hat and ducks into the low-beamed stone cottage.
'Here – you're welcome to this one.'
His host shoulders the thick oak door against the elements.
'It's a kind offer – but I shouldn't deprive you. I take it you have further to walk?'

'Aye – but only to Keswick, like.'

'And from where have you come?'

'Crummock Hall – by Coledale Hause.'

'Ah – that explains everything – I was just watching it on the television news as you knocked.'

'What's that?'

'Come through – it might still be on.'

The older man leads Skelgill into a small kitchen, where a portable television set of ancient lineage is playing. Skelgill darts forwards and squints at the grainy screen, as though he can't believe his eyes. An outside broadcast team is interviewing a youngish man clad in a fur coat with a high collar; rather indecently his torso appears to be naked beneath, for a triangle of dark chest hair is visible between the broad lapels. The caption states, "Breaking News: Lakes Murder – Owain Jagger, *Empty Hollow*". In the background is the distinctive snow-capped front portico of Crummock Hall, a bright-liveried police Land Rover and – to amplify Skelgill's exasperation – a distinctive stocky overcoated figure animatedly briefing two uniformed constables and repeatedly glancing in the direction of the camera and edging subtly into shot. Skelgill lets loose a string of expletives and digs for his mobile phone.

'Excuse my French, Jim.'

He jabs at the handset and raises it to his ear. Distractedly he rakes the fingers of his other hand through his damp hair. In the little sideshow, the plainclothes detective can be seen to pull what must be a phone from his inside pocket and regard it with surprise. Rather tentatively he answers the call. Then, visibly, he jolts.

'Leyton – get that news crew out of there! If the Chief's watching she'll have my guts for garters! You know what that means.'

Skelgill raises a palm to his host, in silent apology for the Anglo-Saxon adjectives that punctuate this broadside. Observant television viewers would notice the sturdy detective glance nervously about, as though he suspects he is under surveillance, then abruptly to back out of frame.

'Er, sorry, Guv – righto, Guv – they caught us on the hop – told the constable on the gate they were pals of Brutus and that he'd invited them – blagged their way in, Guv.'

Skelgill does not waste energy in pointing out the lameness of his sergeant's excuses.

'You've got thirty seconds, Leyton.'

He terminates the call and glares at the television set. The interviewer has evidently asked Brutus some question about his family history. He is at ease before the camera, his permanent semi-smirk tempered by a creased brow to represent the correct degree of mourning. He is presently explaining that Crummock Hall has been in his family for the past three centuries, and how much it means to him, having been a "seminal backcloth" to his childhood. A disparaging retort is just forming upon Skelgill's lips when the screen goes blank. The director reverts to the studio, where an unready anchor is caught applying lipstick. It seems a fearful DS Leyton has obeyed orders and taken the simple expedient of yanking out a plug.

Skelgill is grinding his teeth – but now his host places two steaming mugs on the kitchen table and smiles amiably.

'Tea, Daniel – have a seat. It is quite a celebrity cast they have up there.' He gestures to the television set. 'I'll turn this off, shall I?'

'Aye – thanks.' Skelgill does as he is bidden. 'It's picking your brains I'm after, Jim.'

'Be my guest – I have been snowed in since Friday – it is one small drawback of moving out of town – so I appreciate your company even more than usual.'

Skelgill grins. The pair are old friends. Jim Hartley, retired Professor of History at Durham University, is a contemporary of Skelgill's elders and one-time mentor of a young Daniel Skelgill in the field of fly fishing (rapidly overtaken by the schoolboy's prodigious obsession). They spend a few moments exchanging pleasantries, family news and bemoaning the unsuitability of the climate as far as angling is concerned. In due course Skelgill, taking a thirsty gulp of tea, cocks his head in the direction of the television set.

'Know anything about them, Jim? What he said – three hundred-odd years they've been there.'

'And a low public profile they have kept, Daniel, considering such length of tenure.' He removes his spectacles and begins to rub the lenses with a corner of a paper napkin. 'Although it is not without reason.'

'Aye?'

Now the professor holds up a qualifying finger.

'First, I should say this period is not my forte – fifth to the fifteenth century if you want anything with real authority – but of course I have an interest in all things historical, especially where there is a local connection. The O'Mores made their fortune on the back of the Triangular Trade.'

'Come again?'

'Rum butter, Daniel – Cumberland sausage?'

'You've got me now, Jim.'

'But you know that Whitehaven was once a great port? Even if it is hard to imagine when you see its sleepy marina today.'

Skelgill rubs the stubble on his chin reflectively. 'There's a big enough harbour and fortifications.'

'Ah – that was to defend us when we came under attack from the dastardly Americans, Daniel – a little later during the War of Independence – but in the early 1700s Whitehaven enjoyed its heyday. Great cargoes of rum and sugar and spices were landed. So we owe some of our local culinary tradition to that era – rum being the ideal way to preserve dairy products – and where would Cumberland sausage be without its pepper, mace and nutmeg?'

Skelgill downs his tea and glances at the cooker, where a pot of soup or stew simmers. The professor grins and gets up for the teapot; he returns also with a plate of chocolate digestives, which he slides across to Skelgill.

'So what, Jim – the O'Mores were importers?'

The professor indicates that Skelgill should help himself.

'Well, of course, that may be the sanitised version that they and their fellow merchants would wish to promulgate.'

Skelgill, now munching, remains puzzled.

'Hold on a second, will you, Daniel – let me show you something.'

The older man rises and leaves the kitchen. Skelgill gets up, too. There is a bird feeder outside the window. What he thinks is a great tit and a nuthatch are doing battle, while a red squirrel hops about beneath, gathering any spoils. There is an identification chart pinned on the wall and Skelgill seems pleased as he confirms his supposition. The professor returns and spreads out a large old book on the table.

'Now, look at this.'

Skelgill leans over. The text is set in an antiquated typeface. Most of the double-page spread is given over to a series of precise hand-drawn diagrams. The subject appears to be a ship, its hold revealed in cross section from above, the starboard side, and the stern. Almost the entire surface area of each image is filled with hundreds of tiny elongated black shapes, arrayed in neat rows and fans, and from the side elevation stacked on what might be shelves. The professor waits patiently while Skelgill strives to understand the pattern before his eyes.

'What is it, fish?'

'Human beings, Daniel.'

Skelgill stares in silence but for a hiss of breath between his parted lips.

'Unbelievable.'

He realises – this is a sales brochure for a slave ship – its 'cargo' arranged for maximum stowage. On closer inspection the tiny charcoal figures are meticulously drawn, and clearly human, packed so close as to be touching, their arms necessarily folded over their torsos. Skelgill's teeth become bared as he reads that the space allocated to each man is 6 feet by 1 foot 4 inches (and less for women and children), and that this layout accommodates 470 people, but that 609 are actually carried by the slave merchants. Skelgill pulls himself upright, swallowing with distaste. But his eyes are compelled to return to the illustrations – what thoughts must have entered the mind of the draughtsman that spent his comfortable days at a desk devising such a despicable plan?

The professor is watching Skelgill's reaction closely – he seems to take a certain satisfaction in his shocked demeanour.

'To prevent insurrection the men were kept in irons for the entire passage – it could take two months. There was negligible sanitation. Those that died were tossed overboard to the sharks. Some of the women were taken above decks for the pleasure of the crew.'

Skelgill has a half-eaten biscuit in one hand and now he looks at it as though he has lost his appetite. But his instincts get the better of him and he dunks it in his tea and swallows it with difficulty, washing it down with another gulp, his features contorted in a bitter grimace. His expression is pained as he looks at the professor.

'So how does this all fit together, Jim?'

Tentatively the man pats the book with the flat of his palm, like a steelworker might check a plate for its heat,

'In a sense, Daniel, the Triangular Trade grew up out of a freak of nature – the cycle of winds and currents in the North Atlantic during the age of sail. We were an advanced economy – *the* most advanced economy – our merchant fleet and navy was the greatest on the seas. We produced manufactured goods such as textiles and weapons that were bartered for slaves in West Africa. They were shipped to the New World, carried by the trade winds – and sold to the sugar planters and tobacco growers. The profits were used to buy sugar and tobacco, rum and spices, and the fully laden ships returned to Western Europe on the Gulf Stream. More profits were made, and the wheel of misery was turned again. The merchants never got their hands dirty – indeed it was a fashionable investment among much of higher society.'

Skelgill is shaking his head. His expression might replicate his face as a boy, under the professor's tutelage, the first time he got a precious fly-rod into his hands, inspired by the strange weightless device: that of awe tinged with fear.

'Jim – why did it have to be people?'

The professor inhales over a sip of tea, and then sighs before he makes a reply.

'Daniel – it has always been thus. Do you think Rome was built by paying the Living Wage? Do you know how many thousands of our own antecedents were snatched from our shores by Barbary pirates and sold into slavery in North Africa and the Ottoman Empire?'

Skelgill remains pensive and does not reply. The professor continues.

'The O'Mores were originally Dublin merchants. As they and their business expanded branches of the family tree took root in British trading ports.'

'Whitehaven being one?'

'As I said, Daniel – you might find it impossible to believe, but Whitehaven was once the third largest port in the United Kingdom – in the 1700s it was up there with Bristol and Liverpool and Glasgow. There was a time when it supplied 80% of Ireland's coal.'

Skelgill is nodding grimly. What he learns now corresponds to his dialogue with Fergal Mullarkey. And – of course – to some degree with what Perdita related about Declan's warning. It is on this point that he speaks.

'Among the celebrities – as you put it, Jim – there's the youngest of the five children, Perdita.'

'Rowena Devlin.' There is something sheepish about the sidelong glance that the professor flashes at his guest. 'I must confess to reading the occasional one of her novels. She writes well if simplistically. And her facts are thoroughly researched.'

Skelgill smiles respectfully.

'She didn't sound all that clued up on this Triangular Trade business – least not as far as the O'More family is concerned. She reckoned her Great Uncle Declan had spun her some yarn about a curse put on them by an African witch doctor.'

'Daniel, I suspect the mantle of disrepute is something the O'Mores have been trying to cast off since the abolition of slavery in 1833. That they might deny any such connection in family circles would not really be surprising. And of course this particular cohort is more detached than most – losing their parents so young – and growing up in the distant Home Counties. In any event, it is unreasonable to tar today's generation with the bloody brush of their forebears.'

Skelgill nods ruefully. As a descendent on his mother's side of the notorious Border reivers, Clan Graham, he would almost certainly be taken into custody this very minute if historical misdemeanours were heritable. And the Skelgills – of Viking blood – were probably little better. Notwithstanding, his next remark reveals that some flicker of injustice still burns within him.

'But they live well on the back of it.'

The professor turns out his bottom lip.

'Well – that is true, Daniel. But how many great estates – and even more modest family fortunes – were built on the shoulders of such iniquitous toil? Throughout our great cities and towns – not just our countryside – there are many people today who owe their fortunate lifestyles to the inhuman compliance of their forefathers. But who is going to set the record straight?'

Skelgill folds his arms and rests his elbows on the table.

'What you say about avoiding the family association might be right, Jim. First off – they've none of them got Irish Christian names like the older generation. I guess that started with their mother. Then Martius calls himself Martius Regulus. Cassandra goes by one of her married names, Goodchild. You've got Owain Jagger and Rowena Devlin. Only Edgar has kept O'More in his surname.'

'You make a convincing case, Daniel – although it is curious that the young authoress has chosen the plantations as the setting for her successful series.' The professor taps the tips of his fingers together several times, reflecting his cogitations, stopping when he reaches a conclusion. 'Perhaps she assuages her feelings of guilt – for her plots usually see an immoral master receive his come-uppance – albeit that the slaves can rarely prevail, and at best receive their freedom.'

Skelgill allows a small grin to crease his features. His host is plainly more of a fan of Rowena Devlin's work than he would like to admit.

'There doesn't happen to be a story where the estate owner gets whacked on the back of the head by one of his slaves?'

Though Skelgill's remark is facetious, the professor regards him quizzically.

'I rather imagined you had in mind one of the family, Daniel?'

Skelgill makes a face of resignation and dunks another biscuit in his tea. He leaves it almost too long and has to duck for it as it begins to collapse.

'I wish I knew what I *had* got in mind, Jim.'

'Presumably they are the main beneficiaries?'

Skelgill scratches his head and then makes an attempt to comb some order into his hair, which has suffered beneath the trapper hat.

'It's not so straightforward. They can vote to sell or to keep the place running. They knew that before Declan's murder. If they keep it on, no one gets any money. So there was no guarantee a killer would benefit.'

'Unless he – or she – was confident of the outcome of the vote.'

'If they're being straight, it's still up in the air. They're meeting next weekend to discuss it.'

The professor now folds his hands together and rests his chin upon the bridge he forms.

'Far be it for me to tell you your job, Daniel – I assume you have no clear leads outwith the motive of inheritance?'

Skelgill shrugs with frustration.

'The staff stand to lose their jobs if Crummock Hall is sold. It's hard to see why any of them would do it. They're all long-servers – if it were a grudge, why wait until now?'

'A fair point, Daniel.'

'There's no sign of a break-in or theft. We can't rule that out, but it looks like Declan was struck from behind with his own walking stick while he was winding the clock in his study. You wouldn't turn your back on someone you considered a threat.'

'So where does that leave you, Daniel?'

Skelgill makes a sarcastic scoffing exclamation.

'I'm coming round to the O'More family curse.'

The professor chuckles.

'That sounds like we are back in Rowena Devlin territory.'

Skelgill nods reluctantly.

'Seems Declan called her in to see him – warned her she was stirring up trouble – as far as we know she was the last person to see him alive.'

'So he did not approve of her subject matter.'

'Aye, looks that way. He's got this tidy collection of old books – not a lot of fiction, by the look of it.'

The professor's antennae twitch at this revelation.

'Perhaps there is some clue hidden away there, Daniel.' He hesitates and makes a tentative cough. 'If at some point – you wanted me to cast an eye over them – I should be pleased to assist.'

Skelgill nods willingly.

'I might take you up on that, Jim. The lawyer they've got – Mullarkey – is talking about taking the collection over to Dublin – for safekeeping. Declan died without making a will and it's just about his only asset. Mullarkey's worried if it's left to fester in the house it'll get picked apart and lose its value.'

'That seems a reasonable assumption. You know how one's books once lent are invariably considered to be the property of the borrower.'

At this statement Skelgill looks perplexed. As a man of not many books – a small but no less precious collection of field guides, manuals and maps – the idea of letting someone get their hands on, say, one of his precious Wainwrights is anathema.

'Neither a borrower nor a lender be.'

The professor raises an amused eyebrow at the vehemence of Skelgill's remark.

'You know your Shakespeare, Daniel – Polonius, from *Hamlet*.'

'I'd have said it was my old Ma.'

The professor chuckles willingly.

'Ah – always a wise lady – and how is she these days – not suffering from the weather?'

Skelgill grimaces.

'It'd take more than a drop of snow to knock her off her stride. Happen she'll have the bike out this morning if they've ploughed the Honister.'

Now the professor shakes his head of white hair in admiration.

'As you have demonstrated in your intrepid arrival, Daniel – it takes a lot to stop a Skelgill.'

Skelgill grins a little abashedly. He begins to rise.

'Aye. Even though they don't always know where they're going. But I'd better make tracks or my sergeant'll be putting a curse on me. Thanks for the tea, Jim – and I might just take you up on what you said about the books.'

'You are most welcome, Daniel – it is a pleasure to see you any time – we must talk fishing when the conditions become more inclement.'

Skelgill is nodding, but as he turns a blue tit alights on the windowsill and catches his eye.

'Jim – you're a bit of a twitcher, aren't you?'

Now the professor makes a face of mock disapproval.

'Daniel – I prefer the term ornithologist, or bird-watcher. Birder at a push. The twitchers are another genus altogether. The storm troopers of the fraternity.'

Skelgill grins.

'Aye – well I reckon I saw some waxwings this morning, at Crummock Hall – little flock of them feeding on a border of guelder rose. Is that likely? Pretty rare, aren't they?'

The professor raises his hands in the air, the gesture perhaps a throwback to his lecturing days.

'Ah – they are indeed – and what a fascinating coincidence.' He nods in the direction of his garden. 'I had a flock here until Friday. Twelve birds. They spent three days stripping my ornamental rowans. *Bombycilla garrulus*, the Bohemian waxwing. They sweep across Britain from Russia and Scandinavia when the berry crop fails. The twitchers like them, because once they find a food source, they remain on site until it is exhausted – typically several days. There's a good chance that the party you found was mine. Well done on the identification!'

Skelgill looks pleased with himself – but then a thought must strike him.

'Aye – if only there were an *Observer's* book of crooks, Jim.'

10. KESWICK – Monday 3.45pm

Skelgill lurks behind a rack of the latest hi-tech lightweight cagoules. The crackling gossamer shells are advertised as "100% waterproof" – which is perhaps just as well, for his face looks like thunder. Certainly it is an expression that deters any shop assistant from approaching – they would conclude that the hefty price tags have offended his sensibilities. In fact he is eavesdropping.

Nearby, DS Leyton confers with DS Jones. Upon completing his work at Crummock Hall and passing this way, feeling sympathy for her lonely vigil he has taken it upon himself to provide some company – knowing he can brief Skelgill upon his eventual arrival. In fact his findings have been rather mundane, and the present conversation revolves around the more titillating aspect of the case.

'The missus saw me on the box. She reckoned I looked a bit like *Columbo*.' DS Leyton is tickled by his minor taste of fame. 'Until I got an earful and had to turf the news crew out.'

DS Jones chuckles.

'They'll be back – it's not often we have A-listers around here.'

DS Leyton looks rather browbeaten.

'Next thing – she was giving me grief about getting a selfie – wants to show off Owain Jagger to all her pals on Facebook.'

DS Jones leans towards her colleague conspiratorially.

'You're welcome to this one.' She spins her mobile phone on the table surface.

DS Leyton grunts as he bends forwards. His eyes widen.

'Cor blimey – looks like you're well in there, girl!'

DS Jones smiles coyly.

'I wasn't expecting him to plant a kiss.'

This proves to be the final straw for Skelgill, who breaks cover and storms across the carpeted shop floor. However there is a small flight of wooden steps leading up to the raised café area, and his boots clump a warning. They see him coming, and DS Jones slides her handset from sight – though she cannot hide the telltale blush of her cheeks. His sergeants both rise but Skelgill ignores them and slumps down into one of two vacant chairs, his features grim. DS Leyton, correctly assessing the scale if not the source of his boss's discontent, reverts to a tried-and-trusted tactic.

'There you go, Guv – just got you these. Still nice and hot.'

Two-handed he pushes across the table a chocolate-sprinkled cappuccino and an appetising-looking toasted sandwich. Skelgill glares suspiciously at the offering.

'Where's yours?'

DS Leyton consults his wristwatch.

'If I eat now, Guv – I'll never manage my tea – then the missus'll have a right old Darby and Joan.'

Skelgill stares at his subordinate for a couple of seconds – as though he doesn't believe his explanation. (Or his doubt might just be that such a minor snack could possibly ruin one's appetite.) Then decisively he tucks into the sandwich.

'News.'

His question comes as a surly demand.

DS Leyton retrieves his notebook from his overcoat and thumbs cumbersomely through pages of surprisingly neat printing.

'Top line, Guv – I wouldn't call it news – but since when did turkeys vote for Christmas?'

DS Jones smirks, but Skelgill quashes her with a sharp glance. DS Leyton winces supportively and continues.

'In a nutshell, Guv, it's what we've already been told – most of Sunday we've only got their word for where they were. That's apart from Perdita – who we know was missing between 12:30 and five o'clock – and Cassandra and Brutus – they're sticking to their guns about bunking off to her bedroom for the afternoon. As things stand, Guv – creeping around in a great old place like that – any one of them could have sneaked off and done the murder.'

107

DS Jones is rather apprehensively watching Skelgill. Preoccupied with the toastie, he appears not to be paying attention. As far as she knows, he has not yet apprised DS Leyton of all the facts. It is not unlike Skelgill to leave his subordinates in the dark. Some might say this is typical of his sheer bloody-mindedness, but Skelgill would argue that if you tell a person what to look for, they will find it – at the expense of a potentially more important clue. He will happily investigate any number of byways and seemingly obvious blind alleys, and yet resist arriving at a tangible destination. It is a method that suggests a lacks of a coherency in his thinking – but Skelgill is neither a great thinker nor a man who cares particularly how others regard him. Peremptorily, he contradicts DS Leyton.

'Not Perdita, it couldn't.'

DS Leyton is no stranger to this situation. He also knows that Skelgill's irritation could be entirely irrational, and may stem from anything ranging from the present lack of available fishing, to England's ever-diminishing chances of winning a World Cup, in any sport. But nonetheless he struggles to find a suitable reply. It falls to DS Jones to break the impasse.

'Guv – about the problem of timing – while I was waiting I called Dr Herdwick and explained your findings.'

Skelgill pauses mid-bite.

'Aye?'

'He's digging his heels in.'

She retrieves her mobile phone and carefully manipulates the screen. She holds it so that Skelgill can see, but he gestures dismissively, meaning that she should read aloud.

'He's gone into quite a lot of detail, Guv. He repeats the caveats – but there's this bit: "the progression of all key indicators, *livor mortis, rigor mortis* and *algor mortis* correspond to a prediction centred upon noon – an estimate to which a good degree of confidence can be attached since the examination took place within a few hours of death occurring."'

Skelgill looks unimpressed. He finishes the sandwich and swallows down some coffee. He wipes froth from his lips with each hand and then rubs his palms on his thighs. However, he does not offer a rejoinder, and after a short while DS Jones feels sufficiently empowered to mention what is something of an elephant in the room.

'Could you have been mistaken about the clock, Guv?'

Now Skelgill glares at her.

'Have you got the logbook?'

'In my bag.' She reaches to pat an attaché case at her side.

'Could you be mistaken about the entry?'

Skelgill's tone is harsh. Meanwhile DS Leyton is looking increasingly perplexed.

'What is this, Guv? Am I missing something?'

Skelgill folds his arms and assumes a rather weary pose.

'Leyton – when I first went into the study the clock was stopped at 2pm. The pendulum was lying on the carpet. There was no way it could work. Then the study was locked for an hour before you arrived. But in that time the clock was changed to 12 noon.' Skelgill gestures loosely at DS Jones. 'Show him the book.'

DS Jones extracts Declan's timeworn journal carefully from her bag and lays it on the table. The relevant page is marked with a slip of paper. With the delicately manicured nail of a slender index finger she indicates the most recent entry.

'He went bird-watching between eleven fifty-five and one thirty-five. And he had time to write up his notes.'

DS Leyton shakes his head slowly and makes a 'that's-put-the-cat-among-the-pigeons' face. Then he grins.

'What about a ghost writer, Guv? They say the old place is haunted!'

Skelgill scowls and sinks back into his chair. He gazes across at the display counter, as though he might be assessing what to eat next. He seems reluctant to be drawn by his irrepressible sergeant's banter – but, while his tone remains bleak, perhaps he sees an opportunity to shed the ill temper that has possessed him since his arrival.

'That's it, Leyton – you've cracked it. I'll email the Chief right now. It's the O'More family curse. A poltergeist walloped

Declan with his walking stick, and now it's playing tricks on us by changing the clocks.'

Sensing Skelgill's brightening mood, his subordinates humour him with excessive laughter; he is obliged to accept the credit for his wit. And now DS Leyton takes the opportunity to impart another small snippet – one that perhaps will not entirely be to Skelgill's satisfaction.

'Talk of the walking stick, Guv. I spoke again to Thwaites – asked him if Declan was in the habit of leaving it anywhere else. He said not, but – you know what, Guv – he reckons it sinks in water – that sandalwood, it's so dense. If some geezer did lob it in the lake, it would likely go under.'

Skelgill is still scowling, but it is now more out of curiosity than annoyance.

'Leyton – the lake's half frozen – you'd need a good arm to scop it out beyond the ice.'

DS Leyton makes an expression of agreement. He seems reassured that Skelgill has lapsed into the vernacular.

'Maybe it'll turn up soon as the snow melts, Guv – like you said.'

'Aye – but it's forecast sub-zero all week.'

They all nod reflectively and there is a silence of a few moments. Then Skelgill turns to DS Jones, and addresses her in a more benevolent tone.

'How did you get on?'

DS Jones smiles patiently.

'The Gilhooleys were interesting.' Her face is suggestive of a small degree of martyrdom in undertaking the assignment. 'They weren't keen to let me in – not that it made much difference – the place was like a fridge – a little stone cottage that looks abandoned from the outside. It's down a long track, at the north end of estate – I had to walk the last couple of hundred yards. They don't have a car – they claim they got a lift to the funeral and have been snowed in since Friday afternoon. They're both in their eighties and not what you'd describe as mobile. I'd wager there's next to no chance of either of them breaking into Crummock Hall and committing murder. As soon as I mentioned the O'Mores the old man clammed up – but his wife started on – "Mark my words, lass, we'll take what's our right – see if we don't."' DS Jones mimics the local Lorton accent with *tek* and *reet* and *dunt*.

Skelgill looks at her quizzically.

'What did she mean by that?'

'They weren't very cooperative, Guv. And not a little bit cracked. But when I went to see Foulsyke & Dodd I was able to get more details. The Gilhooleys are tenants on the Crummock Hall estate – they have been for generations. They just pay a peppercorn rent – it's never been increased – that's down to some agreement that was made back in bygone days.'

'So they're onto a good number.'

'You would think so, Guv – at their age they can't be making much off the land – but it looks like their livings costs are next to nothing. I suppose they get their pensions.'

'What about Declan – what did they have to say about him?'

DS Jones shakes her head resignedly.

'Like I mentioned, Guv – beyond repeating the "rightly ours" mantra – they weren't forthcoming. The land agents suggested they might mean the freehold of the property – but there's no provision in law for that – not where there's a tenancy agreement in place. They'd have had more luck if they'd been squatting.' DS Jones is absently twirling a strand of hair. Skelgill watches her closely. He may be thinking that it is no surprise that Brutus – and his infamous alter ego Owain Jagger – might want to kiss her. 'They have no heir – the agents said that's probably been eating at them for a long time – that the tenancy will eventually revert to the estate.'

Skelgill nods – though his eyes are glazed, and it is a few seconds before he asks his next question.

'What else from Foulsyke & Dodd?'

Now DS Jones seems to have absorbed something of Skelgill's abstraction. It is a moment before she releases the breath she has been holding, and inhales again in order to reply.

'At the bottom line the estate is just about breaking even. The chap I saw – Foulsyke – described it as "rather feudal" – but he explained that's the way Sir Sean had wanted it – the tenants know they've been getting a good deal, so they tug their forelocks and pay on time. He believes the income could be doubled if the land were farmed more intensively – they'd be able to justify higher rents. He did mention Declan in that context.'

'How?' Skelgill uses the Scottish how, borrowed from just across the border, that really means *why*.

'The traditional farming methods encourage wildlife – it suited Declan's bird-watching hobby to keep it that way.'

Skelgill nods pensively. He inhales slowly and sighs before he continues.

'Did he put in his four penneth about the future?'

'The agents are hoping the estate will remain in the family – Mr Foulsyke said he plans to call Martius with his recommendations.'

Now Skelgill grimaces.

'Aye – what – send in the contractors to rip up all the hedgerows and plough the meadows? That would be music to his ears.'

Both Skelgill and DS Jones look troubled by this prospect. DS Leyton does his best to mirror their expressions of concern – but being of metropolitan stock his sentiments are less troubled by what seems an academic distinction – after all, surely a field is a field – and, actually, doesn't it look more pleasing filled with a single neat crop rather than a jumble of weeds swarming with creepy crawlies? He decides to toss in *his* four penneth.

'If it's cash they're after, why go round the houses? Surely they'll just flog it and do one, Guv?'

In the absence of anything left to eat, Skelgill gnaws tenaciously on a thumbnail.

'By the look of it, Leyton – none of them's exactly in queer street.'

He pauses and there is another round of silence. It is plain to the trio that this is their next line of investigation: it does not take a Sherlock Holmes to deduce that the death of Declan has opened the door to a potential pecuniary windfall – albeit there could be a more complex motive at play.

'I'd like to be a fly on the wall when they have their vote.'

His eyes drift to the view through a skylight window – although his brooding expression suggests that the darkening sliver of horizon, marked by the distinctive summit of Grisedale Pike, is not where his thoughts lie – and that he is calculating just *how* he might become that fly.

DS Jones makes a little jolt forwards – as if she too has been contemplating this matter and already has a plan in mind. But she refrains from offering a comment, and shakes her head in self-reproach. Her unnatural movement attracts Skelgill's attention, and for a moment he regards her warily. Then he composes himself and clears his throat to speak.

'In the meantime, we need to get them all checked out. Leyton – you take the twins. There's no love lost between them. If there's any closing of family ranks, it's a chink in their armour. Just mention the gerbil.' Skelgill lets out a rather schoolboy-like snigger. Then he smiles somewhat smarmily at DS Jones. 'Jones – take Martius and Cassandra – start with their finances. I'll take Mullarkey and the staff – plus Perdita since she's planning to lodge at Grasmere. I've got a few local contacts I want to tap up, anyway. Kill two birds with one stone.'

DS Leyton seems quite content with this arrangement, but once again DS Jones's features reveal a degree of consternation – that Skelgill is orchestrating affairs with some ulterior purpose in mind. Her suspicions may be reinforced by his next, rather gratuitous remark.

'Leyton – Brutus – another angle – he's obviously gay – leaves him open to blackmail – you know what these showbiz types are like.'

DS Leyton rolls his eyes – it is an unusual expression and one that suggests he is not entirely in accord with his superior; it is more a face of bafflement that Skelgill has crowbarred the notion into the briefing. But while DS Leyton holds his peace – and rather reluctantly nods in compliance – DS Jones is prompted to speak out.

'Guv – I don't think Brutus is gay.' She sets her jaw determinedly in the face of Skelgill's stare. 'Don't you mean Edgar?'

Skelgill continues to glare at her.

'What are you talking about?'

'It's Edgar that's gay, Guv.'

Skelgill remains mulish.

'Who told you this?'

DS Jones relaxes and gives a little sigh. The hint of a knowing smile teases the corners of her lips. Suddenly armed with feminine intuition, she senses her advantage. She glances at DS Leyton to see that he is watching her with interest.

'Guv – I just know – it was really, well – *obvious*.'

Skelgill inspects his palm as if he is recalling Edgar's extended handshake. He looks defiantly from one to the other of his colleagues. Having unadvisedly raised this subject, it would appear he seeks an exit strategy. It arrives from an unexpected quarter. As his eyes dart erratically about the store they fall upon a shock of strawberry blonde hair bobbing beyond the rack of waterproofs he earlier used for cover. The shopper removes a garment from its hanger and holds it experimentally to catch the light. Swiftly, a sales assistant moves in for the kill.

'Hey up.' Skelgill springs to his feet. 'That's not what she wants – can't let them rip her off.'

Without further explanation he strides away and thumps down the steps to the retail floor. The shopper is Perdita.

11. CRUMMOCK WATER – Tuesday 10.30am

'So it was just above Low Ling Crag it went down?'
'Aye, ower yonder.'

Eric Rudd casts an arm like he might a fly, indicating to Skelgill the correct line of sight. While Skelgill is no stranger to Crummock Water, the venerable angler is a local legend, twice his age, and many times more wise. Nowadays the lake is separated from its rather more picturesque neighbour Buttermere by a half-mile-wide outwash plain of rich milk pastures (that may account for the latter's name) – but once they were both part of a single massive glacial body of water, and Eric Rudd gives every impression that he might recall this epoch. Dog-legged Crummock Water is the source of the winding River Cocker, and both *Crummock* and *Cocker* are derived from the ancient Brythonic Celtic word for 'crooked'. Such an adjective befits the hunchbacked Eric Rudd, and the taller Skelgill literally bows to address his gnarled figure.

'That's the deepest part of the lake?'
'Aye, 'undred an' forty foot, lad. Goes down sheer.'
'They'd rowed a good way from Crummock Hall boathouse.'

Eric Rudd shrugs.

'Happen there were a northerly that day.'
'How was the alarm raised?'
'Hillwalker. Gadgee coming off Rannerdale Knotts. He heard shouts for help – could see they were shipping water.'
'What did he do?'

The old man growls throatily, and it brings on a hacking cough. He turns to one side and spits to clear the way for his reply.

'No mobile phones then, lad. Ran as best he could towards Buttermere. But it's a good mile t'first house. It were above half hour before we'd got a boat up there.'

Skelgill nods pensively.

'Too late.'
'Aye, lad.'

'What happened then, Eric?'

'First off – there were talk that they'd swum – but we searched t'banks and there were no trace of 'em. Then some as said yon hillwalker must have invented t'story – attention seeking, like.' He shakes his head and clears his throat once more. 'But t'police checked with Crummock Hall – sure enough they were gone. Missing for a week.'

Now the man stares out across the lake.

'That's what I remember, Eric. All the talk in the village school was how long before the water gave up the bodies.'

'Aye – they allus come back up.'

Now Skelgill allows himself a wry grin.

'I can point you to a couple of cases where they didn't, Eric.'

The old man chuckles, rather wickedly. More than one of Cumbria's lakes have a macabre history in this regard – and may be the repository for who knows how many weighted corpses, slipped over the gunwales down the centuries.

'Aye – keep your hook off t'bottom if you don't want a nasty shock.'

Skelgill raises an eyebrow.

'I'm surprised the boat sank, Eric.'

Now the old man screws up his features; the low morning sunlight casts his complexion as a relief map of the district, his watery green eyes the lakes set deep in the shadowy dale.

'Depends what ballast they had aboard, lad. Teks nobbut a split-shot to sink a float.'

Skelgill nods, but his expression tells he is dissatisfied with this aspect. It seems unlikely the craft was wrought from anything like the same stuff as Declan's fabled walking stick.

'What would it have been, clinker built?'

'Aye, oak most like.'

'Think there's owt left of it, Eric?'

The fisherman shakes his head.

'Nay, lad. She'll be long gone. There's all manner of worms down there.'

Skelgill still looks unconvinced. He suspects there is some complex equation that combines temperature and oxygen concentration and salinity (or lack of) that determines the survival of submerged wood. But if he has in mind an expedition, he must know he would be whistling in the wind – for any such search would be dangerous, expensive and almost certainly futile – and verging on impossible to justify given his present lack of an hypothesis. That he has followed his nose down to the lower reaches of Crummock Water is no basis for action. He has a big nose.

'What were they up to, Eric – any idea?'

Eric Rudd removes his battered tweed trilby and retrieves a half-smoked roll-up from behind one ear. After a couple of attempts he succeeds in lighting it with a match. He inhales and then indulges in another bout of coughing and spitting. Squinting through the bluish smoke he finally addresses Skelgill's inquiry.

'Word was they'd gone fishing – leastways, his nibs. Reckon she just went along for the ride, his young lady wife.' He takes another drag of the unfiltered smoke and exhales as he speaks. 'Course, the Regulus gadgee – he were a townie – happen he didn't rightly know what he was doing – panicked when they got into trouble. He couldn't swim, neither. By all accounts she tried to save him – her scarf were wrapped round his wrist. Happen he dragged her down.'

Skelgill is looking grim faced.

'There's plenty of decent swimmers drowned in the lakes, Eric – you know that. Once the cold shock gets to you – it's like you're inside a sack of taters.'

'Aye, if thou go under lad, that spells trouble.'

Now Skelgill hunches his shoulders and digs his hands into the pockets of his trousers. He takes a step towards the lake and stamps his feet. He is wearing a more conventional outfit than usual and must be cold. He gazes out across the wintry scene, its backcloth the distinctive muscular curves of Mellbreak – a mountain of *"loneliness, solitude and silence"* in Wainwright's book, but a hunting leopard in Skelgill's own little game, prone and poised to spring. Beyond the perimeter ice a drake goldeneye, resplendent in black and white, is defying the laws of nature that they presently discuss. After each dive for food it bobs back up with such buoyancy that it almost leaves the surface, its slick plumage and a little shower of droplets sparkling in the sun. Skelgill breaks out of his reverie and turns to face his old friend. It appears he feels he has gleaned all he can at this moment.

'Long time since we've had this much ice, Eric.'

Eric Rudd inhales viciously on the last vestige of his cigarette – it produces a pulmonary reaction like a misfiring diesel engine, and streams of smoke from the bristling twin exhausts of his nostrils.

'Folk wo' skating on it in '63 – worst winter I can recall. Some were fishing like eskimos – cut little holes. I nivver sin owt caught, though.'

Skelgill makes a sound of amusement.

'Had any char lately, Eric?'

'Aye – afore the freeze set in – couple o' four pounders on a minnow, trollin' like.'

'Nice one. I must give it a crack some time.'

'Thou should – there's more than yan lake int' Lake District, lad.'

Automatically Skelgill begins to counter this statement – but then he breaks out into a grin – for Eric Rudd has cannily subverted his regular aphorism and has a mischievous glint in his eye.

'An' there's more to life than pike, lad.'

Skelgill chuckles and pats his elder upon the shoulder.

'Right enough, Eric.'

'Y'off ter see yer Ma?'

'Aye, I'd better drop in later – if she gets wind I've been knocking about down here I'll get my ear bent if I don't.'

'Get your timing right for dinner, lad.'

Skelgill pulls his right hand from the warmth of a pocket and checks his wristwatch. It is approaching eleven a.m. and his mother is likely still at work. Somewhat cagily he glances at Eric Rudd.

'I should get a shift on, Eric – I need to see a man about a dog.'

The old man winks ostentatiously.

'Aye – I thought thee were reet proper togged up, lad.'

*

'Your donation went down a treat – I handed your cheque to the treasurer last night – thanks very much, er –'

'Inspector –' Perdita O'More interrupts; she holds up her gloved hands, but then she checks herself and catches her breath. She takes a couple of quick paces to get ahead of Skelgill, and nimbly turns to face him, stopping him in his tracks. 'I realise I must refer to you by your title – but, would you mind – there's no need for Miss or Madam or Ms – just call me by my name?'

Skelgill looks a little discomfited.

'Aye – which one, then?'

Now she purrs and swings into step with him; they walk on through the well-trodden snow of the village path.

'Well now – as I told you, I mainly go by Rowena these days – and that's how I've registered at the B&B.'

'Rowena it is.'

Skelgill's features give a hint that he wrestles with some conundrum – perhaps that he is sorely tempted to reciprocate the informality – but the inner voice of protocol prevails and he maintains a semblance of professional distance. His companion, however, appears unperturbed by this one-sided state of affairs, and now she grins somewhat ruefully.

'Besides, after what happened on Sunday I think 'Perdita' is rather tempting fate.'

'Aye?'

'It's a Latin name – it means 'lost one' – or 'despairing' – which is even more depressing. I don't know what possessed Mama to deviate from the Irish tradition.'

'She was an actress.'

'But not at the RSC, Inspector.'

'Happen it was your father's influence?'

Perdita O'More purses her ruby lips and her dark eyes become pensive. She gazes at the ground passing beneath her feet – her sheepskin boots crunch on the ridges of frozen footprints of those who have gone before, and for a few moments it is plain that some memories have been stirred by Skelgill's question.

'I believe – that Dada had limited attention for us. He carried the great weight of the Regulus & Co merchant bank on his shoulders. No one wants to go down in the annals as the son that failed the family firm.'

Skelgill has his hands in the pockets of his jacket, and now he gives a casual jerk of the shoulders.

'He didn't hang about – made sure he had an heir – and plenty to spare.'

Perdita flashes him a quick sideways glance – but if she is looking for some sign that Skelgill is probing, she is met with a rather inane twisting of his features that might actually be an expression of admiration for her late father's fecundity. It prompts the corners of her mouth to turn up.

'It can't be denied – though he ought to have stopped at Martius, so he should.'

Chivalrous on her behalf, Skelgill makes a sound that communicates his disapproval of this notion. Notwithstanding, he takes the opportunity to develop her point.

'He seems well suited to being a banker – not that I can say I've met too many.'

The young woman simpers apologetically.

'By that you mean brash and arrogant, Inspector?'

Her candour takes Skelgill by surprise, and he stares ahead unblinking.

'I was thinking more along the lines that you need the right background. Can't ever imagine how I would have ended up in a job like that.'

'If you are suggesting that high finance and nepotism go hand in hand, I must agree with you.' Perdita nods reflectively. 'But I daresay that applies to many walks of life. It's human nature to favour one's kin.'

They walk on through the crisp snow, silent now. Rather wistfully Perdita casts her eyes to the larch-and-oak-clad fells that rise ahead of them, the forest bare beneath the long rollercoaster ridge that stretches from Hay Stacks to Red Pike. For once the usually striking 1300-foot vertical gash of Sourmilk Gill is indistinct, its frothing beck part-frozen, part invisible being as white as the surrounding snow.

'Inspector – tell me now – how on earth do the sheep survive in these conditions?'

Skelgill looks puzzled. She might as well be asking him why is Buttermere the name of the nearby hamlet, when it is patently the name of the lake? Some things are just the way they are. However his reply, when it comes, would prompt his colleagues to remark upon an uncharacteristically patient explanation.

'The likes of the Herdwicks – the main breed in these parts – to all intents and purposes they're wild animals – they know their own heaf, it's their territory. They can forage by instinct – beneath the snow, even – such as beside a spring where there's warm groundwater flowing. If there's a prolonged freeze the farmer might drag out a bale of hay with his quad. But they don't need much of a helping hand. Come April the shepherds gather them in-bye to lamb.'

Perdita tugs at her collar and snuggles in her new puffer jacket. Its satiny fabric is of a metallic navy hue, and sets off the shining bronzed coils that tumble almost to her waist. She skips playfully ahead of Skelgill. The jacket is cut to the hip; tight charcoal stretch jeans reveal an athletic feminine musculature that draws his gaze.

'I used to adore their little black lambs – many a time I tried to convince Nanny that I had obtained permission to take one home after the Easter holidays.'

It is a moment before he responds.

'What –? Aye – they're cute right enough – but it doesn't last.'

Perdita turns to face him; now her expression is doleful.

'Only in death is there eternal youth, Inspector.'

Skelgill regards her evenly.

'Now that's Shakespeare, I take it?'

She appears a little nonplussed, her lips part. Then she looks away, and speaks softly, her Irish brogue underscoring the note of pathos that has crept into her voice.

'Oh – no – I don't think so – unless I unwittingly plagiarised the line. It was spoken by a character in one of my stories – but I was picturing Mama when it came to me.'

She is just a yard away, and Skelgill can see the tears that well up in the dark pools of her eyes. Her gaze meets his own, and for a few seconds there is an unspoken exchange – however it is one that somehow unnerves Skelgill, for he blinks first, and takes half a pace backwards.

'I'm sorry, lass – I mean – it must still be hard – for you to come back here.'

He glances inadvertently in the direction of Crummock Water. They have crossed the outflow plain and have reached Scale Bridge, the old stone packhorse crossing with its double arch that spans Buttermere Dubs. The lake, a couple of fields hence, is visible only as a horizontal sliver of grey, but Perdita seems to understand that he looks to the site of the tragedy – 'The Accident'.

'Unfinished business, Inspector.'

'Come again?'

She smiles – but it is a wan smile and in the slanting rays of the sun Skelgill sees lines at the corners of her eyes that remind him she is not even a handful of years his junior. Her voice takes on a wistful, dreamlike quality.

'When, as a child, you lose someone close to you, I believe the cut is many times deeper, for you have no meaningful intellect that will intervene to soften the blow – it is a wound that never becomes resolved – but so too the raw love is preserved.'

Now Skelgill wheels away – he stares across the bleak pastures to Buttermere. His gaze settles upon a distant row of distempered cottages; they blend into the snowy backdrop, but for their steep slate roofs and a wraith of grey that rises like a departing spirit from one of the chimneys. He nods, swallows, combs a hand through his hair slowly and methodically, as if to draw away some notion that has possessed his mind. Then purposefully he turns back to face the young woman, and there is a hunted look in his eyes.

'Do you think your parents got on okay?'

It is a blunt question, insensitive even, given the drift of their conversation – but Perdita, rather than be offended, takes it in her stride – perhaps she is even relieved that he moves matters forwards.

'The honest answer is that I don't know – I was too young – even Martius was only nine when they died – and I don't think my siblings wish to remember them as anything but devoted.' She gives a little sigh – a suggestion that this is not all, that this is not the whole picture. 'They had opposing careers that dominated their lives – allowed them precious little time together. And I'm not sure they were a match made in heaven – the analytical thinker and the impulsive artist. Consider Edgar and Brutus if you want to see the same contrast in the flesh. They wouldn't have been the first married couple to experience difficulties, would they now?'

'Who would know?'

Slowly Perdita shakes her head, treading carefully in the snow, as if she picks her steps in the same way as she composes her reply.

'That, I'm not sure. They were both only-children. For each family, Regulus and O'More, theirs is a lost generation – we have no aunts or uncles, cousins or suchlike. Of course, my grandfather would have had some insight – and my great uncle to a lesser degree. Nanny moved back to her native Argentina – to a family of British diplomats in Buenos Aires – I heard some years ago that she had retired and later passed away. Today there is just Thwaites who survives – I suppose he may recall some of my parents' contemporaries.'

Skelgill is pensive – but Perdita tilts her head to one side and regards him keenly.

'Inspector, do you imagine some connection between their deaths and that of Great Uncle Declan?'

Skelgill makes a sudden expiration of breath; the kind of noise that signifies such an idea would be wild conjecture on his part.

'I imagine all sorts of things – but I don't much heed my imagination – most of the time it would just dump me in trouble, and I shouldn't be long in the job.'

Perdita brings her angled brows together.

'Inspector, I think we both know that is far from the case. Your record goes before you.'

Skelgill finds himself conflicted between modesty and preening, and though the latter threatens to prevail, he somehow contrives to play down her praise. And in any event – how does she know about his "record"?

'Happen I have my methods – if only I could work out what they were.'

In a gesture of mock exasperation she tosses her hair until it covers her face. When she parts the veil it is to reveal a look of mischief that belies the underlying gravity of her next question.

'Have your methods eliminated any of *us* yet, Inspector?'

Skelgill seems to tower over her – and all of a sudden she appears small and helpless before him. Indeed, he is compelled to reach out and grip her upper arm. She does not flinch, and lifts her opposite hand to cover his. He draws her closer. His features are strained.

'Rowena – I don't reckon you ought to worry on that score.' He licks his lips, his mouth dry – this is a breach of procedure after all – and now he sets his jaw, barring further loose talk. Yet, seemingly without volition, he raises his free hand to indicate the great snowy bulk that is Whiteless Pike, with Grasmoor beyond.

Perdita gives an answering nod – just a small inclination of her head that shows she understands his message – and he feels the tension drain from her slender frame. He steers her gently around, rather like he is demonstrating a country-dance move, until they face in the direction whence they came.

'Hey up, lass – I think we could both use a hot toddy.'

Perdita offers no objection, and begins to walk with him, closer now, so that they bump shoulders as they negotiate the uneven frozen ground. They have rambled just a few hundred yards from the cluster of slate-and-whitewashed properties that make up Buttermere village, and in five minutes they are stamping snow off their feet in the porch of the inn. For Skelgill, for whom manners are something of a variable smorgasbord, it would not generally be convention to despatch a small, pretty young woman ahead of him into a strange hostelry – exposed to whatever hostile or salacious heads may turn her way – but for some reason he deviates from his rule and pushes open the heavy oak door to allow her to go first. She steps past him, but then hesitates.

'Oh – Inspector – do you mind if we don't?' Now she spins around, blocking his way, and reaches to place a restraining palm on his chest. Skelgill sees the fleeting alarm in her eyes, before she composes herself. 'I've just remembered – I must call my agent in Dublin before 12:30 – my notes and my laptop are at the guest house.'

He tries casually to crane past her for a glance into the bar, from where emanates an inviting wave of beery warmth and woodsmoke and the hubbub of lunchtime drinkers, the occasional clink of a glass and peal of laughter. But she steps hastily out of the porch and Skelgill is obliged to let the inner door swing to in order not to lose sight of her.

'Aye – no bother – I'll run you along.' He casts an arm towards his car, the long brown salt-stained shooting brake in which he picked her up half an hour or so earlier. 'My next stop's in your direction.'

She smiles, at once sweetly and apologetically – it is an effective combination and as she backs away she draws him with her.

'Some other time soon, Inspector – yes?'

Skelgill affects enthusiasm; though it is plain he is a little crestfallen.

'Aye – that'll be grand.'

The snow in the car park is excessively rutted and icy, and treacherous underfoot. Perdita waits for him to catch her up, and then unprompted she links arms for support – though he is wearing only ordinary leather brogues and is no better equipped than she. Self-consciously he glances behind at the building, but the windows of the inn are bereft of watchers. Perdita leans against his shoulder, her head bowed as she concentrates upon the uneven ground. But her expression is one of consternation: for what she does not mention is that, tucked into a dark corner of the old beamed bar room – with a female for company – she glimpsed her brother.

*

It must be that old habits die hard, for Skelgill pays a passing visit to the outdoor privy beside the coalhouse at the rear of his mother's cottage. He has circumnavigated the terrace and entered by the rear gate, knowing the back door will be unlocked, and his mother – if she is home – most likely banging about in the kitchen. However, there is no sign of her bicycle – a decrepit boneshaker that she resolutely refuses to replace, despite continual offers from he and his brothers. These days of course there is an internal bathroom – a luxury she did accept from her offspring, part and parcel of them clubbing together to buy out the lease, a heritable estate of the most modest proportions, the freehold secured in perpetuity following the premature death of her spouse.

Skelgill enters to silence, but there is a delicious waft of lamb stew that he tracks to a pot simmering on the traditional range cooker. He lifts the lid and inhales, closing his eyes as the aroma rolls back the years. Eric Rudd would be nodding sagely, that he has timed his visit for dinner, as advised. Skelgill withdraws his hand quickly, conditioned to expect a sharp rap across the knuckles from a wooden spoon. He checks his watch – it is past 12:30 and his mother would ordinarily have returned by now – but then of course there is the snow, the roads are only partially clear, and it will have impeded her progress; though she may be engaged in a chinwag en route. He drifts across to a Welsh dresser, their sole family heirloom. Its upper shelves display photographs, and his eyes dart about, until they come to rest upon a portrait of himself – a mud-streaked sun-bleached urchin beaming precociously beneath a basin haircut, triumphantly holding aloft a trout parr hooked on a handline in the nearby beck. His age would have been seven years – about the time of 'The Accident'. He stares pensively for a few moments, and then beats a decisive retreat upon the polished oak. He swivels on his heel and sets off in search of his mother.

He marches somewhat more sedately than his regular pace, back towards Buttermere. He passes the gateway of the B&B where Perdita may be cavorting with the characters of her latest romance – the property is hidden among trees, conifers that still carry snow in their branches. The garden bordering the lane is walled – a necessary precaution in these parts, for sheep know the meaning of self-service. Skelgill notices little movements in a trained cotoneaster – it is a flock of waxwings busy with the fruits – perhaps the same avian party that was previously feasting at Braithwaite, and subsequently Crummock Hall. Such speculation is interrupted, however, for the roar of a tractor gathers beyond the bend. As it swings wildly into sight, Skelgill is obliged to press himself against the wall. He raises a palm to the farmer – but the man seems to be on a mission, he cannot spare a hand to return Skelgill's greeting, and instead makes a rather desperate backwards movement of the head, the whites of his eyes flashing disconcertingly. The great mechanical beast thunders past, a bouncing trailer in tow – and now Skelgill is hailed by the shriek of a passenger – for aboard, clinging gamely to the tailgate, handlebars of a bicycle protruding beside her, grey hair flapping in the wind, is an old woman, grinning and gap-toothed. As he is left marooned in their wake, she cackles gleefully and flicks a v-sign of dubious intent. It is his mother, 76-year-old Minnie Skelgill, née Graham.

12. CRUMMOCK HALL – Tuesday 1.30pm

'Where are you, Guvnor?'

'Crummock Hall – I'm using their landline.'

'Right you are, Guv.' DS Leyton sounds apprehensive – as though he anticipates an impossible question and the inevitable reprimand for his failure to know the answer.

'I thought I dialled Jones's extension.'

'You did, Guv.' DS Leyton hesitates for a second. 'She's on a day off.'

'What?'

'It's on the holiday chart in your office, Guv – remember last week you were saying – what with the year-end coming up – use it or lose it?'

In fact Skelgill had uttered a rather less repeatable version of this statement, airing his disapproval of "layabouts" who prioritise their holiday entitlement and drop their colleagues in the proverbial. He had made particular reference to "that flash Harry" DI Alec Smart. Now he emits an exasperated gasp.

'This is a murder inquiry, Leyton.'

'Perhaps she had a family commitment, Guv – her old Dad's been in and out of hospital lately. She's not said a lot about it.' DS Leyton does not sound happy – he suffers under the same unforgiving regime as his female colleague.

There is silence on the line while Skelgill swallows and digests his frustration. After a few moments DS Leyton finds the hiatus too unnerving and offers a suggestion.

'Is it something I can look at, Guv?'

Skelgill begins to make an unintelligible noise – indicative of disparagement – but then he evidently undergoes a change of heart.

'What you can do, Leyton, is dig out the coroner's inquest report of the drowning of Edward Regulus and Shauna O'More.'

This may not be a simple task, since these records are filed manually and kept in out-storage somewhere about the county – normally the local coroner's office requires a week to retrieve the documents. However, DS Leyton evidently sees no benefit in underlining any such hurdles.

'No bother, Guv – are you coming in later?'

'Who knows, Leyton.' (There is another period of silence.) 'What have we found by way of fingerprints in Declan's study?'

'Hold on, Guv – I've got that right here.' DS Leyton can be heard clicking away at his computer. 'That there birdwatching logbook, and the pendulum and the winder for the clock – all just Declan's prints. The key to the garden door had Martius's thumbprint on it.'

'Aye – he admitted that.'

'The key for the internal door – that was too messed up to get anything, same as Declan's fountain pen. And the glass that was lying on the carpet – no prints at all, Guv.'

'Leyton – there's always prints on a glass. It's the best place to look for them.'

DS Leyton makes an apologetic *ahem*.

'I'm just going by this report from Forensics, Guv.'

Skelgill is in no position to object further, but this item of relative trivia seems to trouble him. Again he ruminates in silence, and again DS Leyton is obliged to make the running.

'Had a couple of interesting leads on the O'Mores, Guv.'

'Aye?' But Skelgill remains distracted.

'First thing that popped up on my screen when I searched for Edgar's accountancy practice – he's being sued for negligence by a bunch of his rich clients.' (Skelgill makes no comment, but that DS Leyton can hear his breathing suggests he is at least listening.) 'Seems he'd advised them on this great wheeze to dodge National Insurance – paying their bonuses into an offshore trust – but the taxman objected and took 'em to court. It ran for years – went all the way to the House of Lords and they ruled in favour of HMRC. The clients had to pay back all the tax they avoided, plus – and this was the killer – eight years' compound interest at some punitive rate. So now they've raised a class action against Edgar's firm for multi-million damages.'

'He'll have insurance, Leyton.' Skelgill's tone is unreasonably dismissive.

For a moment DS Leyton is a little deflated. Gamely, however, he conjures a counter argument.

'But that don't always help, Guv. You know what insurers are like for finding loopholes. One of our kids put a light sabre through the brand new telly a couple of months back – we've got accidental damage cover but the company wouldn't have none of it – said attacking Darth Vader's no accident.'

Now Skelgill makes a scoffing noise, as if to signify that his sergeant's incongruous analogy proves his point. But DS Leyton is not finished.

'There's more, Guv – wait 'till you hear this.' He pauses, perhaps for dramatic effect; but Skelgill sounds like he is yawning, and DS Leyton is obliged to reveal his hand. 'The offshore trust was held in the British Virgin Islands – by none other than Regulus & Co merchant bank.'

DS Leyton makes a humming noise, redolent of self-satisfaction, but falling just short of an overt expression that he rests his case. Skelgill – as might be predicted – remains obdurate and does not comment. Eventually he asks a rather banal question.

'So what are you proposing?'

'I've had a word with a contact in City of London Police, Economic Crime Directorate – old mucker of mine – we were on the same intake, years back. He said he'd find out what he could without making any waves – so's not to let 'em know we're sniffing around.'

'Fair enough.'

'Thing is, Guv – I was thinking – if Edgar and Martius have cooked up something together – wouldn't it make sense if I took Martius instead of Brutus?' (Skelgill does not reply, so DS Leyton continues.) 'Google "Owain Jagger" and a shedload of celebrity gossip comes up – he's leading the life of Riley.'

'So what, Leyton?' Skelgill's voice is rising.

'I just thought, Guv – with Cassandra being a bit of a socialite and all – put the pair of them together and they're right up DS Jones's street – all this social media malarkey – it's more her generation.'

DS Leyton is treading on eggshells – and not just in subverting his superior's instructions.

'Leyton – she's twenty-six – that's not a different generation – your bairns are a different generation. You'll be applying to draw your slippers next, man.'

Of course, his sergeant makes a reasonable point – not least since he has unearthed a pecuniary connection between Martius and Edgar – but Skelgill is haunted by lurid fantasies that revolve around Brutus, aka Owain Jagger. And when his emotions hold sway, a logical hearing is unlikely – it takes something that appeals to his baser needs to provide an effective diversion. Unbeknown to DS Leyton this now arrives in the shape of a tray of antique silverware, Darjeeling tea and scones with jam and cream.

'Leyton – that's Thwaites here for me to interview.'

Skelgill peremptorily hangs up the call.

*

'It's just you and the staff left, Thwaites?'

Skelgill mumbles these words through a mouthful of dough, and waves the intact portion of his scone in a semi-circle to illustrate his meaning. He reposes on one of the sofas in the drawing room, and has induced Thwaites to take a seat opposite. It is the first time he has had a proper look at the butler in broad daylight, and the man's frailty is emphasised by his faded outfit, worn at the knees and elbows, lank grey hair and pallid complexion. As the afternoon sun's rays stream through a long mullioned window set in the south-west corner of the room, spotlighting a myriad of tiny dust motes, the old retainer resembles a Jamesian ghost, ephemeral and insubstantial. Only his dark eyes, shining like horse chestnuts newly broken out of their involucres, reveal some sense of a more vital life force within.

'That's correct, sir. Master Martius went yesterday before luncheon as you know, and Miss Cassandra and Master Brutus and Master Edgar took a taxi last evening to Kendal, to catch the London express from Oxenholme. Mr Mullarkey departed early this morning – his office had managed to book him on a flight from Liverpool that took off at midday. Miss Perdita has decided to lodge in the vicinity, sir. She arrived by ferry from Ireland in her motor car, and there is no point in her going home, as she would have to be back in two days for Mr Declan's funeral.' Now he looks a little remorseful, and perhaps his professional pride has been offended that she has moved out. He pulls himself together, however, and puts positive spin on the matter. 'She thinks she'd be better able to write – in what you might call more homely surroundings than rattling about in this big place, sir.'

Skelgill regards the old man with a certain agonised indecision. An onlooker would presume he doubts the butler's statement – but in fact what troubles him stems from his own sensibilities. While a career as a diplomat was never going to be his (and not just because of his station in life) – and while the culture of the Cumbrian farming community in which he is steeped is to call a spade a spade – he holds back – he plainly harbours some sympathy for the elderly retainer, a man with a modest background akin to his own, a man wounded in the service of Queen and country, and a man who has devoted his entire working life, well beyond normal retirement age, to his feudal employers. But Skelgill is Skelgill, and a policeman at that, and there are limits to his capability as regards beating about the bush.

'I need to put it to you, Thwaites – it's come to my attention – that concerning yourself there is an undisclosed matter – of paternity.'

The watchful brown eyes become those of a rabbit caught in the headlights, widening to reveal yellowed sclerae and bloodshot rims, and the frail figure seems to shrink within his butler's outfit, the fingers of his off-white gloves twitching involuntarily.

'But – why – what – w-who has been saying something, sir?'

The man's stammer seems to disconcert Skelgill and he swivels at the waist and stares out of a window, as if some movement has caught his eye. Indeed, he rises and stalks across for a better view: there is nothing new to observe, other than that the guelder rose bushes – as foreseen by the professor – have been stripped of their fruits and abandoned by the voracious waxwings. He remains staring, however, upon the snowy scene.

'Let's just say a little bird told me.'

Thwaites makes no reply; he seems petrified, grey as stone, unmoving in situ. It must be plain to Skelgill that his shot in the dark has found its target – yet he seems disinclined to press home his advantage. After a few moments he turns around, but remains at the windows, leaning against the sill. He digs his hands into his pockets, and lifts one shoe and inspects its scuffed toecap; he expels a reluctant sigh.

'Thing is, Thwaites – it was commonplace in those days – you'd be far from the first to be born the wrong side of the blanket –'

Skelgill suddenly becomes conscious of the other man's movement – it is nothing major, but a distinctive start that is out of synch with his present demeanour. He glances up at Thwaites, contriving a sympathetic expression – but Thwaites has set his jaw and now presents a surprisingly defiant countenance.

'But, sir – my father was an American airman.'

'What?'

'His name was Hal, sir – Harold O'Rourke. I'm named after him, sir. He was a nose-gunner on the Flying Fortresses. He was stationed at RAF Silloth for a time – a special assignment helping out on the Wellingtons – and that's when he met my mother. He was shot down over the North Sea and listed missing in action. She never got to marry him, sir.'

Now it is Skelgill's turn to be rocked. He gazes blankly at Thwaites but then turns back to look out of the window, perhaps to conceal his consternation. That his lunchtime picking of his mother's brains might have provided him with misinformation, he had not bargained for. She is sharp as a tack, with a memory to match – however, she was just a slip of a girl, of an age with little Harold Thwaites when these events might still have retained some salacious currency in the local grapevine. Of course – Minnie Graham might not be wrong. That Mary Ann Thwaites had a less than virtuous reputation is in a sense confirmed by her fleeting liaison with the American. It need not have stopped with him. That she was provided with protected employment and an estate cottage by Padraig O'More was reasonable evidence on which to base the supposition that there had been some relationship – Padraig O'More might have believed (indeed been *induced* to believe) that he was the source of her out-of-wedlock 'trouble'; and perhaps even Mary Ann did not know who was the father-to-be. But if Aerial Gunner O'Rourke downed over Doggerland was responsible, then any embryonic theory of Skelgill's concerning Thwaites' as-yet-unasserted claim of succession as a half-brother to Sean and Declan O'More is likewise shot down in flames.

While such thoughts assail Skelgill's mind, his body is working to dispel any outward impression that he has been knocked off his stride. But a twitching of the shoulders is suggestive of an inner turmoil – something, perhaps a subtle aspect of Thwaites' reaction, is telling him not to consign this idea to the trash. He swings about to find the butler watching with furrowed brow. Skelgill waves an arm in an offhand manner.

'Not to worry Thwaites – if it turned out to be an issue – you know we can sort it with a simple DNA test. If we swabbed yourself – cross-referenced it with one of the family – that would soon clear up whether you were both related to her grandfather.'

This hypothetical prospect seems to bring on a repeat bout of Thwaites' initial unease. He swallows, with difficulty, his prominent Adam's apple jumping like a trapped frog in the saggy gullet of a pelican. He inhales wheezily and now looks pleadingly at Skelgill.

'I shouldn't like to offend the family's honour, sir.'

Skelgill regards him reflectively for a few moments.

'Aye – well – like you say – doesn't sound like there's any need for all that palaver.'

Thwaites bows his head with excessive servility.

'Very good, sir.' He sounds as though he is taking an order for drinks.

Skelgill breaks away from the window and strides to the grand piano where the family photographs are arranged. Thwaites watches his progress. Skelgill beckons him to follow.

'What you can do, Thwaites, is tell me who would have known Edward Regulus and Shauna O'More.'

Thwaites rises arthritically from the sofa; for a moment he seems in danger of toppling forwards, until of a fashion he straightens up and gains his balance. It strikes Skelgill that the old man himself could be doing with a walking stick, though it would not befit the duties of a butler. He shuffles across to where Skelgill is examining a print he has selected. It is a portrait of a group of men in tweeds, casually armed with expensive shotguns and lounging around the rear of a Land Rover Defender, labradors and working cockers milling at their feet.

'That's Mr Regulus there, sir.' Thwaites indicates with a trembling gloved forefinger. 'That would have been a shooting party – Mr Regulus used to bring his important clients up from London.'

'So these are not his friends?'

Thwaites shakes his head doubtfully.

'I don't recall any regular friends, sir – of Mr Regulus, or of himself and Miss Shauna as a married couple. It wasn't very often that they came here together. There was a London crowd – but they were both well known in their particular spheres and had a lot of what you might call acolytes, especially Miss Shauna, being such a public figure. And as for business associates, Mr Regulus would invite different ones each time, as a rule, sir. I should say he only visited on average twice or thrice a year, sometimes just for a weekend. Although Miss Shauna was born here she'd moved away to drama school at an early age – I don't she think had such an affinity with Crummock Hall. And Mr

Regulus was very much a city person. It was the children that stayed for longer periods, for their school holidays, sir.'

Skelgill nods pensively. He waves a hand rather hopefully at the collection of photographs.

'Is there anyone here that jogs your memory, Thwaites?'

The butler glances jerkily from one composition to another. His expression has the pained look of an eyewitness who is desperate to help but is unable to pick out a suspect. Finally he turns his attention back to the picture that Skelgill still holds. Skelgill angles the frame so he can better see.

'My memory's not so good these days, sir.' Nonetheless he stabs with an index finger. 'That gentleman might be Mr Mullarkey – the elder – I think he was an uncle or great uncle of the present Mr Mullarkey – but I believe he passed away, and that was why the young Mr Mullarkey took over, sir.'

Skelgill scrutinises the image. Thwaites refers to one of seven or eight men in the shooting party; he looks a good generation older than the rest of the laughing group, and is positioned a little to one side. And certainly he bears a small resemblance to Fergal Mullarkey – there are the round protruding ears, and the same pattern of hair loss (though it is difficult to discern any colour due to the faded nature of the photograph). Skelgill makes a doubting face, but nonetheless digs his phone from a pocket.

'I'll ask him.'

Now Thwaites stands by obediently while Skelgill composes a photograph and hands him the original. Skelgill extracts Fergal Mullarkey's business card from his wallet and squints to read the small print of the mobile phone number.

'What is it, +353 for Ireland?'

'I believe so, sir.'

Skelgill gives a little grunt of approval. 'Look at that – full signal.'

He taps in a brief note and transmits it along with the image, watching his handset with scepticism until it advises him the message has gone. He puts away the phone and then takes the picture back from the butler. He checks the reverse of the frame, but there are no markings of any kind.

'When do you reckon this was?'

'I should say in the spring of the year of The Accident, sir – or perhaps the autumn before.'

Now Skelgill replaces the framed original on the grand piano. For a moment the butler looks like he would wish to rearrange the positioning, for Skelgill's work is rather slipshod. However, his training gets the better of him and he suppresses any such inclination.

'On the day of the drowning, Thwaites, they went fishing. Was that usual?'

Thwaites seems a little reluctant to answer this question; his breathing appears to be troubling him.

'It was Mr Declan's boat, sir. He'd had it made ready the night before. But Mr Regulus was the headstrong sort, if you know what I mean, sir? Mr Declan was not too pleased when he discovered they'd taken it.'

Skelgill's expression has darkened at this revelation.

'What about when he heard what had happened?'

Now Thwaites seems positively embarrassed on behalf of his late master.

'He wasn't one to declare his emotions, sir – especially when it came to affection. If he complained at you it was his way of showing he cared, in a funny sort of way.' (Skelgill exhibits a flicker of recognition in response to this notion, but remains silent.) 'It's difficult to remember too much about the time, sir.' He pauses for thought, as if to illustrate his dilemma. 'I do recall the police coming with his fishing rod – asking him to identify it – he was awkward about that, because they'd wanted to keep it – as some kind of evidence, I suppose.'

Inevitably this statement sparks Skelgill's curiosity.

'Tell me about it.'

'The rod floated, you see, sir – they found it long before they found the bodies.' Thwaites looks discomfited. 'Of course, sir – it was never used again – Sir Sean put a stop to all boating and fishing after that – but it's hanging in the main hallway if you wanted to see it? That's just outside, sir.'

'Aye – why not.'

It has not escaped Skelgill's notice where there is fishing equipment displayed around the walls, and indeed he makes a beeline to the correct item. It is a traditional seven-foot split cane fly rod, with a cork grip and equipped with a brass reel stamped *Hardy Bros, Alnwick*. Skelgill needs no invitation to take it down from its brackets, adroitly unfastening the twisted wires that hold it in place.

'They don't make them like they used to, Thwaites.'

'No, sir – I should think that applies to a good many things.'

Skelgill weighs the rod in his hand, and turns it to examine the reel. It is set up right-handed, as most rods would be – but that does not stop Skelgill from experimentally stripping out half a dozen yards of line, the ratchet of the reel protesting like a chorus of cicadas in the great echoing hallway. He releases the fly from the hook keeper.

'Thing is, Thwaites – this isn't a boat rod.'

'No, sir?'

'Best thing about split cane – it's ideal for fishing on a beck, where's there's overhanging trees – tuck a short roll cast into the places where trout lie like no other material.'

'Really, sir?'

'Aye – watch this. See that Indian rug at the end of the hall?'

Thwaites has no time to reply and can only lurch aside as Skelgill lifts the rod left-handed, and in a smooth movement draws it back at a low angle, avoiding the ceiling and loading the tip with line. Without interruption there is sudden swish – the rod has come alive, like a rapier in the hands of a skilled swordsman – and a curling loop of line is projected down the long hallway, the invisible leader with a final elegant flourish turning over to deposit the fly gently in the centre of the rug, some twenty feet away.

'My word, sir – that's very impressive if you don't mind me saying so.'

Skelgill settles for a shrug of affected modesty; now he inverts the rig so he can reel in – with a final deft flick he retracts the leader and grabs it just above the fly. He inspects the lure with interest.

'Greenwell's Glory.' (The butler looks a little nonplussed.) 'You don't fish, Thwaites?'

'No, sir – never, tried it sir.'

Skelgill dangles the fly for the man to see.

'It's the name of the pattern. Invented by a vicar from County Durham in the eighteen hundreds – for trout streams. If you ask me, Declan was planning to fish the outflow of the Cocker – or Buttermere Dubs, at a push.'

Thwaites nods obediently.

'I couldn't really say, sir. I recall he sometimes fished Bassenthwaite.'

'Lake.'

'Sorry, sir?'

Bassenthwaite Lake. Bassenthwaite's a settlement.'

'Of course, sir – that's right.'

Skelgill looks like he is about to trot out his little maxim – but must realise there is a danger of the conversation drifting into an unproductive backwater.

'Did Edward Regulus fish much when he came here?'

'Not as I recall, sir – as I mentioned, he was a city person, you see – I think he liked the idea of country pursuits – but he didn't have a great deal of practical experience.'

'Reckon that was the cause of the accident?'

'What else could it have been, sir?'

Skelgill shrugs.

'Happen they had an argument – an altercation – swamped the boat?'

Thwaites looks troubled.

'I suppose it's possible, sir.'

Skelgill notes that the old retainer doesn't reject the idea out of hand.

'How did they get on together?'

'It could be a little combustible at times, sir. Mr Regulus was accustomed to getting his own way – and of course Miss Shauna she had what you might call a fiery temper when it came to standing up for herself – that's in the O'Mores' nature – young Miss Perdita being a case in point – though a proper little lady she's turned out to be, sir, and artistic like her mother.'

He reflects on this analysis with some satisfaction. Then suddenly he seems unnerved to find Skelgill watching him closely. He folds his hands in front of him in the servant's pose of attention, and waits to be addressed. Skelgill duly obliges.

'Still – they must have been alright if they went fishing – the last thing you do if you want to avoid someone is go out with them in a boat.'

Thwaites is forced to accept this logic – certainly he offers no rejoinder – and his mind would not be trained to work like Skelgill's, who could imagine half a dozen reasons why you *would* take someone out in a boat if you wished them ill.

Skelgill hands over the rod for Thwaites to return to its place on the wall. For a moment the old butler apes Skelgill's original action, and weighs the rod in his hands as though he is thinking about giving it a whirl. But he frowns when he realises something is amiss.

'The winder seems to be on the wrong side for me, sir – I'm afraid I'm left-handed.'

Skelgill grunts approvingly.

'Don't worry about it, Thwaites – sign of intelligence.'

13. HEADQUARTERS – Wednesday 11am

It is not every year that winter coats the countryside in such abundance – in fact on this scale it is more of a once-in-a-decade event – and Skelgill is unaccustomed to the view that greets him each morning from his office window. As the late dawn unveils the bleak beauty of the snowscape he observes a phenomenon that seems to fascinate him: that, while under ordinary conditions the rolling farmland rising to the distant Howgills is a flat and amorphous vista blending browns and greens and greys with no particular landmarks, beneath its blanket of snow it is transformed into a detailed diagram – almost a 3D map – in which every tree and brake and wall and barn is meticulously inked in black upon white; up to the naked eye's limit, even every sheep is visible. If there is an analogy to be drawn, perhaps he wishes for some magical lycopodium powder – like that used for fingerprinting of old – that could be sprinkled about Crummock Hall to bring out the salient details of this case. But there is a complication – a fourth dimension – he has encountered a time-warp; events stretching back over decades and even centuries might hold some import and inform his rudimentary theories; thus the amorphous landscape prevails in his own mind's eye.

'Got that coroner's report, Guv – courier just dropped it off with George at the front desk. Had it copied for us.' DS Leyton's tone is matter of fact; clearly he is not expecting praise for whatever heroic endeavours have circumvented the system.

Skelgill does not respond immediately, instead he remains standing at the window, gazing out. But his sergeants have arrived in tandem, and while DS Leyton brings news DS Jones bears supplies from the canteen, and these turn his head: aromatic bacon rolls and piping hot teas. Skelgill is quick to exchange places: he regains his seat and pulls a plate and a mug from the tray, she assumes her station beneath the window, taking just a black tea. DS Leyton carefully positions a copy of the report on the desk – but not so close as to suggest that

Skelgill ought actually to read it. He, too, helps himself to comestibles.

'Thanks, Emma – good on you, girl.'

'You're welcome.'

Skelgill, already tucking in, raises an eyebrow in her direction, which may be a token acknowledgement, an obligation felt in light of DS Leyton's more profuse thanks – however it might be deduced that he still resents her absence yesterday.

'Bacon's a bit on the streaky side this morning, Guv.'

Though there is a certain verisimilitude in what DS Leyton says, in fact it is a conversational point (perhaps raised to snuff out the flicker of disharmony) rather than a well-founded complaint. Skelgill, ducking into a double-handed bite, looks up critically.

'Leyton – if you can't finish it, I'll have yours.'

Now DS Leyton clearly feels under pressure – he realises he has made a slip and must disappoint his boss – when it comes to his stomach, Skelgill ranks quantity before quality.

'Ah – well, Guv – I'll give it a chance – reckon I've got one notch still spare on the old belt.'

Skelgill gives a disparaging toss of the head, and then indicates the coroner's inquest report – meaning he wants to know what it says. DS Leyton hoists his plate onto the filing cabinet beside his regular seat, and brushes flour from his fingers before locating his own copy.

'I've had a quick butcher's, Guv. Top line: verdict of death by misadventure – no suspicious circumstances. Both parties drowned. No lifejackets worn – nor any found. Sir Sean Willoughby O'More gave evidence that Shauna O'More was a competent swimmer, but that he believed Edward Regulus was not. Her silk scarf was wrapped round his wrist, and it was suggested she'd tried to tow him to safety but it proved too much for her.'

Skelgill is munching pensively, regarding his subordinate through narrowed eyes. Of course, he knows this detail, but at the moment he shows no inclination to mention it. DS Leyton continues.

'It was recorded that because the boat was never recovered, it was impossible to say whether there was any third-party liability – but, after all, it belonged to Crummock Hall – it's not like they rented it from one of these boat-hire companies.'

'It belonged to Declan, Leyton.'

'Straight up, Guv?' Beneath DS Leyton's inquisitive frown it is apparent that he is trying to guess what Skelgill expects him to make of this. He dives for cover back into the document. 'It was also noted that they were inexperienced on water – however, the conditions were calm and the witness who raised the alarm reported that the boat hadn't capsized – it was sinking.' Now he scratches his head rather absently. 'You'd think it would float even if it filled with water, Guv – then you could just hang on to the side?'

Skelgill treats his sergeant's question as rhetorical, and does not offer a reply. But now DS Jones weighs in with a more direct inquiry.

'Guv – I know this is a daft question – but how would a boat fill with water?'

Skelgill pounces upon the opportunity to show his expertise, as long-standing skipper of a tub not dissimilar to that which went down with the Regulus-O'Mores. He holds up a quelling palm while he gulps tea to clear his throat.

'Any wooden boat leaks to some degree – but usually we're talking minor. It all depends how you've looked after it. See – wood swells when it's wet – on a clinker-built boat that swelling can break the internal structures of the strakes where they're pinned by the copper rivets. Let the boat dry out – the wood shrinks – except now it's damaged. When it's soaked again it can't expand to its original size – so you get little gaps that won't reseal.'

DS Jones is nodding thoughtfully.

'Surely it would be obvious if it leaked?'

'Not if it were holed an inch above the waterline. Might have been overlooked with just Declan using it – then two folk get aboard and maybe take a load of gear – wine bottles, picnic hampers, whatever – that causes the draught to increase – now it's holed *below* the waterline.' He pauses to allow the facts of Archimedes' Principle to sink in. 'Water trickles down the hull and gathers beneath the bottom boards. Be easy not to notice – especially if you're a novice. So the draught grows by the minute. Then maybe there's another leak, a bit higher up, and this comes into play – now you've got water ingress in two or more places. And if there's no baler – she's filling to the gunnels – what do you do?'

His tone is ominous, and DS Leyton shudders, self-confessed landlubber that he is. But DS Jones correctly interprets the peculiar workings of Skelgill's ego.

'What would *you* do, Guv?'

Skelgill gives a casual but self-important shrug of his shoulders.

'If I had a non-swimmer in the boat – I'd make sure their lifejacket was inflated. Then row like the clappers towards the nearest shallows. If you must sink, may as well make it somewhere you can salvage the boat from.'

Skelgill's disproportionate concern for his craft does nothing to allay DS Leyton's fears, and he remains disconcerted by the prospect.

'Guv, from what the eyewitness said – sounds like they were panicking – they weren't going nowhere – only down.'

Skelgill does not respond – instead he becomes submersed in a brown study. He consumes the last remnants of his bacon roll in silence. There is a rather sinister question that has been threatening to bob to the surface of their discussion; now DS Leyton rather candidly dredges it up.

'Reckon there's more to it, Guv? Some connection with old Declan? Think he could have known about the condition of the boat?'

Skelgill blinks a few times and gazes rather vacantly at his sergeant. Then he wipes his lips on his cuff.

'You tell me, Leyton.' It is a frustrating response, however he tempers it with some unexpected praise. He pats the hitherto uninspected document lying upon his desk. 'Good job on getting this – last time I spoke to that archivist it was like drawing teeth.'

DS Leyton looks suddenly pleased with himself – but it is a short-lived indulgence, for he realises Skelgill's commendation is a backhanded compliment aimed at DS Jones. Now Skelgill regards her with a certain impatience – unfairly so if he alludes to her day off, when she could not be expected to work. Yet such an assumption would be to underestimate her diligence, intelligence and – not least – her speed-reading proficiency. As Skelgill inhales to speak she interjects.

'About Declan, Guv.'

'What about him?'

'It occurred to me that we've got a kind of diary – a slice of life at least – I was looking at his nature log – first thing this morning.' Skelgill is scowling doubtfully, but DS Jones presses on, undeterred. She holds up her copy of the coroner's inquest report. 'In here it states that when the police contacted Crummock Hall to check if Edward Regulus and Shauna O'More were missing it was 1pm.' She pauses for dramatic effect – though Skelgill remains disinterested. 'According to his logbook, on the afternoon of the drowning Declan went bird-watching between two o'clock and four. From the entry you wouldn't know it wasn't just an ordinary day. And – incidentally – the coroner's report also notes that he did not give evidence at the inquest because he was too ill to attend.'

These revelations certainly have the effect of stunning DS Jones's colleagues into a silence. Skelgill seems reluctant to show any particular reaction – but DS Leyton's broad fleshy features become twisted into a mask of consternation. It is he that speaks first.

'Cor blimey – that's bang out of order.' He rattles his sheaf of papers. 'This says Sir Sean mobilised all the staff and led them down to the lake – they were frantic, searching the banks in the area the boat was last sighted. And old Declan goes bird-spotting!'

Now the two sergeants turn to Skelgill to await his pronouncement. He gnaws rather distractedly at a thumbnail.

'We've heard he was a recluse.' He spits a sliver, real or imaginary. 'All Declan knew was they were missing, not dead.'

This appears to be the sum of what Skelgill has to say on the matter – it is typical that he refuses to be drawn; like a patrolling pike eschewing a juicy bait, he acknowledges its presence but mistrusts the particular swim in which it dangles, conditioned by the scars of some narrow scrape of old. Yet DS Jones – who could be excused for trying to curry favour – has a point that is both apposite and thought provoking; DS Leyton might have procured the elusive coroner's report, but it is she that has made something of it. Could Declan have been complicit in 'The Accident' – and might such a possibility provide a connection to his untimely death?

However, their conference is about to be turned topsy-turvy: Skelgill's office door opens uninvited, and the mustelid-like features of DI Alec Smart become insinuated in the crack. He sidles in like a grinning cartoon character with the power to slip through improbably small gaps, taking care not to besmirch the designer suit that clothes his angular frame.

Skelgill's expression blackens, and he looks like he is about to berate DI Smart in no uncertain terms for his unwelcome entrance – but the interloper is quickest to the draw.

'Tasty line for you, Cock – no strings attached.' He addresses Skelgill directly, his nasal Mancunian drawl imbuing his words with a guileful undertone. 'Chief forwarded me your initial report on your little celebrity difficulty.'

Skelgill folds his arms and sinks against the back of his chair, his knotted brows a wall of dark distrust. That DI Smart has invoked the rank of their senior officer – and painted the case as problematic – succeeds in putting him on the defensive. Now DI Smart gains in confidence, and takes a couple of casual steps into the centre of the floor.

'Not exactly your bag, eh, Skel? City slickers and celebs and not a country bumpkin to be seen.'

Skelgill seems tongue-tied and can only glower more fervently. DI Smart preens, brushing at the lapels of his merino jacket and inspecting the shine on his outrageously pointed footwear.

'She knows it's right up my street – soon sort it with the right team *under* me.'

Head still bowed, his salacious grin widens and he flashes a sidelong glance at DS Jones. She squirms uncomfortably beneath his eviscerating scrutiny – and not least his blatant and somewhat lewd double-entendre. Today she wears more comfortable attire for desk-based work – indeed she has arrived in Skelgill's office in what might be a trendy Aran sweater, perhaps anticipating her superior's habit of keeping open the windows, whatever the weather. However, her lithe lower limbs are sheathed in her trademark stretch jeans, and it is this feature of her anatomy that attracts DI Smart's flagrantly roving eye. Now he winks at her – and tugs at his tie and casts about as though he is looking for a mirror in which to admire himself.

'Chance for someone to get their glad rags on – jaunt to London I reckon, rub shoulders with the glitterati.'

His intimation is plain to his fellow officers – and quite likely he has made a play to the Chief to take over Skelgill's case. That he is not gleefully bearing news of a proclamation to this effect, however, suggests any such attempt has been rebuffed – for the time being, at least. Skelgill might not be best versed in regard to high society, but he does have local provenance on his side – and perhaps this is recognised by the powers that be. Skelgill must detect that the balance of power still rests in his favour, and at last contrives a rejoinder of sorts.

'Aye, well – happen the right team's in place already, Smart.'

DI Smart shrugs indifferently, but in a way that at once openly admits defeat and suggests that any such victory of Skelgill's will prove to be in vain. He digs his hands into his pockets and whistles a couple of bars. It is clear that any meaning is lost on Skelgill – but DS Jones patently identifies what is the theme tune of *Empty Hollow*, in which 'Owain Jagger' of course stars. Unnoticed by her two male colleagues, whose eyes are upon DI Smart, her cheeks redden.

'Like I was saying, Skel – got a little line for you. Your report states that the four O'Mores that live down south have returned to London.' Now he pointedly looks at DS Jones, who is compelled to shy away and examine her notes. 'But your posh soap star Brutus was spotted incognito in a local hostelry yesterday.'

'Which hostelry?' The pressure cooker that is Skelgill's pent-up ire has him hissing this question before he can contain himself.

Now DI Smart comes over rather coy.

'Couldn't tell you for sure, Skel. My pretty little source doesn't want to compromise herself.' He edges away until he stands in the doorway; now that he has dropped his bombshell he wants to stand back and admire the results. 'Trust me – I'll let you know if I get any more – always happy to help, Cock.'

He winks again – this time at the angry-looking Skelgill – but as he turns to depart he leers at DS Jones and taps the side of his nose, palpably compounding her discomfort. With a click of his heels he is gone, leaving the door open and only the sound of his footsteps diminishing down the corridor. True to form, he has bested Skelgill in the verbal exchange; rather like a rogue hyena that inveigles himself into a rival clan to plunder their resources, disorient the males and impregnate the females, he retreats cackling before the incumbents can muster a counter-attack and drive him off. DS Leyton, who has been ignored throughout the whole episode, reaches from his seat and slaps shut the door. Skelgill thumps a fist down upon his desk, causing the tray to rattle and his mug to jump alarmingly.

'Divvy.'

Naturally he employs a somewhat more graphic version of this Cumbrian slight, with a clutch of Anglo-Saxon adjectives thrown in for good measure. His belated retort is meant to restore his wounded pride in the eyes of his tribe. His colleagues have their eyes lowered sheepishly, and there is an awkward silence before DS Leyton eventually moves himself to speak.

'I meant to warn you DI Smart was sniffing around, Guv – he was going about yesterday afternoon like a cat with the cream.' He rubs the top of his head rather absently. 'Think he's right, Guv – that Brutus didn't go back to London?'

Skelgill gapes at his sergeant – disapproving of his disloyalty in attaching credence to DI Alec Smart's teasing morsel. However, his expression becomes somewhat introspective; he pauses to examine his rough-skinned fisherman's hands, tilting his palms to reflect the light, in the pose that an angler displays his catch for a souvenir photograph. He glances briefly at DS Jones, as though he seeks her confirmation. There is a residual blush around her sculpted cheekbones and trepidation in her dark eyes. She looks like she wishes he would not question her – and in the event this comes to pass. Skelgill intertwines all but his index fingers and makes a little church, or maybe a pistol.

'He mentioned staying in the area – I didn't take him seriously. Thwaites confirmed that the three of them left together last night by taxi – Cassandra, Edgar and Brutus. But that doesn't prove he took the train with the others.' Now Skelgill turns to DS Leyton. 'I'll leave it with you.'

DS Leyton shifts somewhat uncomfortably in his seat, but his reply is accommodating.

'I'm onto it, Guvnor.'

Now DS Jones clears her throat, and uncrosses her legs and leans forwards. Her movement attracts the attention of her colleagues.

'Guv – I have a friend – I shared a flat with her at Uni – she stayed in London and went into journalism. I spoke with her yesterday – she's a junior features editor on *Celebz*.'

Skelgill regards her cynically – but it is a look she recognises that he employs when he is concealing a deficit in his knowledge. For some reason she pauses, as if to put him to the test – but now DS Leyton chips in.

'*Celebz* – the missus gets that delivered – she's a right old sucker for gossip – likes to know who's knocking up who.'

In fact he uses a rather more crude expression, but his artless manner causes DS Jones to giggle rather than take offence. Skelgill, however, is dismayed that there can be a whole industry devoted to the promulgation of celebrity couplings, and – worse – an audience with an insatiable appetite for such inane trivia. DS Jones hurries on with her story.

'My contact is sending links for various articles – some not published – they've got masses on "Owain Jagger"' (she makes the parentheses around Brutus O'More's stage name with her fingertips) 'but also references to Cassandra – and Martius – where he's appeared at VIP charity dinners, that sort of thing. She's also on good terms with one of their top reporters – it struck me that if we wanted some questions asked it might be a way to get under the radar.'

Skelgill is now regarding her broodingly – but DS Leyton seems enthused by this notion.

'Right enough, girl – people clam up the second you say you're a copper – but if they think they're going to be in a magazine or on the telly there's no stopping 'em.'

Now Skelgill is quick to interject.

'Aye – you'd know all about that, Leyton.'

Skelgill refers, of course, to DS Leyton's own minor aberration in this regard, with the camera crew outside Crummock Hall. His sergeant squirms with what might be both intentional and comic irony – for the paradox proves his point. Skelgill disregards his protest and addresses DS Jones.

'See what comes of it – pass anything about Brutus to Leyton.' DS Jones begins to remonstrate, but Skelgill speaks over her. 'You didn't mention Perdita.'

DS Jones takes a moment to reply.

'I asked about her, Guv – but it seems she keeps to herself in Dublin. *Celebz* is restricted to the London scene. I could try again – see if they've got an Irish correspondent?'

Now Skelgill folds his arms and hunches his shoulders as though he is suddenly feeling the cold.

'She's the least of our worries, Jones.'

14. THE SECOND FUNERAL – Friday 11am

Skelgill acknowledges Perdita as she passes. None of the rest of the family party has noticed him, despite their entrance to St James' Buttermere being an altogether less choreographed affair than a week ago. Their attire lacks the formal precision displayed for Sir Sean's funeral – most have opted for the practical expedient of warm overcoats and sensible boots, perhaps a mutually agreed decision to dumb down. (However Skelgill recognises Brutus's rather effeminately styled fur, worn for his TV interview in which DS Leyton infamously appeared as 'Columbo'.) Nor is there the packed congregation of starched-shirt dignitaries representing the various trusts and charities of which Sir Sean was a benefactor, nor dutiful tenant farmers from the estate, nor star-struck locals hoping for another glimpse of their gentry *in absentia*. Perhaps it is that the funeral has not been announced, or perhaps it is the weather – or perhaps it is just superstition, mutterings in the village over carefully nursed pints and elbow-smoothed shop counters, and between shepherds conferring upon their crooks across snow-capped stone walls. Although on reflection Skelgill might imagine that murder is a reason folk *would* come. He counts just seven other attendees, whom he knows as elderly locals – two batty – who have scant connection to Declan that he can think of, but probably little else to do on a frozen snowy Friday morn in December. There is no trace of the Gilhooleys.

Perdita flashes him a wry grin – though before he caught her eye she appeared troubled, and the smile fades as she proceeds up the narrow nave in company with her siblings; they walk in single file in descending age order – a long-standing habit of theirs, perhaps? Behind them comes the small coterie of estate staff, led by Thwaites; Skelgill notes they move with a little more alacrity than before, when Declan, assisted by a combination of Thwaites on one side and his walking stick on the other, determined the speed of the procession and in fact rendered a pace with an appropriate degree of solemnity. Finally, like a loyal sheepdog that hangs back to nip any strays, the lawyer Fergal Mullarkey brings up the rear of the cortege.

Now the organ heaves into life and Skelgill starts. His 'regular' pew beside Wainwright's window is at the very back of the small church and the two-centuries-old instrument with its dark carved oak surround and gilt-painted pipes is crammed into the corner directly behind him. The tune is *Crimond* and its haunting melody envelops him – almost literally – and perhaps together with the un-sung words of the Shepherd's Psalm transports him to a mystical *Arcadia*. After a short while, however, his gaze begins to wander – for one marvellous contemporary feature of this most modest place of worship is its collection of intricately stitched hassocks that hang neatly on the back of the pews, a humbling labour of love that captures in its meticulous detail characteristic aspects of the locality, along with associated Christian imagery, each and every one sewn with magnificently understated grace. Skelgill notes a nativity scene; and three angels like paper-chain dollies; a stunning facsimile of the arched stained glass windows of Mary and Martha; there is the church itself, viewed from a little higher up the lane to Newlands Hause, with Blea Crag for a backdrop; a remarkably lifelike Herdwick tup and another portrait of a noble Blackface of uncertain gender (since both sexes are horned); for his part – for his own hassock – Skelgill has a snowy upland landscape that he can't identify, but it holds his attention for he realises it features a team of four or five roped figures marching through the snow, bearing a stretcher in their midst: the mountain rescue. He grins ruefully – perhaps it is the coincidence (he had not noticed this hassock on his visit a week ago), or it could be their standard-issue outfits of smart red cagoules, black over-trousers and white helmets – if only!

Subconsciously he reaches for his trapper hat that rests on the bench beside him, and begins to turn it over in his hands, like a worshipper with rosaries – but his musing is abruptly interrupted when at the end of the short pew there suddenly appears a man, who regards him inquisitively and slides into the seat. In return Skelgill engages in surreptitious sidelong surveillance. The fellow is a little breathless, as if he might have jogged up the hill from the village. Youngish – certainly younger than he, maybe around the thirty mark – there are, however, aspects of his appearance that cry out "middle-age" – indeed middle age in a bygone era. He is below average height, and slight of frame; his brown hair is neatly trimmed and side-parted, and thoroughly combed into place. There is a military moustache – of the handlebar type – and small dark eyes set among regular and not unpleasant features. Beneath an oversized greatcoat (out of which he now struggles) is a traditional ensemble of navy blazer, black trousers and brogues, and a white shirt buttoned at the collar and worn with a hastily knotted old school tie. All in all, it is the impression of a pukka chap one might meet by invitation for lunch at his Pall Mall club.

He catches Skelgill looking at him, and nods politely and makes a grimace of apology, though this would appear to be in relation to his lateness rather than any invasion of Skelgill's personal space (which may be a reasonable complaint of Skelgill's, given there are so many unoccupied pews from which to choose). Skelgill responds with a rather cursory nod of his own and edges a couple of inches closer to the window, which is indeed suggestive that he would rather have the stall to himself.

While the service for the recently departed Declan follows a similar pattern to that of his identical twin only a week earlier, it is by necessity a more brief affair, not least for the lack of any real substance that the family have been able to provide for the eulogy. The vicar does his best to make a decent fist of the task, but it proves thin on facts and heavy on hyperbole, clichés and platitudes. Indeed phrases such as "greatly missed" and "dearly beloved" contrive to combine all three figures of speech. Certainly Skelgill's attention wavers, and one by one he repeatedly scrutinises the family party, as though he is occupying himself with a peculiar game of eeny, meeny, miny, mo.

Not that there is a great deal to see. Unlike his perspiring neighbour they are hunched in their coats – the church is little warmer than the freezing outdoors – and if Skelgill were performing a comparison he is restricted to the backs of their heads, as they are ranged across the first two rows of pews. There is Martius, fair, with his Sandhurst officer's cut, and beside him Cassandra, the closest match in colour, her shoulder-length hair tinted with bronze and gold. Then the contrasting identical twins, Brutus with his full head of dark, wavy locks, casual yet no doubt skilfully coiffured, Edgar mousy and utilitarian short back and sides. Next and most striking is Perdita's unruly abundance of strawberry blonde ringlets, which from time to time she draws back from her face. Behind the family are the servants – Fergal Mullarkey perhaps excepted from this class definition, he instantly recognisable by his bald crown ringed by its band of ginger – and Thwaites with his lank grey hair combed and plastered in place with macassar or some other such oil.

The perpetual winner of Skelgill's little diversion appears to be Perdita, for after each pass his focus invariably comes to rest upon her – although perhaps it is her tendency to be most often fidgeting that draws his gaze. However, when the service concludes and the family retreats down the stone-flagged aisle, it is apparent that he intentionally makes eye contact and begins to move to intercept her. However, he finds his way blocked by his strange young-yet-old neighbour who, in picking up his coat contrives to spill a jangling assortment of car keys, coins and pipe-smoking accessories, obliging Skelgill first to wait, and then rather grudgingly to stoop down and join in the recovery process. By the time the man's scattered property has been gleaned from the salt-bleached floorboards, it is clear they will be the last two left in the church.

'Thank you, Inspector Skelgill – so kind of you.'

His accent is a rather exaggerated English public school strain of received pronunciation, and he utters these words as Skelgill hands over the last errant pound coin – only for Skelgill to stop mid-action: the stranger knows his identity! Before Skelgill can speak he has procured a wallet from the breast pocket of his jacket and is pressing upon him an ornate business card. As Skelgill squints suspiciously at the inscription, the man narrates in the avoidance of doubt.

'Tobias Vellum, Aloysius Vellum & Co, Antiquarian Books, Charing Cross Road, London.' Skelgill is perplexed – but now he is obliged to reciprocate as the fellow shoots out his right hand. 'Call me Toby, please, Inspector.'

Skelgill is agitated. The door is closing behind the last of the Crummock Hall contingent. He steps forwards in a way that conveys his desire to leave – but the newcomer procrastinates, an eager expression animating his moustache.

'Can I help you, sir?'

Save shoving him in the chest or shoulder-barging him out of the way – which Skelgill looks quite inclined to do, and perhaps it is only respect for his surroundings that prevents him – this rather strained diplomacy appears to be the only avenue of escape available to him. And, certainly, Toby Vellum wastes no time in taking up Skelgill's invitation to treat. His delivery is somewhat breathless, and perhaps this is just his normal state.

'Well it would be immensely appreciated – if you could, Inspector.' He clears his throat in a formal manner. 'I realise it is a little unconventional – but first I ought to explain I am the latest of the Vellums – only assumed control of the family business a few months ago – pater has succumbed to cataracts – an inconvenient ailment in our line of business – and he rather struggles with the internet.'

'That's Aloysius Vellum, is it?'

'Oh heavens, no – my father is Gerald. Aloysius Vellum perished at Balaclava in 1854. We're an old established firm, nine generations – we've been supplying books to Declan O'More for over sixty years – my father and grandfather before me.'

'Aye.'

Rather in the way of *snow* to Eskimos, Skelgill has many variations of the word *aye*, its meaning ranging from plain "yes" to something more akin to the outright denial, "is it heck as like" – but this *aye* is rather more subtle, a non-committal response that might be interpreted along the lines of, "okay, so you're just starting to make sense and I am interested but I am not going to act like I am or show that there is a gap in my knowledge, so you had better carry on with your explanation." Such is the economy and elegance of intonation.

It works. Not that Toby Vellum needs any encouragement.

'Naturally I wanted to pay my respects on behalf of the firm, Inspector,' (now Toby Vellum looks a little embarrassed, and pauses to catch his breath) 'but since it is a 600-mile-plus round trip from town I was really hoping for a glimpse of Declan's collection – in case there is any way we can be of assistance – I shouldn't like the family to be short-changed when it comes to valuation – I have first-hand knowledge of the market value of many of the books that we have procured.'

'It's a crime scene.'

'I quite understand, Inspector – I have been in touch with the Regulus-O'More family – through their representative Mr Mullarkey – and he informed me in no uncertain terms of the position.'

There is now something of a pregnant pause. Toby Vellum is obviously hoping that Skelgill will give a little ground, but Skelgill stands firm, as if he is putting the man's aspiration to the test.

'So I wondered, Inspector – if there is any possibility that you might chaperone me – I would not need to touch anything – indeed a few judiciously taken photographs ought to provide all I should require to compile a catalogue.'

While Skelgill's conventional detective's nose undoubtedly smells, if not a rat, then an ulterior motive, his unconventional detective's mind is asking what skin is it off that same nose if Vellum & Co want their pick of the books?

'Aye.'

This *aye* is an altogether different one, and draws a response from Toby Vellum that is at once surprised and delighted. He gives an involuntary gasp of satisfaction – and looks like he might even be tempted to offer up a small prayer. He pops the pound coin into the slot of a collection box.

*

There is a somewhat low-key wake in progress when Skelgill enters Crummock Hall with Toby Vellum in tow. As they pass the drawing room guided by Thwaites it has its doors ajar and the respectful hubbub of conversation emanates from within – until, that is, a sudden shriek of hysterical laughter strikes a discordant note: an unruly duet of Brutus and Cassandra. Thwaites looks scandalised by such lack of decorum; however Toby Vellum flashes Skelgill a rather sardonic grin. Skelgill dismisses Thwaites when they reach the hall outside Declan's study, and lifts the barrier tape for his charge to duck beneath. As a further expedient the police have fitted lock blockers – both to the internal and external doors and Skelgill first extracts the device before unfastening the lock proper with its old cast iron key. These security measures notwithstanding, he enters coiled as if in readiness to spring upon some interloper – perhaps he has not entirely dismissed the fanciful notion of there being a secret passage – despite having thoroughly checked every possible structure to satisfy himself there can be no such thing.

'Ah, sandalwood.' Toby Vellum, who has taken several paces into the centre of the room, pauses with eyes closed and head tilted back, his hands held out as if he is sampling the ether between his fingers and thumbs like it is fine quality cloth. 'And the glorious smell of old books.'

He turns to find Skelgill regarding him with suspicion, and he feels the need to explain.

'Sorry, Inspector – for some reason I was expecting something – unnatural – you know, since the death occurred in here?'

Skelgill's next reply of "aye" is one that hints at distraction, and Toby Vellum wastes no time in approaching the massed ranks of shelves that line the wall ahead of them. He rocks before them in a kind of awe, like a small child that has been let loose in a Victorian sweet shop, hands clasped and eyes bulging, suffocating in the ecstatic indecision of whether to gorge upon aniseed balls or to feast upon golden toffee humbugs.

'I'd appreciate if you didn't touch anything, sir.'

Skelgill's tone is rather harsh – as though he expects Toby Vellum is about to lose control and pounce upon the shelves, dragging out book after book, discarding them carelessly each time he spies a better one.

'Certainly, Inspector – I quite understand.'

Indeed, he is true to his word, and begins to stoop and rise and sway rhythmically from side to side – a new incarnation – his hands now circling, his fingers fluttering, like a pianist, a virtuoso, lost in the movement of some great symphony that plays in his head. There is a good half-minute of air-piano, until finally he comes to his senses.

'Just a few shots, Inspector – as I had hoped, it looks like I shall be able to capture everything I need – most of the books are easily recognisable from their spines.'

Skelgill watches in silence as Toby Vellum pulls out a compact digital camera from a pocket of his greatcoat and methodically sets about snapping a section at a time.

'Some of these yours, were they, sir?'

'Oh, absolutely, Inspector – certain volumes I recognise having sourced personally in the past few years – although I imagine when I cross-reference our files I shall discover many more.'

'What sort of records have you got?'

Toby Vellum makes a sharp intake of breath, a prelude to an apology.

'We are rather Dickensian I'm afraid, Inspector. When they invented computers they passed us by. All of our billing is still manual – we just have great dusty old ledgers – and paper invoices – for our bookkeeper – *hah-ha!*'

Skelgill manufactures an affable grin – perhaps surprisingly he seems to find the anachronistic fellow tolerable company – and he affects to be amused by what must be a rather hackneyed joke in the trade.

'When was the last time you supplied a book to Declan O'More?'

Toby Vellum inhales in a way that indicates it involves some racking of his brains.

'I should say it was in August this year – a first edition *Familiar Wild Flowers*, series 1 to 5 bound in a 3-volume set – published by Cassell, 1890 if I recall correctly.'

Skelgill raises an eyebrow.

'How did that come about?'

'My father has an encyclopaedic knowledge of the genres in which our regular clients specialise – as you can see, in Declan's case it was primarily natural history and the local environment – so he would contact him when something of interest came on the market. Less often Declan might get in touch with an inquiry – something he wanted us to locate.'

Skelgill regards the shelves rather broodingly. Toby Vellum busies himself with photography, occasionally expressing an "ooh" or an "aah" as he spots some particularly edifying title, *Interesting Rock Lichens of Granite Tors*, perhaps.

'I thought it was all going digital these days – with your e-readers and apps and whatnot?'

'Thankfully, Inspector that shall never apply to antiquarian books.' He addresses the shelves and sweeps a proprietorial arm. 'How wonderful to be surrounded by such craftsmanship – and of course one's book collection is one's very own autobiography. It tells a story of a man and his life.'

Skelgill looks like he is pondering how this notion would apply to him: his haphazardly filed though fiercely guarded compilation of field guides and maps with their squashed mosquitos, and oil-thumbed how-to manuals, and piles of dog-eared magazines, spanning his interests from fishing and fell-running to real ale and *Triumph* motorcycles.

'What would that set of Wainwrights fetch?'

Toby Vellum looks suddenly alert, and his face assumes a mask of professional caution.

'Ah – that was more my father's bag – I should need to consult our records and do a bit of research. Is it something you are interested in acquiring, Inspector?'

Skelgill looks surprised – and sheepish – that his covetousness has been revealed.

'I've got them all – mostly modern editions, like.'

Toby Vellum nods thoughtfully.

'The proof of the pudding will be in the eating – the price they command when they go to auction.'

Skelgill now seems perplexed – that Toby Vellum apparently knows something he does not. Has he received word of a planned sale?

'I thought the idea was to keep the collection together – that it's worth more that way?'

Toby Vellum in turn appears puzzled. And now maybe increasingly guarded.

'I should be very surprised if that were the case, Inspector. As I say, collections are so personal – it would be rather like buying out the entirety of someone's wardrobe. Unless the purchaser is looking for wallpaper – but in that case it would be far cheaper to buy books of a lesser pedigree, or faux books – they can look just as well if it's only for décor.' He strokes his moustache pensively. 'No, I should say maximum value would be realised by breaking the collection down into its constituent parts, individual sets, perhaps grouped into interests – British birds for instance.'

Skelgill does not answer, but Toby Vellum is clearly a confident chap by nature, and in possession of a sharp mind to boot.

'You are not by any chance thinking that Declan's death had something to do with his books, Inspector?'

His expression is curious, for he looks slightly horrified – perhaps it is the realisation that his all-enveloping passion could be connected to the despicable event.

'Seems it's his only asset – and a valuable one.'

This is a surprisingly candid admission from Skelgill, and it is hard to imagine that he makes it without some Machiavellian purpose. However, his countenance is that of a local country copper baffled by an unfathomable mystery; that flails about and clutches at this insubstantial straw. Toby Vellum lowers his camera and turns to face Skelgill; he blows out his cheeks and now looks for all the world like a pupil in a school production playing the part of a false-moustached adult who has been confronted with shocking news concerning the parson's wife and the verger.

'But, Inspector – surely that would point the finger at the beneficiary?'

Skelgill shrugs somewhat helplessly.

'Aye – except there isn't one. At least, not as far as we know.'

'Oh – well – oh dear.'

'Aye?'

'Well – I was just contemplating, Inspector – I mean – this is pure speculation – and rather wishful thinking – but imagine if he had left them to us – to Aloysius Vellum & Co!'

Now he looks entirely disconcerted.

'That's not likely, is it, sir?'

Toby Vellum slowly scratches his head, and replies in a distracted manner.

'Well – actually – no I rather think not – but I suddenly imagined that – well, say you knew that – and you've allowed me in here – and I've been jolly well swooning over his books – it wouldn't have looked very good.'

'Happen if you'd have known they were coming to your firm you might have been a bit more restrained, sir.'

Toby Vellum thinks about this and grins rather inanely.

'Yes – I believe you are right, Inspector.'

'Still – I wouldn't mind you letting us know what you reckon it's all worth – when you've done your valuation.'

'Why, certainly, Inspector – you shall be the first to –'

Before he can complete his sentence there comes a sharp knock upon the study door. Skelgill scowls – it means someone has crossed the police tape in the hall – and holds up a hand to indicate that he will deal with the matter. It would appear to be neither the self-important, self-styled Martius Regulus, who last time simply burst in, nor Thwaites, who has the polite servant's habit of making a cough and calling out

"Sir?" – indeed, when Skelgill opens the door he is met by the gratuitously grinning clownish countenance of Fergal Mullarkey, who immediately begins to apologise.

'Sorry to butt in, Inspector – the buffet has just been served – the family wondered if you would like to join us while it is still hot?' He cranes to see around Skelgill into the study. 'And young Vellum there, of course.'

Toby Vellum grins rather self-consciously, and Skelgill is quick to note the unspoken exchange between the pair, tradesmen as they are, their firms long-standing purveyors of their respective services to the O'More clan. He might wonder if there is a little contest of pecking order – surely a solicitor would rank himself above a bookseller? – albeit that Toby Vellum's business card boasts a string of letters after his name the equal of Fergal Mullarkey's, in quantity if not in quality. And there might also be an element of reproach – for it occurs to Skelgill that through his good offices Toby Vellum has managed to gain access to the book collection when, for all he knows, such an opportunity has been denied by the family. However, all this is in a fleeting moment, and Fergal Mullarkey brings with him the waft of piping hot sausage rolls (at least that would be Skelgill's guess), and Skelgill's stomach makes up its mind on behalf of both of them.

'Aye – we're done in here.'

*

If Skelgill feels like a gatecrasher at the wake he is sufficiently thick-skinned not to notice those disparaging glances cast in his direction; undaunted he forages along the trestle table that has been set up in the drawing room. His dedication wins the approval of the portly maid who serves the finger buffet, content that at least one person appreciates the efforts of the staff. Certainly the Regulus-O'Mores do not exhibit any great appetite (preferring liquid sustenance), and it is only the muttering coterie of black-clad undertakers who, in a shadowy alcove, like Skelgill have seriously availed themselves of the facility, balancing full plates with one hand and rather surreptitiously knocking back glasses of sherry with the other.

When Skelgill turns with his own plate amply stocked he finds himself a singleton. Beside the piano a cornered Toby Vellum is on the receiving end of a lecture from Fergal Mullarkey. The family members have divided into two groups. Martius and Edgar confer beneath the portrait of their great grandfather, Padraig Willoughby O'More; Cassandra and Brutus engage in a more animated conversation upon one of the sofas by the hearth, heads together they whisper and giggle and give every impression of being liberally oiled. Perdita sits opposite them; she seems relaxed, if a little detached from their hilarious wrangling. Skelgill saunters across to gaze out of the windows. It is another cold, clear day, and the mercury has struggled to rise above freezing – certainly in the now-shaded garden all looks frosty. He is chewing pensively, staring at the border of guelder rose bushes – now merely inauspicious bare brown twigs stripped of their festive scarlet baubles – when there is a light tug upon his sleeve.

'A penny for your thoughts, Inspector.'

The soft Irish accent seems to infiltrate his reverie like a ripple over sand, and it is a moment before he swallows and slowly looks upon Perdita's upturned countenance. If he has not noticed her beauty to date then he cannot fail now to be captivated, for the solemnity of the occasion seems to lend to her a tragic allure. He appears a fraction overawed.

'I was just thinking about bird-watching.'

'Of taking it up?'

'No – no.' Absently he combs the fingers of his free hand through his hair. 'I've got enough daft hobbies to last a lifetime.'

He doesn't add anything more and there follows a slightly awkward silence. But Perdita is unfazed, and she seems to be taking some pains to choose her words. Over her shoulder Skelgill notices that Thwaites, holding a decanter top and bottom in his white-gloved hands, is looking at them rather anxiously, and seems to be trying to decide whether he may come across and interrupt. In the event – to his evident chagrin – he is diverted by a request from the maid and sidles crablike from the drawing room, casting a somewhat anguished glance back in their direction. Now Perdita finds her voice.

'Remember we said, "some other time", Inspector?'

'Aye?'

She grins impishly – now cheered it seems.

'I thought, perhaps – to escape from this rather stifling atmosphere – would you accompany me on a walk down to Buttermere? We could slip out unobtrusively.'

Skelgill's first reaction is to glance about the room, as though concerned for eavesdroppers – but then he leans back and examines her footwear: she still has on the *après ski* snow boots she wore for church. She moves to allay any objection he might make.

'I shall be fine with these if we stick to the road – but oughtn't we go – before it gets dark?'

Skelgill regards her through narrowed eyes. There is a hint of admiration in his expression, for she closes like a skilled saleswoman.

'Fine by me – my car's there anyway – I hitched a lift up with that Vellum character in his *Spitfire*.'

She inclines her head by way of understanding. Then her manner becomes a little more conspiratorial.

'Just one thing, Inspector – I believe there are two pubs in the village – would you object if we tried the other?'

Skelgill shrugs.

'Good ale, all the same.'

'And good company, I hope?'

She affects to be offended by his priorities. He reddens a little.

'Aye – right – I meant –'

But now she interrupts him with a little peal of liquid laughter, and she moves towards him and stares at him quizzically. He is obliged to speak.

'What is it?'

She touches her chin lightly, a glint in her brown eyes, like she is daring herself to act. And then, before he can recoil, she reaches and wipes something from his chin and slowly sucks it from her fingertip. She giggles mischievously.

'Cranberry sauce, Inspector.'

15. THWAITES – Saturday 8am

'Guvnor?'

'Aye.'

'It's me – Leyton.'

'What do you want?'

Skelgill's voice, crackling and hoarse, sounds like he has just woken.

'Where are you, Guv?'

'Where am I?' Now he could be asking himself. He clears his throat with some difficulty. 'Buttermere.'

'Stay at your Ma's, Guv?'

There is a momentary hiatus before Skelgill replies.

'Get to the point, Leyton.'

Skelgill has inserted a graphic adjective before the noun. His irritation, elevated at the outset, now rises to cause DS Leyton to become even more tentative.

'It's the butler, Guv – Harold Thwaites.'

'What about him?'

'He's dead, Guv.'

*

By the time Skelgill reaches Crummock Hall it appears its occupants have been roused and have gathered in the drawing room. He pokes a cursory head around the door to see them clustered on the sofas before a weak fire, tousle-haired and bleary-eyed and wrapped in dressing gowns, cupping mugs of coffee that may be fortified with the cognac that is conspicuous in their midst, cap off and half consumed. They pay little heed to him, or that he wears the same outfit in which they last saw him at the funeral – if indeed they paid any attention then. But he wastes no time and stalks away; the staff quarters are situated on the upper floor of the old stable block, converted in Edwardian days, when Padraig Willoughby O'More acquired the first motor car in this part of Cumberland. Skelgill is taking the narrow stairs two at a time when a shadow falls across his path.

It is the bulky figure of police pathologist, Dr Herdwick. He stands, arms akimbo, a battered leather Gladstone bag held at one side, his rough-hewn features twisted in mock censure.

'What kept you, lad – thought this was your local patch?'

Skelgill affects a simper but does not offer an explanation. The doctor seems intent upon descending, and there is a momentary awkwardness. Now the doctor sets his jaw.

'That said, don't reckon there's owt for thee, lad.'

'What do you mean?'

'Carbon monoxide poisoning – died between midnight and two.'

Skelgill suddenly winces and raises a hand to his brow as though he suffers a jag of pain.

'Are we talking suicide?'

The older man shakes his head decisively.

'We're talking poor ventilation, lad. Plus a coal fire.'

Of course, while it is for Skelgill and others to establish such practical facts, his medical colleague is no stranger to events of this nature, and Skelgill knows better than to question his judgement without basis. He notes, however, that the doctor's reply does not dismiss outright his suggestion. He takes a step upwards.

'I'll have a butcher's, as that Cockney layabout Leyton would say.'

'Enough to spoil your Saturday morning, eh, lad? I might just go and join that lot in a brandy. Decent stuff they keep, these toffs.'

Skelgill flashes a wry grin and presses himself against the bannister to allow his well-padded colleague to descend. As they squeeze past one another, the doctor holds up a little device – it is a portable detector.

'Safe in there now.'

He departs with a chuckle, and seems to Skelgill to be muttering something about "hair of the dog".

*

The first thing that strikes Skelgill about the little bed-sitting room is the extreme cold that enfolds him as he cautiously pushes open the door. Although the time is past eight a.m. the sun has not yet risen; the sash window has been flung up – presumably by the doctor – and an empty black rectangle admits freezing air. Somewhere beyond a robin regales him with its mournful winter song. He fumbles for the light, and finds a Bakelite toggle switch that activates a naked bulb dangling from the cracked ceiling. To his immediate right is a plain oak wardrobe, warped and standing a little askew, beneath the window a modest dresser with a few unremarkable accessories, and directly ahead the brick hearth. The single bed with its nightstand and shaded table lamp is on the left behind the door. At the end of the bed Thwaites' threadbare butler's outfit is neatly arranged upon a valet stand, a hollow ghost watching over the old retainer.

Skelgill is sniffing extravagantly – though he knows carbon monoxide has no odour – and all he can detect is the faint hint of soot from the grate, where the fire is apparently extinguished. But first he turns his attention to the bed. Dr Herdwick has pulled the top-sheet over the old man, and Skelgill hesitates before inspecting the corpse, perhaps debating whether he need do this at all. It would seem to be his duty – and is not a task from which he ordinarily shies away; however on this occasion it is with a pained countenance that he lifts the covers.

If a dead man can be reassuring, however, then Skelgill seems to take some solace from what he sees. The elderly butler lies at peace, his long years of service now over, his travails at an end. His usually pallid complexion is rosy – healthy, even – and Skelgill recalls a little ditty from his mountain rescue first-aid training (for carbon monoxide poisoning threatens campers and cavers alike, who use their burners in enclosed surroundings). It refers to one of the classic symptoms, *"when you're cherry red – you're dead."*

He replaces the coverlet and turns with an expiration of breath to inspect the room. He shivers, and pulls his jacket about his torso, and then decides to close the window. He notes that the casement is fitted with self-adhesive foam draught strip; it is yellowed with age, and partially compressed, but nonetheless forms a tight seal: the sash, once lowered, does not rattle, despite his best efforts. The glass still bears some condensation, perhaps Thwaites' last breath intermingled; the paintwork is flaky and stained with black mould where such droplets have drained over the years.

He checks the door. It too is taped for draughts, both jambs and the head, but there is a good three-quarter inch gap at the foot: it would afford ample ventilation provided there was a half-decent draw on the fire. However he notices pushed against the side of the wardrobe a traditional tapestry door draught stopper, washed-out silk embroidered with a bird pattern. He prods it with his toe; it feels sand-filled and must have been swept aside by the maid, when she came to wake the ostensibly oversleeping butler. Skelgill stares broodingly at the object: the faded flocking birds appear to be corvids.

Now he crosses the room to the small hearth and stoops down before it. A pair of antique brass firedogs guard the grate, and across them rest matching irons. Skelgill lifts the poker and stabs at the fused mass of cinders; it shatters to reveal no glowing embers – indeed there is fresh glistening anthracite, matching that in the copper scuttle. It is a further indication of the incomplete combustion that produced deadly carbon monoxide, when much-maligned CO_2 would have been a blessing. He replaces the poker and rises with a little groan. Still facing the hearth he flexes his ever-troublesome spine. Then he realises he is looking into a tarnished mirror, and some fresh pain has him pressing his temples. He does not approve of what he sees, and with a grimace he turns and departs, taking the key from inside and locking the door behind him.

*

'They're all packing, Guv – this one's really spooked 'em – they're like rats leaving a sinking ship.'

Skelgill scowls somewhat disparagingly but does not comment. Together with his sergeants he has temporarily commandeered the kitchen; traditionally laid out with its long work table, great hearth where a wood fire smoulders, and a log-fired range, it is by far the warmest room in the house at this time of the morning. The cynic might suggest Skelgill has chosen the location for other reasons – and indeed he has prevailed upon the cook to provide them with appropriate sustenance before dismissing her. Now both he and DS Jones watch DS Leyton, who continues.

'Can't blame 'em, I suppose, Guv – and we've got no cause to detain anyone.'

'Have we not?'

Skelgill casts a look upon his subordinates that is at once expectant and censorious. It is DS Leyton that responds first.

'They were supposed to have their meeting about Sir Sean's will last night, Guv – but it turns out Perdita went AWOL so they couldn't do it.'

Skelgill raises a hand in reflex, but then he merely rubs at one eye with his fingers.

'She's been lodging down at Buttermere, Leyton.'

DS Leyton looks suddenly deflated – as if in Perdita's hitherto unexplained absence there was cause for suspicion. DS Jones, on the other hand, is curiously animated – though at first she represses her response, until the words seem to escape of their own volition, together with an almost hysterical laugh.

'She's never here when they die, Guv.'

'Happen she had nowt to do wi' eet.' Skelgill's retort is snappy, doubly emphasised by his lapse into the vernacular.

But now DS Leyton seems to realise he might be operating on a different wavelength, and determines that he must tune in to the conflict that troubles his colleagues.

'Guv – what are you pair saying? That there's something suspicious about Thwaites' death? I thought Dr Herdwick insists it's accidental.'

'Aye – and he reckons Declan died when we know he was out bird-watching.'

Skelgill glares at DS Leyton, who folds his arms and frowns with consternation. For a while they all three sit in brooding silence. It seems the invisible tensions that bind them also pull in disparate directions, and hinder any coherent progress. In the end it is DS Jones who speaks.

'Why didn't he die every night?'

Taken literally, her words are nonsensical, but from Skelgill's reaction it is apparent she makes a profound point. He watches her, his eyes unblinking through narrowed lids. After a moment she shrugs in the manner of one resting their case, and Skelgill turns his gaze upon DS Leyton.

'Let's get that maid back.'

DS Leyton nods and rises and jerks a thumb behind him.

'Won't be tick, Guv – reckon she's in the scullery.'

True to his word DS Leyton returns within a minute followed by the stout woman Skelgill had last set eyes upon stoically serving the buffet. He indicates a chair opposite.

'It's Betty isn't it?'

The woman nods once rather apprehensively.

'I'd rather stand if it's all the same, sir.'

Skelgill makes what he probably considers a sympathetic face, although by most people's standards it is a less-than-endearing expression.

'We shan't keep you long, Betty.' It looks for a second that he is searching for a diplomatic form of words, but if so these elude him and he reverts to blunt type. 'Mr Thwaites died of poisoning from carbon monoxide – caused by his coal fire and the lack of ventilation.'

Again the woman gives a single nod, and her own expression remains fixed, suggestive of her having already heard this information. But she offers no comment.

'What we can't understand, Betty – is why it happened last night – why not before? He was a man of habit, wasn't he?'

'He was that, sir.'

'Do you clean his room?'

There is now a fleeting look of alarm in her eyes.

'I clean everywhere, sir – the whole of Crummock Hall, including the servants' quarters. There's only me that does, sir.'

Skelgill nods encouragingly.

'So you'd notice anything different?'

She remains anxious.

'I don't know, sir – I don't know what you mean.'

Skelgill suddenly rises and indicates to his colleagues to do the same.

'We'd just like you to take a look for us, Betty – we can get up these back stairs, can we?'

He leads the way and the woman automatically begins to follow him – although her discomfort is apparent; understandably she is reluctant to return to the room. DS Jones places a kindly hand on her shoulder and guides her by the elbow as they mount the staircase.

Skelgill unlocks the door of Thwaites' room and flicks on the light switch, although it is ineffectual now that insipid northern daylight prevails and shows the modest quarters to be even more austere than before. He crosses the floor to stand beside the hearth. The maid has slowed almost to a stop and shuffles to one side of the door, her back against the wardrobe. Considerately, DS Jones and DS Leyton range themselves in front of the bed, so as to block her view as best they can of the human form beneath the covers. Skelgill meanwhile indicates with a circular movement of one hand the arrangement around the grate.

'He normally burned coal, did he?'

The woman seems a little relieved by this question – that she is not in fact going to face some sort of impossible third degree – but actually be questioned on facts with which she is familiar.

'We use coal in all the bedrooms, sir – the fireplaces are too small for logs – happen they don't give out a deal of heat, or last so long.'

Skelgill nods encouragingly.

'Did he light a fire every night?'

'He's been complaining something terrible about his chilblains, sir – since this cold snap set in. I've had to clean out his grate every morning for the last three or four weeks, sir.'

Skelgill inclines his head in the direction of the window.

'I take it he kept the window closed?'

'Yes, sir – at least, I've never come in to find it open in the morning.'

Skelgill begins to look like he is struggling for something else to say, then he realises he is turning over the key with the fingers of his left hand. He holds it up for inspection.

'What about locking his door – what did he usually do?'

Now the maid shakes her head with some determination.

'He never locked it as far as I know, sir – perhaps when he were getting dressed. There's no reason for anyone to lock their rooms –'

She stops abruptly.

'Aye?'

'Least – not until – Mr Declan, sir.'

Skelgill nods, understanding her point.

'So the door was unlocked this morning?'

'Yes, sir.'

'Was it like him to sleep in?'

'Oh, no, sir – we thought he must be ill – he's had a bad chest lately, sir. And the cook, she sent me to check on him – and I found him – but he weren't –'

Now for the first time she glances briefly at the bed, but quickly averts her eyes, and looks back at Skelgill. She begins to shift her weight from one foot to the other, a sign that she would like to leave.

'Anything else, Betty – that you notice?'

She makes a cursory sweep of the room, now avoiding the bed. Too quickly, her gaze returns to Skelgill. She shakes her head. Skelgill glances at his subordinates, but they are both watching the woman, and appear to have nothing to add or ask.

'Aye – well, thanks, Betty – we'll let you go.'

The woman now turns, with more alacrity than she has demonstrated thus far – but in doing so she catches her left foot on the sand-filled draught stopper and gives a little shriek. She begins to put a hand to her mouth, but then for some reason she resists the urge and makes to continue on her way.

'What is it, Betty?'

Now she turns rather hesitantly. She cannot very well deny the cause of her concern.

'The snake.'

'The snake?'

She points to the embroidered object, with its faded pattern of Hitchcockian birds rising against an ominous sky.

'To block the draught – it belongs in Mr Declan's room.'

Skelgill digs his hands into his pockets; he gives the impression of being a little disinterested, but that he is indulging the woman's concern.

'It wouldn't be needed.'

However the maid seems perplexed – that a long-standing domestic arrangement has been violated.

'I noticed it were gone yesterday evening, sir – I had to get some extra blankets from the press in Mr Declan's room – Miss Cassandra and Master Brutus were wanting them because they weren't warm enough the weekend before. I thought it was one of the family took it – I never imagined Mr Thwaites would have it for himself.'

'Maybe he borrowed it earlier in the week – when there was no one else here?'

Now she shakes her head decisively.

'I'm sure I would have seen it when I came in to vacuum yesterday, sir.'

Skelgill does not reply – but he nods in a way that seems to indicate he is certain she is right – and the matter is now explained.

'What was his state of mind, Betty?'

'I'm sorry, sir?'

'How's he been lately? His behaviour. Was he much affected by the deaths of Sir Sean and Declan?'

175

'Naturally, sir – we all were.' (She makes it sound like she has already got over it.) 'Mr Thwaites didn't seem too bad after Sir Sean went – we all knew it was coming, I suppose. But he'd not been himself since Mr Declan died – which is the other way round to what you'd have expected – Mr Declan being what they call the cantankerous sort, sir.'

'Why do you think that was, Betty?'

She ponders blankly for a moment and then glances past DS Jones and DS Leyton to the bed.

'It must have been – finding the body, sir – that's enough to disturb any soul.'

She visibly shudders, and Skelgill holds up a palm, akin to a gesture of farewell.

'Well, thanks, Betty – that's helpful to know.'

Paradoxically, now she regards him expectantly, as though she anticipates sympathy for her own plight, but he simply waits until her long years of servitude kick in and she performs a little curtsey and removes herself. As her steps fade away Skelgill gently closes the door and manoeuvres the draught stopper into position. He steps back to admire his handiwork. Now DS Leyton pipes up.

'Think that was the final nail in the coffin, Guv?'

Skelgill looks askance at his sergeant – that he would employ such a turn of phrase in the company of the deceased.

'Steady on, Leyton.'

'Sorry, Guv – what with that bird pattern an' all – murder of crows they call 'em, don't they?'

'They're not crows, Leyton – they're jackdaws.'

'Hang about, Guv – they're all the same thing aren't they? Crows, rooks, ravens, jackdaws – all black and strung up on farmers' fences whenever I see 'em.'

Skelgill is suddenly pensive, and he seems unmoved by his sergeant's loose speculation. Then he turns to DS Jones.

'Can you make your phone into a torch?'

She looks surprised and gives a little start, having been largely an onlooker since they arrived in Thwaites' room. However she reaches into the back pocket of her jeans.

'Sure, Guv – what for?'

'For one – I haven't worked out how to do it on mine.' Skelgill takes the handset now that she has activated the light setting. 'For two – no Leyton – they're not all the same.'

And with that he ducks into the hearth and, with scant concern for his attire, jams one elbow in the grate and thrusts his hand that holds the torch up into the flue. Almost immediately he makes a little gasp of discovery. Now he braces himself against the back of the hearth and reaches up with his other hand. There follow a couple of contortions and accompanying grunts and snorts, and then suddenly he slides down and pitches forwards onto the hearthrug. DS Jones darts in to rescue her phone – just as Skelgill deposits before him a tangled mass of twigs, straw, string, tufts of sheep's wool, strands of horsehair, pieces of tinfoil, shiny crisp packets, strips of coloured polythene and lengths of frayed blue baler twine.

'Struth, Guv – what is that?' DS Leyton's jaw falls agape.

Skelgill brushes off his hands and then runs his fingers through his hair – to questionable effect – for they are stained with soot and smeared with oily grime.

'See Leyton – only jackdaws nest in chimneys.'

The three of them crowd around for a close-up view. The semi-disintegrated structure does not much resemble a bird's nest – but nonetheless Skelgill's analysis seems convincing, with authenticity provided by the dried fragments of guano that are stuck to many of the components. There are even some flakes of eggshell, very pale blue and speckled with chocolate brown and grey. Now DS Jones is the first to speak.

'It was blocking the flue, Guv?'

'Aye.' Skelgill shoots her a sharp glance. 'Must have been dislodged by a clod of snow that's fallen down the chimney.'

DS Jones nods pensively, while DS Leyton glances across at the form lying cold beneath the bedcovers.

'Cor blimey, Guv – it's like that draught stopper brought bad luck.'

Skelgill nods slowly.
'It's one way of looking at it, Leyton.'

16. FROZEN – Saturday 1pm

Skelgill stamps his feet and rubs his hands together; he seems fogged by indecision, wreathed as he is by the clouds of his breath that hang in the air. He hovers beside his car outside the B&B at Buttermere. Like her siblings, Perdita has flown the nest – in her case, according to the landlady of his acquaintance, to return to Dublin. He digs his hands into his trouser pockets and slowly rotates on his heel, surveying the scene around him, a frozen landscape so still it could be a panoramic Christmas card. Through a gap in a belt of pines he has a view of Crummock Water, the shaded eastern fellside of Mellbreak rising beyond. Despite the clear skies the sun this time of year is no Sugar Ray, packing a punch too weak, steadily outpointed by the earthly elements. If the freeze continues for much longer the creeping ice might bridge the neck of water between Low Ling Crag and Hause Point – permitting him to walk out to the spot where the long-lost rowing boat decays 140 feet down. He stares broodingly; in ordinary circumstances this Saturday afternoon would most likely have found him upon his beloved Bass Lake, aboard his own craft, straining his sinews to winkle a winter pike out of its lair. But the weather – along with events at Crummock Hall – conspire to thwart him and he has not fished now for over a fortnight; his boat immobilised by pack ice at Peel Wyke harbour. Of course, the rivers on the whole keep flowing, for the ground water that produces them runs at a few degrees above freezing – but most species that he would covet are now out of season until the spring; he might have to lift down his cobwebbed beachcaster and head for the coast.

Skelgill's being stymied impacts not just upon his mood; it also affects his job. He is not a police officer that wants to pore over forensic reports and retire to ruminate clutching a pipe or sipping *sirop de cassis*, or to prop himself upon the crutch of the clichéd corporate incident room of gory photos and sensationalised press clippings assembled by a team of eager runners. Skelgill's detective work is kinaesthetic in form – he must experience the evidence and evasion with his own five senses – and his method of problem solving enlists a mysterious sixth that he freely admits he neither comprehends nor commands – a subconscious synthesis of facts and intuition that probably has its workings nearer to his stomach than his brain. Gut feel, as his contemptuous critics might say. It finds its own way at those times when he is relieved of stress and hassle, yet occupied in some mildly repetitive deliberative mode. Angling often provides such conditions – thus at the moment he is doubly icebound. To solve the crime he must understand its nature – but he can't answer this question until he can work out what it is. Like a cryptic crossword clue that seems unfathomable, gobbledegook, a riddle that all the staring at in the world will not help.

He clambers into his car and sets off in rather pensive fashion. As he slows for the cattle grid at the end of the driveway he notices the waxwings have gone, though there are still berries upon the abandoned cotoneasters. He slots his mobile phone into its hands-free clip and raises an eyebrow that there is a signal. Presently the lane, the winding B5289 to Lorton and Cockermouth, converges with the eastern shore of Crummock Water, and in half a mile he pulls into a passing space beneath Rannerdale Knotts that gives him a view directly out over Hause Point. The signal is weaker now; he calls DS Leyton.

'Alright, Guvnor?'

'Leyton – what's the latest – on the four you and Jones are covering?'

'We're just pulling a report together – for when you get back in?'

His tone is hopeful and he expresses the statement as a question.

'Who said I'm coming in?'

'I just assumed –'

'Get hold of Jones and call me back from my office. Stick me on loudspeaker.'

'Straightaway, Guv?'

'Make it twenty minutes – I need to do something.'

'Wilco, Guv.' DS Leyton hangs up with a sharp intake of breath that is indicative of a tough ask.

Skelgill leaves his engine idling and cautiously rounds to the back of his car, treading in tyre ruts that scar the frozen surface. He hauls up the tailgate and drags his battered aluminium Kelly kettle clanking from beneath a pile of outdoor clothing. Then he puts it aside for a moment while he has second thoughts and pulls his orange cagoule around his jacket and dons his tartan trapper hat. He rummages in storage crates and with a grunt of satisfaction locates a dented Kendal mint cake tin decorated with a scuffed design of alpine scenery. Inside are little polythene pouches, and from these he extracts a couple of dog-eared tea bags, half a dozen sugar lumps, and a rough measure of powdered milk, which he inserts successively into the round spout of the kettle. This is not the conventional way to use the device – but then convention and Skelgill make an oxymoron. And now he carries the improvisation a stage further. He takes a couple of tentative strides into the virgin snow towards the lake and squats down to trap the tall cylinder between his knees. He begins to feed handfuls of snow into the spout – a tricky job since its diameter is no more than two inches. However, he succeeds to his satisfaction and returns to the vehicle. Vigorously he rubs his hands and curses the cold, and wrings and shakes them before he continues. Next he jams the pot-like firebase into the crunchy snow-ice, and settles the kettle upon it, pressing down until the arrangement seems to be stable. Then he begins tearing sheets of newspaper, the local advertiser, and twisting them into tight spills, which he drops into the hollow centre, or chimney, of the kettle. From the vehicle he produces a stainless steel *Sigg* bottle and a box of long cook's matches. He pours a dose of methylated spirits into the flue, and follows it with a lighted match. There is a small explosion and concomitant swearing as Skelgill almost has his eyebrows singed, and immediately purple and then orange tongues of flame begin to lick out of the mouth of the chimney. He busies himself with making more paper spills, adding them one at a time to replenish the fuel supply. There begins a hissing

– it is the compacted ice liquefying beneath the firebase, and Skelgill adjusts the balance. Snow being considerably less dense than water, when after a couple of minutes it melts it must fill only a tenth of the cylinder, and Skelgill gingerly feeds in additional handfuls, muttering oaths each time he burns himself. He maintains a rumbling boil with a steady supply of spills.

After about five minutes he decides his snow tea is ready, and hauls the kettle off its base and carefully pours the precious brew into a chipped enamel mug. He kicks over the firebase and tosses the kettle into deeper snow and leaves them to cool. He slams shut the tailgate and carries his mug round to enter on the passenger side. He delves into the glove box and seems surprised to find half a packet of chocolate digestives. Now that the car is closed up, the interior quickly heats. He winds back the seat and looks over the semi-frozen expanse of Crummock Water to his left. He works his way steadily through the biscuits, slowly becoming immersed in the warming sensation of the hot sweet tea and velvety dunked melted chocolate. It is not exactly fishing, but he seems happier than he has been for some time. In the manner of an addict getting his fix, there is some mesmerising experience, and perhaps he is imagining himself at Whitehaven West Pier casting with optimism into the Irish Sea.

Indeed some revelation seems to come to him, for his gaze, for several minutes glazed, abruptly sharpens and there is a strange light in his grey-green eyes: no longer the hunted, but the hunter. Gut feel fuelled by his snack, perhaps? He gulps the last of his tea – grimacing a little as he swallows the soft slugs of biscuit base that lurk in the dregs – and with a sudden purpose clambers across into the driver's seat and sets off. He is whistling *Danny Boy*.

There follows, however, a momentary setback in his new-found momentum – literally so, for he curses and slithers to a halt after only twenty yards and reverses, wheels spinning furiously to find their grip in the packed snow: he jumps out and retrieves his Kelly kettle and its base. He sets off again, and when his phone bursts into life he looks entirely perplexed.

'That's us, Guv?'

'What is?'

DS Leyton senses some incongruity in Skelgill's manner.

'Twenty minutes, Guv – you said to give it.'

'Aye.'

This "aye" infers that Skelgill has already forgotten about the call, and that he has better things to do. DS Leyton, meanwhile, is obliged to play for time.

'DS Jones is just powdering her nose, Guv – she won't be two ticks.' He makes a rather curious humming sound that might be a soccer chant. 'You watching the game tonight, Guv?'

'Which game?'

'World Cup qualifier – they're saying England could win it this time round.'

'Aye – and I'll do a morris dance on the Chief's desk waving St George's cross hankies and wearing three lions grotts.'

DS Leyton chuckles. Skelgill employs the local slang for underpants.

'Never know, Guv – she might join you. Maybe she's got an outfit of her own.'

'You can't dance in cast iron, Leyton.'

DS Leyton is about to reply but Skelgill hears a door closing and instead DS Jones's slightly breathless voice comes on the line.

'Sorry, Guv – DI Smart just asked me to run a computer analysis for him.'

'You told him where to shove it, I hope.'

'In a manner of speaking, Guv.'

Skelgill huffs.

'I'm on the move – the signal could drop anytime.'

There is a short silence and it could be deduced that the two sergeants glance uncertainly at one another. DS Leyton strikes up.

'I'll go first, Guv.' He clears his throat in the rather formal way of one preparing to deliver a valediction. 'Starting with Edgar – and this business with the writ. My pal Billy down in the Economic Crime Directorate, he's had a butcher's at the documents filed with the court. It don't look like there was anything criminal – just unprofessional – negligence, know what I mean?' (Skelgill grunts, sounding displeased.) 'Like you thought, Guv – he's got director's liability insurance but they're contesting the cover – so he's between a rock and a hard place. What Billy reckons is that, even if the insurance pays up, he's gonna lose the case. So that'll be his reputation down the Swanee. His best bet is to settle out of court and make it go away – no bad PR, like. For that, he'd need a couple of mil in readies.'

Skelgill is silent – but that probably indicates he is mulling over what DS Leyton has said. DS Leyton assumes he should continue.

'Moving on to Brutus, Guv.' There is now a longer pause and Skelgill can hear a rustling of papers, which might lead him to suspect his subordinates are conferring over some point. 'Just finding the page, Guv. Here we go. Thing is – with him being this celebrity – *Owain Jagger* – it's knowing where to start.' He coughs again, more affectedly this time. 'About what you mentioned, Guv – I went through the paparazzi shots of him. First off, I would say he's usually got a dolly bird on his arm.' (Another pause; perhaps for an apologetic glance at his colleague.) 'But given we're looking for a financial angle – there was one thing that struck me.'

'What, Leyton?' Skelgill is becoming impatient.

'You know I've got family connections – turf accountancy?'

'Your uncle's a bookie, Leyton.'

'Correct, Guv. So I'm tuned-in to the old gee-gees – and I noticed a good number of photos of Brutus at race meets. Now, your Ascot, your Epsom – you'd expect that – they're on the nobs' social calendar and he'd get corporate hospitality – plus they're handy for Town – but he's also been to the likes of Newmarket for the *Guineas* – that's out in Suffolk – and he was at the *St Ledger* – fair enough, it's one of the Classics – but that's Doncaster, Guv – thick end of two hundred miles from London.

And there's others out in the sticks, not always big meets – Market Rasen, Wincanton.'

'So what are you saying, Leyton?'

'On the q.t. – I spoke with my connections – the word is, he's more than an interested spectator. He bets big – cash on the course. It's not like online gambling. There's no records kept, no questions asked – but given a couple of days I can probably find out if he's on a streak. Winning – or losing, more like.'

Skelgill is silent for an inordinate period. Perhaps he is recalling what seemed at the time a throwaway remark during their interview with Cassandra: *"Oh, I'm not the gambler in the family."* After a minute he responds.

'Okay – follow it up. Look – I need to shift. Jones – just give me the summary.'

There is a squeal as she edges her chair closer to the telephone.

'Sure, Guv. Firstly, Martius. I've also tried to follow any lines that might have commercial implications. Regarding the offshore investments linked to Edgar's clients, I've still got a DC working on that – the Virgin Islands' tax haven status means the normal channels of enquiry are almost impenetrable – so we're working with Interpol's money-laundering unit to see if they can shed any light on it. However, their initial view is that Regulus & Co merchant bank is unlikely to have lost out in the transaction. They merely received and transmitted the funds. More significant might be what happened in the financial crash – or after it, rather. I came across a report that Regulus & Co had – if not exactly failed – performed poorly in the IMF stress tests. Subsequently there was a press release from the bank itself – stating that Regulus & Co had significantly increased its liquidity from a number of private sources. Again it's hard to scratch beneath the surface – but I realised there's the public register of property ownership. I checked for Martius's home in Surrey – it's the ancestral Regulus family estate – there suddenly appeared at the same time a mortgage of five million pounds.'

In the background DS Leyton whistles.

185

'Jeez, Guv – how the other half lives, eh?'

'Make it half per cent, Leyton.'

There is a pause while they each consider this revelation.

'That's all for Martius at the moment, Guv.' Skelgill neither comments nor commends her, so she continues. 'As for Cassandra – wow – there was more than I expected. She's romped through three high-profile marriages in ten years – and probably done pretty well for herself along the way. But this party-planning outfit of hers seems a bit odd. It's a limited company – she's registered as the sole director and shareholder – and her accounts haven't been filed for the last two years. She stages spectacular events that attract pages of coverage – but I just wonder if she's been making a loss to win business. I found an article where a competitor was complaining about unfair practices – they'd lost out on a big tender for a fashion awards after-party. Looking at her lifestyle, she's obviously high maintenance – there's a lot trips abroad – French Riviera, Milan, New York, the Caribbean – including the British Virgin Islands. And then about two months ago a gossip column reported that she'd given up the lease on her own flat in Knightsbridge and moved into a penthouse apartment overlooking Hyde Park – it belongs to a financier. The piece was pretty thick with innuendo – he's a non-dom and only spends a month a year in the country – he's twice her age, and the journalist used the expression *sugar daddy* more than once.'

Skelgill grimaces. He has remained silent during DS Jones's exposition, and has in fact turned into the entrance to the long winding driveway of Crummock Hall, halting the car, knowing he will probably lose the signal if he presses on beneath the towering bulk of Grasmoor. Perhaps the manoeuvre has distracted him, or more profoundly that his subordinates' words have provided genuine food for thought – however, he squints anxiously ahead, suggesting his first priority is to motor on. His sergeants can be heard exchanging muffled whispers, before DS Leyton comes back on the line a little wheezily, close to the microphone.

'Can you hear us, Guv?'

'No need to shout, Leyton.'

'Sorry, Guv.' DS Leyton's voice wavers. 'Couple of other things – just quickly?'

'Aye.'

'You asked me to check out that bookseller down Charing Cross Road?' Skelgill does not reply in the affirmative, so DS Leyton keeps going. 'Seems all above board – but I was just trying the name Vellum, doing an internet search together with Regulus-O'More – and this photo came up from an old school yearbook. Stone the crows – there's Edgar with the Toby Vellum geezer that you met! Edgar's a prefect – Toby Vellum's what they call in those public schools his 'fag' – you know, Guv, his gopher, like?'

'I know what a fag is, Leyton.'

Skelgill sounds remarkably unfazed, given that his sergeant has unearthed a potentially intriguing connection. Yesterday in the drawing room – albeit for a short while – he witnessed Toby Vellum arriving in proximity with the Regulus-O'Mores, and there was no indication of any relationship, long lost or otherwise. It seems unlikely that Edgar, at least, would not have recognised him. And surely Toby Vellum would have had no qualms about identifying himself? Yet his introduction to the family by Fergal Mullarkey had been met with cursory nods and those present returning to their conversations.

'What do you reckon, Guv – should I follow that one up?'

'Aye – as you like, Leyton – what else was there?'

DS Leyton hesitates – perhaps a touch deflated his superior's apathy.

'Er – about Brutus, Guv – what DI Smart said about him being in the Lakes – when we thought he'd gone to London?'

'Aye?'

'Drawn a blank so far, Guv. I've talked to all our regular press and radio contacts – you'd think they'd have been tipped off if a celebrity were knocking about – but nothing – nor anything coming up on social media. I've tried all the main hotels and guest houses – I wonder if it was a case of mistaken identity – or someone pulling a fast one on DI Smart to make a few quid – oh –'

'Not very likely, Cock.'

The voice that interjects has an unmistakable grating drawl – it is none other than DI Smart himself.

'And here's me bringing you the latest news – in case you missed that, too, Skel?'

That he is aware of Skelgill at the other end of the line suggests a certain amount of eavesdropping has occurred prior to his ingress. Skelgill can hear nothing from his sergeants, who are presumably cringing in silence. Now he is faced with the dilemma of blanking his rival – at risk of passing up some nugget – or the ignominy of swallowing his pride. In the end he responds with the best compromise he can muster, though Alec Smart will take pleasure in that he utters it through gritted teeth.

'I'm losing the signal, Smart – if you want to tell me something.'

'Seems to me like you're losing more than your signal, Cock.'

DI Smart sniggers, and Skelgill can hear the rattle of his heels on the tiled office floor, as if he is performing a little tap-dance of triumph.

'That crowd you're *investigating* –' (DI Smart pronounces the word as if it is in parentheses, to mock their efforts) ' – were having a cosy little chat together at The Island this morning.'

He refers to a large modern hotel that is situated close to the M6 motorway junction for Penrith, and a short distance from the mainline railway station. It would be the obvious choice for travellers to convene prior to going their separate ways. Skelgill curses silently under his breath – that he might have overlooked something so obvious in hindsight. But unlike DI Alec Smart, whose modus operandi depends upon an evanescent legion of mercenaries, spies, snouts and would-be supergrasses, Skelgill largely eschews the paid informant on grounds that treachery begets treachery.

'Aye.'

This is an unconvincing effort to suggest he might already be abreast of these facts – and again DI Smart cackles, sensing Skelgill's discomfort.

'Half an hour they were plotting, Skel – I can even tell you who ordered *Americano* and who drank a *Manhattan*.' He gives a short hysterical laugh. 'Then four of them took a cab to the station and the other pair left together by car – cosy – that lawyer chap and your pretty little writer.'

Skelgill scowls fiercely – then abruptly he leans forwards and cuts off the call. He waits, his face like thunder. Broodingly he watches the clock on his dashboard. It is only two minutes later when his phone rings again.

'That's him slung his hook, Guv.'

'Make sure he's not outside, Leyton.'

'Already have, Guv.'

'What else did he say?'

There is an awkward pause – long enough for Skelgill to picture his colleagues exchanging discomfited glances.

'That was about it, Guv – he said he's got a meeting with the Chief.'

Skelgill makes a derisive scoffing sound.

'It's no big deal, Leyton – as for the family – we know they were due to discuss the will – they didn't want us cramping their style. That's why they cleared out of Crummock Hall.'

'Fair point, Guv.'

Now there is another bout of silence, which DS Leyton eventually breaks.

'How've you been getting on, Guv?'

'Eh?'

'I mean – with Perdita and the Mullarkey geezer – anything we should know?'

Skelgill, unseen by his colleagues, glowers and folds his arms. It is a reasonable suggestion – that his team pool their knowledge – but he seems unprepared for the question (or maybe unwilling to provide the answer).

'I'm working on it, Leyton.'

The pregnant pauses are coming thick and fast – heralding a minor baby boom – but DS Leyton seems determined to put a positive spin on their predicament.

'Still, Guv – darkest hour before dawn, eh?'

'What?'

Skelgill's tone is irate, though DS Leyton seems not to notice.

'It's what they say, Guv – that it's the darkest hour before dawn.'

'No it's not. It starts getting *light* in the hour before dawn. It's called nautical twilight. The darkest hour's in the middle of the night, Leyton.'

'Oh, right, Guv.'

Skelgill crunches his car into gear and sets off at a hair-raising rate along the snow-and-ice-covered track that leads to Crummock Hall. He loses the signal but does not appear concerned.

*

'Mrs Gilhooley? You must be frozen.'

The diminutive old lady glares suspiciously at Skelgill. Her eyes are uncannily pale, set close astride a hooked nose, there is lank grey hair straggling about a shrivelled countenance, and a moth-eaten blanket gripped at the throat by gnarled fingers that shake, perhaps with cold. She resolutely blocks the narrow doorway of the cottage, though in summoning a reply she appears torn – for this tall rangy stranger in a peculiar hat hauls a sack of coal over his shoulder.

'Weez thon, woman?' The hoarse cry of an angry male voice emanates from within.

She ignores the demand of her spouse to identify the newcomer, and juts out a chin that is pointed and unfortunately hairy. Brutus's childhood analogy from Brothers Grimm was perhaps prophetic.

'Tha yan o' Minnie Graham's bairns?'

'I heard you were short of fuel.'

That Skelgill's reply is patently oblique does not seem to concern her. Indeed, in its evasiveness it is perhaps music to her ears. Her eyes narrow shrewdly: bargaining mode.

'What'll tha tek fer it?'

Skelgill shrugs – as much as a person can shrug with a half-hundredweight on their back.

'I'd take a brew.' He manufactures a friendly grin. 'There's two more in the boot, love. Call it community service. Ask no questions.'

At this hint of chicanery, of the Robin Hood variety, the old woman cackles with approval.

'Weez thon?' The shout of *who is it* comes again. 'Yer lettin' in draught, woman!'

She gives a curt toss of the head and steps back to admit Skelgill. He enters an unlit oblong room that has the makings of a kitchen to his right and a parlour to his left. Of what he can discern in the twilight, conditions are both spartan and shabby. Wizened and hunched and gripping a trembling walking stick between his knees, Old Man Gilhooley huddles in a threadbare wingback armchair, one of a pair angled towards a small hearth, where an inadequate log fire falters. The man does not look directly at him, but turns his head in birdlike fashion, disquietingly so, and Skelgill wonders if he might be blind.

'Tis yan o' they Grahams frae Buttermere. He's brung us coal.'

'Ne'er trust a Graham.' The old man's retort is sharp and venomous and he spits into the fire.

Skelgill breaks into a broad grin – such vilification seems to delight him, as though it is a compliment of the highest order – and humps the sack down upon the hearth.

'I'll get a blaze going for you.'

The old man stares vacantly and now Skelgill can see that his eyes are opaque with advanced cataracts. Again he rotates his head while Skelgill produces a lock-knife and slits open the sack and begins to face up the smouldering log-pile with large chunks of coal.

'He's staying fer a cuppa scordy.'

The man reacts to his wife's explanation with a rather unpleasant smacking of his lips, suggestive of distaste – or perhaps thirst on his own part. Now the woman addresses Skelgill.

'Pipes is froze. T'only watter's int' well.'

Skelgill lifts a sooty palm, though he declines to respond to the plaintive note of appeal in her voice. She loiters for a second, before pulling on another blanket and lifting up a pail from beside the apron front sink. She hobbles out, banging the door behind her.

'Where've thee chaffed that frae, lad?'

This is the first hint of an acknowledgement that Skelgill's mission is benevolent. That the goods are stolen is taken as read.

Skelgill chuckles.

'Crummock Hall estate.'

The man does not respond, but as Skelgill snatches a glance he sees that a grin of satisfaction has spread across the aged countenance – and yet it is suddenly jerked away, as if it is incompatible with deep-seated muscle memory.

'They owes us a sight more than a sack o'coal.'

'There's another couple in the car.'

Gilhooley snorts with indignation.

'Three sacks – three 'undred sacks – all the coal as is still left in Haig colliery – wunt cover it.'

Skelgill nods sympathetically (an act probably unappreciated) and continues with his work. His application is paying off, for hungry flames are licking between the coals. The old man can sense the burgeoning heat, and leans over his stick, his features stretching like a stroked cat.

'They'd tek shirt off back o' likes o' us, lad.'

The implied commonality between the Gilhooleys and the Grahams has the makings of a small olive branch, albeit Skelgill is unaware of any inter-clan antipathy (though he kens well enough the infamous reputation attached to his own matriarchal lineage).

'Aye.' Skelgill edges back a little as the fire grows. 'What did they take from the Gilhooleys?'

The old man makes a sudden sharp hawking noise. He raises a bony finger in the approximate direction of Crummock Hall.

'Gilhooleys ought ter be livin' ower yonder – not them thievin' O'Mores.'

'How's that?'

Gilhooley fixes his clouded eyes upon Skelgill – it is a look of rage.

'Jipped us – of us *inheritance*.'

He more or less shouts the latter word and it leaves him wheezing.

'What is it?'

The man's ire is palpable – as if it ought to be obvious – indeed, that the whole of Lorton Vale, nay Cumbria, should know of this injustice.

'Us *inheritance!* Arv telt yer already!'

'Aye. So you did.'

Skelgill is assessing how to bridge this semantic impasse, but now it is the old man who cocks his head in the direction of the door – again the birdlike movements, as if he is listening for clues that will signal the approach of his spouse. Skelgill has noted that the well is thirty yards away, down a difficult slope where the water table must be more reliable; they have time yet. Abruptly, Gilhooley begins to claw at his clothing – he wears a misshapen and horribly stained fisherman's sweater from which his scrawny neck protrudes like a tortoise from its shell. He hooks scaly, yellowed fingernails into the collar and extracts some object fastened upon a cracked leather thong.

'Tek a deek.'

Skelgill widens his eyes in the gloom, ducking closer for a better look. He grimaces as the old man's foul breath hisses in his face. Gilhooley can't hold the object still – a concave metal oval about two inches across – quite possibly gold, though heavily tarnished – ringed by six or eight broken claws and what appear to be the remnants of feathers, quills threaded through tiny holes around the perimeter of the plate, plumes worn down; indeed what barely recognisable matter survives is blackened and thick with human grease and grime.

Skelgill is about to speak when the latch rattles. With an alacrity that belies his apparent infirmity the old man conceals the battered amulet and resumes his hunched stance. The woman, lopsided under the weight of the pail, targets her spouse with an accusing stare.

'What's crackin' on?'

Gilhooley is either well used to repelling her cross-examination or – as DS Jones suggested – is just a touch mad.

'Where's us scordy, woman?'

'How could I 'ave med yer brew – I've only just fetched watter?'

The old man hawks again, and spits with renewed venom.

'Away then, woman!'

Skelgill is still crouched beside the armchair. He stands up and ostentatiously stretches his spine, and then addresses Mrs Gilhooley.

'That's your fire going, love – I'll get your other sacks.'

The old man completely ignores him. It seems their confederacy is to remain clandestine – unless it has already slipped his mind. Skelgill is obliged to shut the door against the cold, but he lingers on the step – however, the recalcitrant couple seem only to be trading vicious insults. He heaves the second, and then the third sack, propping them either side of the door. Then he trudges back to his shooting brake and drives away.

The trackway that had defeated DS Jones's efforts to reach the cottage by car is treacherous, but Skelgill has been more cavalier and now he retraces the undulating course, slipping and sliding and employing the basic principle of the rollercoaster, not to stop on an upslope. When he reaches the junction with the lane, he halts and checks his phone. There is a signal, and he consults his contacts and taps on "Jim H". The answer comes almost immediately.

'Daniel – how are our waxwings faring?'

The professor's voice is a little muted, as though he has Skelgill on loudspeaker.

'They were at Buttermere until Tuesday, at least.'

'Ah – they are sweeping southwards. The twitchers' grapevine is full of new reports across the Midlands.'

Skelgill pauses for a diplomatic second or two – but he is eager to get down to business.

'Jim – this Crummock Hall affair – do you know of any connection with a family called Gilhooley?'

'Gilhooley? And O'More?' The professor can be imagined tapping together the tips of his fingers. 'They sound as though they may share a common provenance.'

'Aye – happen there was some ancient dispute over property.'

'Then it might have its roots in Ireland, Daniel – I have an old friend, a history don at Trinity – I can drop him an email – how urgent is this?'

Skelgill has extracted his road atlas from the pocket behind the passenger seat, and is presently tracing a route that takes his index finger into North Wales.

'Just whenever you've got a minute, Jim.'

'I am online at this moment, Daniel.'

'Aye, well – if it's no bother – in fact, you couldn't just look up something for me?'

'Certainly – what is it?'

'Crossing times – for the fast ferry from Holyhead to Dublin.'

17. DUBLIN BY NIGHT – Saturday 8.30pm

Skelgill circles the Edward VII post box in the manner of one who suspects his eyes may be deceiving him – a trick of the streetlight neon, perhaps, that makes the familiar red appear – well, *green*. He glances about warily – as though he might be looking for the candid camera concealed to capture yet another gullible English tourist. When he turns back a leprechaun will be perched on the top.

'It really is green, Inspector.'

Now he swings about – a grinning Fergal Mullarkey has a hand upon his shoulder.

'We Irish might hold high political ideals – but we're a pragmatic bunch. No point in throwing out the baby with the bathwater.'

Skelgill is nodding rather vacantly.

'First time in Dublin, Inspector?'

That Skelgill has barely set foot outside his lodgings before being accosted in this fashion – in a city of well over a million inhabitants – seems to be an illusion that comfortably eclipses the emerald pillar box. However, a few seconds' reflection enables him to qualify the ostensibly unlikely odds. After all, he has chosen his accommodation – a modest hotel on St Stephen's Green – for their close proximity to the addresses in his notebook. Perhaps Fergal Mullarkey, upon his return to the country, has made a visit to his offices – or maybe he lives nearby?

And yet there is something curious in the tenor of his greeting, which lacks the note of surprise that the 'coincidence' might merit. It is more like he has come across Skelgill in a corridor of Crummock Hall engrossed by a stuffed otter. And Skelgill falls in with this mode of inappropriate familiarity. The entire cameo is suggestive of a certain amount of mutual suspicion, of cards being kept close to one's chest.

'Just as well I saw that before I've been to the pub.'

'Ah – you're heading for Temple Bar, Inspector?'

Skelgill manufactures a wry smile.

'I figured there was a decent clue in the name.'

Fergal Mullarkey chuckles.

'Perhaps I may chaperone you?' He checks his wristwatch. 'I have a – an appointment – at The Morrison at 9 p.m. – it's literally the other side of the Liffey from Temple Bar. I can steer you away from the rather less salubrious quarter – unless of course you are looking for a lively night?'

'Just a quiet pint.'

'In that case it would be a pleasure – walk this way, now.'

The lawyer sets a brisk pace – no problem to Skelgill – and seems content to point out various landmarks along the way, largely connected with the Easter Rising, and precluding the need for any more searching conversation. Five minutes have passed when Skelgill falls momentarily behind – they have entered a secluded backstreet square, and a parked *Triumph* motorcycle draws his attention. When he looks up he sees that Fergal Mullarkey is unaware that he lags, and is already on the next side of the square. Skelgill begins to cross diagonally, passing close by a young woman who waits on the corner of the central island, beneath the orange glow of a streetlamp. She wears a close-fitting corset top and a tight short skirt, and sheer nylons and high heels – she looks dressed for clubbing and must be freezing. She engages him with penetrating blue eyes, heavily mascaraed, and he breaks stride as he inhales her musky fragrance. But Fergal Mullarkey halts – and the abrupt ceasing of his footsteps alerts Skelgill. The girl allows a hint of a smile to play at the corners of her scarlet lips. He nods a little self-consciously and hustles on to where the lawyer awaits.

'Queer place to stand for a taxi – you'd think the main road would be a better bet.'

Fergal Mullarkey glances sharply at Skelgill, as if suspecting him of being disingenuous.

'I don't believe it's a taxi she's looking for, Inspector.'

Skelgill is about to reply – then it must strike him that he has been slow on the uptake. As they walk on he glances briefly over his shoulder – the girl, a shadow now, might be watching as she lights up a cigarette. He opts for silence.

'You'll be running the gauntlet if you come home this way home, Inspector.' The Irishman produces a salacious wink. 'Nearly there, now – just after this next corner.'

And sure enough they round into a narrow street to be greeted by a pub sign immediately on their side of the terrace. Fergal Mullarkey shoulders the door upon a busy hubbub that reaches out to embrace them and does not diminish as they enter. He seems to be known, for he catches the barman's eye and makes a two-fingered gesture which is met with a curt nod, and he leads Skelgill beyond the servery to a section of stalls where they find a free table.

'When in Rome, Inspector?'

'Come again?'

'I've ordered you a Guinness.'

Skelgill scowls.

'I'm a real ale man, myself – but I shan't offend the locals.'

Fergal Mullarkey looks like he is offended, but responds in a conciliatory tone.

'I don't believe we pasteurise it over here – so you might be pleasantly surprised.'

Skelgill glances about uneasily. The room is warm and he busies himself with shedding his jacket. Fergal Mullarkey, however, gives no indication that he intends to remove his smart *Crombie* overcoat. There ensue a few moments of stilted silence, until the lawyer speaks again.

'I imagine this is too much of a happenstance to suppose you're on a weekend city-break, Inspector?'

Skelgill looks away and rubs the end of his nose between a thumb and forefinger. It is an uncharacteristic gesture and it might be deduced he is concocting an explanation.

'Aye – there was something I needed to follow up.' He says this in a way to suggest Fergal Mullarkey is not that 'something'. Now his gaze returns to his companion. 'But –

while I'm over here – there is a matter your firm could help me with.'

'We are at your service, Inspector.'

Perhaps curiously, Fergal Mullarkey does not ask what. Could there just be a hint of strain in his eyes that belies his casual helpfulness? Skelgill is obliged to explain.

'It might be a wild-goose chase – but you mentioned you've been the solicitors for the O'Mores since the year dot?' (Fergal Mullarkey is nodding cautiously.) 'If you've still got old records of property transactions – I wouldn't mind having a look through them. Especially dating from around the time they moved to Cumbria – Cumberland as it was then.'

Now the lawyer seems to relax, though he taps the top of his bald head doubtfully, and in his reply he sounds a note of pessimism.

'That would be three hundred years ago.'

'Too far back?'

'Yes – well, no – that is, whatever is extant, we'll have it, alright. That's not the trouble.'

At this juncture the bartender arrives bearing their drinks. Skelgill casts a sceptical eye, but he is thirsty and there's no denying that the black stuff looks appetising. He takes an exploratory sip. Fergal Mullarkey does not touch his. Skelgill smacks his lips approvingly and moves in for a more substantial gulp; it produces a knowing smile from the lawyer.

'The difficulty is more for the person who has to read through the material – we're talking handwritten scrolls and parchments – it's not like you can tap a word into the search box and – *click* – there you have it.' He folds his hands and rests them neatly upon the table. 'I can let you in tomorrow if you would like – you'll get far more peace on a Sunday – you know what a rowdy bunch lawyers can be.' He has a mischievous glint in his eye. 'Unless you've other plans, that is?'

Skelgill looks like he is not expecting such cooperation.

'What about you – have you not got anything better to do?'

'I do have commitments – I'm an elder of the church for one thing – but I reside close to the office, Inspector.' He looks like he expects Skelgill to know this. 'I can let you in and leave you to it – if you've no objection. You still have my mobile number?'

Skelgill has his nose buried in his pint, and nods his gratitude. Then he raises a finger to indicate he has thought of something.

'The photograph I sent you – did you have any joy with that?'

Now Fergal Mullarkey looks perplexed.

'I have not been in the office since Thursday morning – was it by mail?'

Skelgill shakes his head – he seems taken by the Guinness and is squeezing in another mouthful between sentences.

'I texted it – from Crummock Hall – on Tuesday it would have been – I meant to ask you after the funeral.'

Fergal Mullarkey's clownlike countenance exhibits a decidedly blank expression, reminiscent of Pierrot. He reaches into a coat pocket for his handset, though he merely gazes at the screen rather than interrogate it further.

'Are you sure it transmitted, Inspector? I've been having a devil of a job getting messages in and out of that place. The walls are so thick – never mind the mountains.'

Skelgill nods and locates his own phone. He thumbs through his recent activity. He is about to turn the handset to show it to the lawyer – but then he seems to have second thoughts.

'Aye – you're probably right – only way to get a decent signal thereabouts is to climb the fell.'

Fergal Mullarkey nods sympathetically – though he does not ask what the photograph concerns. And now Skelgill seems content to let it pass. Fergal Mullarkey looks again at his phone and gives a sudden start.

'Jeepers – I shall be late – my apologies, but I must fly, Inspector.'

As the lawyer rises from his seat, Skelgill leans forwards and stretches out a protesting palm.

'Your pint?'

The beer is untouched. Fergal Mullarkey makes a resigned face.

'Would you be my guest?'

Skelgill sinks back into his chair. His own glass is considerably more than half empty. He shrugs phlegmatically.

'Don't mind if I do.'

*

Having consumed the second pint more steadily, Skelgill dons his jacket and heads out into the night. Unheeding of Fergal Mullarkey's words of caution he casually retraces his steps into the dimly lit square – but when he looks about he finds it bereft of life, just a few parked cars and the echo of traffic from a neighbouring street. The motorbike is gone, the girl, too. He dawdles now, and opens the maps application on his mobile – and then almost immediately picks up the pace as he gets his bearings. He decides upon a zigzagging course back towards St Stephen's Green – and it is not long before he finds himself emerging upon the bustling pedestrian thoroughfare of Grafton Street, bright with dazzling Christmas lights and thronged with merry revellers, mainly younger than he. This is not his natural habitat, and yet he seems content to stay on the route, despite the occasional jostling from the exuberant crowd. He pauses to look at the overhead decorations – there are the illuminated words *Nollaig Shona Duit* – and he is wondering what they mean when a raucous English voice rudely hijacks his thoughts.

'When's Shona gonna do it, eh Paddy?'

The speaker roars with laughter – and Skelgill is not sure if it is being assumed that he is "Paddy." A gang of twenty-something stags, seven or eight strong, sporting white England soccer shirts and steeped in alcohol if not Irish tradition is spilling from a bar, perhaps having been ejected. They bellow and screech with coarse London accents and break into what is

201

obviously a practised chant of "Shona, Shona, show us your tits!" repeatedly sung to a popular football rhythm. Skelgill can see the signs of disapproval – and apprehension – from those citizens unfortunate enough to be in the gang's immediate proximity, though understandably no one wants to provoke them. They argue about which direction to head, and then begin to move away from Skelgill, several of them swaying drunkenly and hanging around their mates' necks. Now they strike up an offensive sectarian chant, one that succinctly combines religion and politics – and this seems to be a step too far for some of the locals – for there is the beginning of a skirmish. This is just what they want. Skelgill hears the breaking of glass and – while a minor fracas occupies the main cohort – he notices that one thug (something of a tattooed bruiser with a pony tail and the nickname 'Horse' appliquéd on his shirt) has a young Irish man, considerably smaller, pinned against a shop front about twenty yards away and is waving a broken bottle in his face. The lad's girlfriend shrieks with terror. But before Skelgill can react a cry suddenly goes up and there is the chatter of police radios and an approaching siren – and the stag party scatters into side streets and alleys. The remaining thug discards his broken bottle but head-butts his quarry for good measure – and then splits in Skelgill's direction. He gallops more or less straight at Skelgill – as if he means to barge him out of the way – but Skelgill at the last possible moment steps adroitly to one side and trips the snorting brute, who flies headlong on the pavement – extracting a cry of anger from him and astonished gasps from onlookers. His horrible curses make it plain he has revenge on his mind – but Skelgill is upon him in a flash, jamming a knee into his kidneys and wrenching an arm up his back that has him squealing like a stuck pig.

'That's your holiday over, sunshine.'

Through his agony, the thug reacts to Skelgill's accent.

'You're English – you traitor!'

While the unedited version of this accusation includes several odious expletives – it is the word "traitor" that makes Skelgill see red, and with his free hand he takes a grip of the pony tail and raises the thug's head and then smashes it down into the concrete – producing a rumble of approval from the watching crowd, and several men now move in to assist. But there is a pattering of footsteps and pell-mell come two panting Gardaí – they drop down beside Skelgill and are ready with handcuffs. Skelgill backs off, reaching into his hip pocket for his warrant card – for it seems he will have some explaining to do.

'I saw him, officers.' As the hooligan is dragged to his feet, spitting blood and teeth and displaying a broken nose, a middle-aged Irishman has intervened. He points distastefully at the bloodied football shirt. 'He threatened a boy with a broken bottle – then he ran and tripped and hit his face on the ground. He's drunk as a skunk.' He turns and gestures to Skelgill. 'This gentleman went to detain him. I saw it all. If you need my name for a witness.'

'Sure, I saw it, too – the fellow went flying, nose first it was. Self-inflicted.'

'Aye, face-planted – so he did, officers. Drunken disgrace.'

There are more people stepping forward, pointing disparagingly at the thug and regaling the police with complaints about the behaviour of he and his cowardly gang. Before Skelgill knows it he has been separated from the Gardaí by his newfound allies – he gets the idea (and he thinks probably so do the Gardaí); he brushes his hands and straightens his jacket, and wanders off casually along the street. He feels a couple of appreciative pats on the shoulder as he goes.

After about a hundred yards he pauses outside a pub – it would be understandable that he might welcome a stiffener following the violent incident – but as he wavers he finds himself drawn to a neighbouring retail outlet. Perhaps it is something in his peripheral vision, a subliminal impression – because, uncannily, before him, as large as life, is Perdita. He starts – and realises that he is looking at a full-size cardboard cutout: for it is a bookstore, and the entire window display is dedicated to the launch of her new novel. *"Slave to Desire – The Raunchiest Rowena Devlin Yet!"* It is a provocative headline – and he has to admit

203

that in her alluring cat-eye make-up and revealing outfit her PR team have created a persona to rival the provocative title.

Skelgill glances at his watch. Again he hesitates. Then he strides into the pub – to emerge only two minutes later. Turning decisively in the direction of St Stephen's Green, he seems to know where he is going.

*

From his vantage point in the quiet cul-de-sac Skelgill observes a taxi pull up across the street. He takes half a pace backwards, deeper into the shadows. He shivers a little; there might be no snow in Dublin, but the temperature is certainly below freezing. He watches as the passenger pays the driver and disembarks – a female, her head covered by the hood of a crimson coat. Indeed, like Little Red Riding Hood she scampers up the flight of stone slabbed steps – and becomes silhouetted against the great white-painted main door of the Georgian townhouse. She enters with her latchkey and a minute later the tall three-over-six sash window to the right is gently illuminated from within. He can see at an angle into the room: there are bookshelves either side of a chimney breast. Another minute passes and the woman now appears in sight, bearing a tray, which she sets down low. Then she attends to the fire, apparently adding some fuel. Finally she approaches the window and takes a seat facing the street; there must be a desk just below sill level. She begins to write.

Skelgill strolls across the uneven cobbles. He halts at the railings that prevent pedestrians from falling into the area. Now he watches. The image before him is remarkably close to that he has recently admired in the bookshop – except this is the real thing, and the writer has her head bowed in concentration – maybe some new lines that came to her that she just had to get down – or a diary or journal – or an urgent letter perhaps – whichever it is, her concentration is intense. Skelgill seems quite content – the street is free of traffic, and for the time being there are no passers-by to suspect him of being a peeping tom – and when in due course she looks up and makes eye contact he remains inscrutable. Her dark eyes show no sign of alarm – or even surprise – and her introspective expression begins to soften into a welcoming smile. She puts down her pen, and calmly rises.

'Inspector – you'll catch your death out there!'

In the twenty seconds it has taken her to reach the door, Skelgill has not moved – but now he pulls himself away from the empty window.

'Aye – happen I should know better.'

Perdita waits patiently for him to approach; though she has the door wide open, as he enters the carpeted hallway he feels the comfort of central heating. She seems taller in extravagant stilettos and a close-fitting mini-dress in navy lace, beneath a leather bolero – and neither has he seen her looking quite so elegant. She removes the jacket to reveal that the dress is sleeveless, with a choker neck. She drapes it on a chair and puts out a hand.

'Yours too, Inspector?'

He obliges, and then she leads him into the room on the right where he had observed her movements. Despite the high and ornate ceiling it exudes a cosiness, enhanced by subdued lighting concealed in the wall units, and a flickering fire – which to Skelgill's eye is surprisingly well set, given her recent arrival. There is the desk at the window, and the bookshelves either side of the fireplace, where various literary collections are interspersed with tasteful ornaments and framed photographs. On the walls to his left and behind him are large abstract seascapes that look like original oil paintings. On the mantelpiece a line of what must be scented nightlights burn, for there is a fragrance that he recognises as sandalwood. Before the hearth is spread a great rug in broad stripes of aquamarine and teal that merge with one another, and ranged around it comfortable-looking sofas loaded with floral cushions in cobalt blue and lemon. All in all, the impression is of a boutique hotel, vibrant and contemporary yet cleverly complementing the classical architecture of the room.

'Beautiful place, you've got.'

'Thank you, Inspector – it dates from the late eighteenth century.'

She does not seem inclined to take any credit, despite that his reference can only be to the decor. She indicates that he should take a seat upon one of the sofas, close to the fire, beside which there is the tray upon an upholstered footstool. On the tray is a decanter of glowing golden spirit and two rocks glasses charged with ice. Skelgill suddenly looks alarmed.

'You're expecting company – I should get on my way.'

The girl bites her full lower lip, perhaps to conceal the semblance a smile.

'Remember what I told you my Great Uncle Declan said about me, Inspector – well, maybe he was right about my acting on intuition.' Now she allows the smile to break out. 'And, in any event, in Dublin I am *Rowena*, my alter ego.'

Skelgill can only assume she spotted him across the road when her taxi drew up – it seems improbable and yet what other explanation can there be?

'Aye – happen I can't knock that – much as my boss would like to ban the word intuition from all police work.'

She giggles playfully and now rather to his surprise sits close beside him and reaches across to pour the drinks.

'Whiskey okay – the real Irish McCoy?'

'I guess it's the only chaser for Guinness.'

'Ah – so you were out on the town?'

'Just a stretch of the legs. I thought I'd get my bearings – I've –' Now he hesitates. 'I'm meeting your family lawyer tomorrow to go through some old papers.'

If he has been hasty to manufacture an excuse for his presence, it does not appear to unsettle her – and she neither questions him on this point, nor seems perturbed that he has gravitated to her home. She raises her glass and he obediently follows suit.

'Sláinte.'

'Aye, cheers.'

They both drink. Skelgill takes a substantial mouthful, but Perdita is more circumspect – the whiskey is neat after all –

and she watches him with a gentle smile as he tries to mask his reaction to the fiery liquid. It takes him a few moments to recover the use of his vocal cords.

'You speak Irish?'

She shakes her head, and he notices how alluring is her mass of soft strawberry blonde ringlets, inviting one's touch.

'Just a smidgen – as I mentioned, my schooling was in England – and France – and by the time I came back here I figured I was too late to learn the Gaelic. I know that Dublin means *Blackpool*.'

He frowns in a good-natured way, as though he suspects she might be ribbing him. They take more sips in silence before Perdita settles her glass two-handed upon her lap.

'You must be thinking we all shipped out in haste.'

Her question could be considered as subtly probing, however, she says it as a statement, an apology almost, and Skelgill shrugs in a way to suggest it is not for him to judge – and perhaps she appreciates this – for she relaxes back into the corner of the settee so that she may better regard him.

'On my part – you know, I honestly couldn't face going back there this morning. It is such sad news about dear old Mr Thwaites – coming on top of everything else. And despite not really knowing him – I mean, as an adult, having so rarely visited – he was always very kind to me – right from when I was a tiny child. I guess I got singled out for special treatment, being the wee one. You know – he unfailingly remembered to set out my cutlery left-handed? Sure, he seemed pleased by that.' She gives a little ironic laugh. 'Over here you get called a *ciotóg* – the strange one.'

Skelgill is looking at her with an undisguised intensity – but now he transfers his gaze to her glass, and then to his own; and then they both grin wryly, and clink southpaw.

'It's "cuddy-wifted" in Cumberland – and maybe I don't have to tell you, a cuddy's a donkey.'

'We left-handers are supposed to be more creative, Inspector.'

'Aye – so they say – except I've not got a creative bone in my body.'

Perdita frowns disapprovingly, and rises to this challenge on his behalf.

'Who said creativity resides in the bones, Inspector – surely it's the realm where the soul wanders free?'

She takes a decisive gulp of her drink. Skelgill reaches for the decanter and offers a refill and she does not demur.

'You –' Whatever he is about to say he checks himself and starts again. 'I – I saw the shop window display – the promotion for your new book.'

She peers rather coyly from behind the strands of hair that are beginning to stray across her face.

'Strictly speaking, my new book is over there.' She gives a casual flick of the hand in the direction of her desk. 'Such are my publisher's lead times that I completed *Slave to Desire* almost a year ago.'

Skelgill drinks and swallows quickly.

'So does the new one have to be raunchier still?'

Now she laughs, a liquid peal, tossing back her head to reveal the pale unblemished skin of her throat.

'Oh, my – the marketing department *has* gone to town, now! And that's not half of what the photographer wanted me to do.'

Skelgill raises an eyebrow.

'I seem to be the only person who doesn't read them – I'm beginning to get the gist of what I'm missing.'

Perdita is amused; she kicks off her stiletto heels and pulls her feet up onto the sofa to make herself more comfortable; her legs are bare and the hem of her dress, gathered at the centre, slips higher and draws Skelgill's gaze. She seems unaware – or unconcerned – but for his part he begins to realise that the delicate and intricately woven fabric is partially see-through, and raises intriguing questions about what – if anything – she could possibly be wearing beneath. She drinks and regards him over the rim of her glass with a beguiling flutter of her eyelashes.

'It's no *Fifty Shades*, I'm afraid, Inspector – my romantic liaisons tend to take place off camera – I think the suggestion that something is *possibly* going to happen is often far more tantalising than the graphic detail.' She pauses to watch his reaction. He is now studying his drink, swirling the fast-melting slivers of ice. 'But when my heroes and heroines are thrown together by turmoil and tribulation I shouldn't like them to resist temptation.'

Her tone is wistful, and now she drains her glass and leans forwards, touching him upon the shoulder with her right hand – then gracefully she rises and takes a step back.

'There is something I should like to show you – if you'll excuse me for a wee second?'

'Sure.'

Barefooted she glides across the room, closing the door behind her. Skelgill waits for a moment and then he too stands; however, rather than follow her he stalks to the window and looks out – the street is empty; a sheen of ice glistens on the railings. He turns his eyes to the open notebook on the desk. There is a fountain pen beside it; evidently she prefers the traditional method, for lines of flowing longhand fill the pages. It seems she halted mid-sentence, and the top is off the pen. He replaces it, and then notices a familiar business card, that she is using as a bookmark: "Tobias Vellum, Aloysius Vellum & Co." For a second he frowns – but, then, she is a writer with an interest in books, Vellum a bookseller with a connection to the family, and pushy to boot. Why wouldn't she have his card?

He crosses to the shelves; there is an eclectic mix of classics – contemporary and traditional, from Highsmith and Updike to Dickens and the Brontës – with a smattering of popular fiction – but it is the photographs that capture his attention. Though books may be their owner's biographer, for Skelgill, these images offer a far more intriguing insight into the life and character of Perdita – and *Rowena* – for she appears in a range of guises and situations, from lustrous literary events to casual holiday scenes, and she is revealed in the easy and intimate company of males and females alike – though there is no

209

consistent companion. He steps across the hearth to continue his perusal, the candles gutter at his passing – and now one particular portrait strikes home. Beneath a snowy mountainous backdrop a rosy-cheeked Perdita – younger, perhaps in her university days – stands victorious between two other girls, each of them displaying a medal. They support skis in crooked arms and have sunglasses pushed back upon their bandanas. Behind them is a signboard that marks the name of the piste; it says simply, *'La Face'*. The exclusive resort of Val d'Isère might be alien territory to Skelgill – but no one with his mountain credentials would fail to recognise what is the most celebrated and notorious black run in the entire French Alps. He stares, teeth bared, his mind electrified.

But now a creak of the door handle interposes between his slip-sliding thoughts and their subconscious substrate – instinctively he pulls a book from the shelf, and by the time Perdita enters he appears engrossed in its content. He turns casually – she is waiting in the doorway – and now she laughs, an outrageous note of amusement: for he has inadvertently selected the first volume of the erotic trilogy she referred to just a moment earlier! Skelgill rather sheepishly replaces the book.

'Inspector – sorry to keep you waiting – but it struck me – ' She pauses, and crosses one leg in front of the other, and tilts her head a little to the side. 'You were interested when I told you about the bibles that my Great Uncle Declan gave to each of us for our Christenings – and I said I keep mine always at my bedside.'

'Aye.'

Skelgill's "aye" is one that even he does not recognise.

'I thought perhaps you would find it more edifying to see it in situ.'

18. THE ARCHIVES – Sunday 8am

'Successful night, Inspector?'

Fergal Mullarkey is waiting on the steps outside his offices, part of a Georgian terrace characteristic of the area. Like Skelgill he is muffled and gloved against the bitter cold, and his beady blue eyes peer out from beneath a bowler hat. His choice of words seems to set Skelgill on his guard – as if he suspects the lawyer of knowing his movements – and the detective hunches his shoulders and casts about uneasily, as though the surroundings might inspire some suitable rejoinder.

'I headed back after I'd drunk the second pint.'

Fergal Mullarkey gives an unconvincing nod of acknowledgement.

'I certainly wasn't expecting your call at this time of the morning.'

'I'm a bit of an early bird.'

Skelgill's tone is unapologetic, and perhaps overly taciturn, given that the man is doing him a fairly sizeable favour. But the lawyer is undeterred.

'To catch the worm – *hah-ha!*' He produces his trademark grin. 'No worries – sure, it suits me to get the job done – in fact, if you're willing, I'll give you the code to reset the alarm, and you can let yourself out whenever you're finished.'

He does not reply: while Fergal Mullarkey wrestles against a series of locks with a great jangling bunch of keys, Skelgill has noticed a brass plate bolted to the grey sandstone wall beside the door. Its inscription reads, "Mullarkey & Shenanigan, Solicitors."

'Never fear, Inspector – there have been no Shenanigans here for a very long time.'

He chuckles, albeit it in a rather forced manner, for this must be an incalculably hackneyed quip.

Skelgill follows him inside; the general impression is not dissimilar to the residence of Perdita Regulus-O'More – for, indeed, these offices comprise several conjoined townhouses, commonplace in central districts, a natural evolution as original occupiers gradually flitted to suburbs more suited to a lifestyle with the new-fangled horseless carriage. The décor is businesslike, with plain carpets and neutral walls ornamented with certificates of proficiency. Fergal Mullarkey leads them up a broad staircase to the third storey, and along a corridor to the rear of the property, at the end of which there is a door on either side. To the left a small plaque denotes "Boardroom", and corresponding on the right is "Meeting Room"; it is into the latter that they go.

The chamber is bright – the walls are bare and reflect the early morning sunlight – and there seems to be a tang of turpentine in the air. Much of the available space is taken up by a large oval table, ringed by chairs, but Skelgill's gaze falls upon a coffee maker in one corner, sitting upon a glass-fronted refrigerator in which are visible cartons of milk and packets of chocolate chip cookies.

'Just make yourself at home, will you, Inspector? Grab a coffee while I pop down to the archive and see what I can unearth.'

Skelgill frowns and clenches his fists at his sides.

'Can't I give you a hand?'

Fergal Mullarkey shifts his weight a little uneasily from one leg to the other.

'To be honest with you, Inspector, I think we would just get under one another's feet. There is only a narrow gap between the rows of racking, and you wouldn't really know what you were looking for.'

'How about carrying it up?'

'We have a dumbwaiter adapted for the purpose – it is somewhat antediluvian, but it does the job.' He moves across to the door. 'Oh – and for reference – the gents' loo is back the way we came, at the top of the stairs.'

Left to his own devices Skelgill wraps his jacket around a chair and balances his hat and gloves on top. Then he makes a coffee, taking several attempts to get the hang of the unfamiliar device. It requires sachets to be slotted into a concealed flap, and a certain amount of patience, which is a quality that only seems properly to visit Skelgill when he climbs into his boat. He finally succeeds having dissembled the front of the machine and effected a modification to the mechanism with the stem of a teaspoon. He ambles to the window with his steaming mug. The view to the rear is of a low-rise arrangement typical of Georgian town planning, once the stables and grooms' accommodation, now converted into desirable mews properties and perhaps equally sought-after city centre garages. However, the scene is haphazard, in that various extensions and conversions have been added down the years, and one such appendage is attached to the lawyers' building. It occupies two storeys, and juts out as a flat roof just below the window. The felt is cracked and has been repaired in places with great daubs of bitumen, and patches of ice reveal where standing water must ordinarily collect. Skelgill casts a critical eye over the sash window, and then gives it a shake; it is loose in its frame – and then he notices that the two-piece brass catch has been removed and is lying together with its screws in the corner of the sill. He realises that the woodwork has a new coat of gloss paint – it is still tacky to the touch (and this accounts for the smell). He lifts the lower sash – it would be easy enough to climb out – or for a burglar to climb in – but what does enter is a rush of cold air about his thighs, and he slams it back down. He glances around the interior of the room; there is a PIR high in the angle above the door – it flickers red as he moves about – so he supposes that even were someone to scale the extension, the alarm system would catch them.

There is no sign yet of Fergal Mullarkey. Skelgill decides to visit the bathroom – although all he does is look around and scrub his fingertips of gloss paint. He retraces his steps and stands silently in the corridor. Gauging by the positions of the doors, the Boardroom would seem to be of similar proportions to the meeting room. He tries the handle, but it is locked – and now he hears clunking and whirring noises, followed by the tread of feet upon the staircase. He slips back to his coffee and is seated when Fergal Mullarkey backs in and rather breathlessly dumps two weighty legal storage boxes upon the table. However, the lawyer beams triumphantly.

'Here you go Inspector – that's everything from 1700 to 1750 – should comfortably cover the period you're after.' He lifts the lid off the upper box and extracts a manila file, and then opens this upon the table and slides it across to Skelgill. 'But – as I warned you last evening – it is all in longhand.'

He grins rather inanely and then he dusts off his hands and takes a step backwards towards the door.

'Well – I shall bid you goodbye for now, Inspector. The alarm code is 1916 – not so tricky, *hah-ha!* – just press the 'exit' button after typing it in – and there is a good strong Yale on the door that when you pull it shut should suffice until tomorrow morning.'

Skelgill, already scowling at the page of impenetrable gothic scrawl before him, glances up distractedly.

'Aye – no bother – I'll send you a text when I'm done.'

'Ah – excellent idea – and are you heading directly back to England this afternoon?'

The answer is yes but for some reason Skelgill plays it cagily. He glances casually at the legal boxes.

'Reckon I'll see how I get on.'

Fergal Mullarkey nods – but now he hesitates – he feels the top of his head in an exploratory manner – as if he is checking that hair has not magically returned since his last inspection.

'And, er – just how is it going? Overall, I mean – are you any further forward with the investigation into Declan's death?'

Skelgill looks up quickly.

'Aye – much further.'

His reply carries a note of indignation, that Fergal Mullarkey would assume otherwise, and the lawyer's mouth falls slightly open.

'Oh – well – jolly good.' (There is more checking for hair.) 'You see, Inspector, the family are rather impatient to get the books over here into safekeeping. Since Declan has died intestate, it may take some months to resolve his will – and irrespective of what they decide about the future of Crummock Hall, now that Thwaites is sadly no longer with us it looks like the place is going to have to be mothballed. The heating system will be drained down – and there is a grave risk that the collection could deteriorate if it becomes damp. Here in our own library we have controlled ambient humidity and temperature, and ample space. I have explained to them, however, that until the police have finished with the crime scene there is little we can do.'

Skelgill is listening evenly – though now he homes in on one particular remark.

'So they've not settled yet?'

'Concerning the fate of the estate?'

'Aye.'

Fergal Mullarkey shakes his head.

'I suppose it is understandable – it is not a decision to be taken lightly.'

'What would you do?'

Skelgill's bluntness seems to catch the lawyer unawares. But, though his pale cheeks flush, to his credit he provides what would appear to be an honest answer.

'Well – if I am being frank, Inspector, it is in our interest that they keep the estate in the Regulus-O'More family – they represent a sizeable client measured over a period of years – and, of course, there is a sentimental aspect in our long association.'

Skelgill nods.

'When do you think they'll make up their minds?'

Now Fergal Mullarkey contorts his pliable features into a resigned grimace.

'I was rather anticipating they would have decided yesterday, Inspector – but of course – events took over – you understand?' (Skelgill nods; he means the unfortunate passing of Thwaites.) 'We shall be reconvening next week.' Somewhat reverently he folds his hands on his breast. 'Let's hope it is the last funeral for a long time.'

'Aye – I'll second that.'

Now the lawyer edges closer to the exit.

'Oh – and these documents – don't worry about putting them back in their boxes – you see, you're not the only person who wants to peruse them.'

Now he flashes Skelgill a look that is emphatically conspiratorial.

'Aye?'

'Our mutual friend, Perdita – or perhaps I should say *Rowena*, given the nature her interest – I understand she has an idea for her next plot – and wishes to add a touch of authenticity. She is calling in tomorrow – although I fear she will be disappointed – I fancy that history will not live up to her vivid imagination when it comes to her characters' romantic liaisons.' He taps the side of his nose in a suggestive fashion, and smirks. 'For my part, I must head off and lay out the hymnbooks.'

Skelgill nods and raises a hand, as if in farewell – but in fact his gesture becomes a detaining index finger.

'Just one thing I've been wondering about?'

'Inspector?'

'How did you recognise me last night?'

For a moment Fergal Mullarkey looks nonplussed – he is clearly unprepared for this question, and he glances anxiously about the room – and then his gaze falls upon Skelgill's discarded garments. He waves a hand loosely at the chair.

'Inspector – there can only be one hat like that in the whole of Ireland.'

He chuckles fretfully and raises both palms in an apology-cum-wave and makes what might be considered a hasty exit. Skelgill is left staring at the door, but after a few moments he turns his attention to the file that lies open before him on the table.

It takes him under a minute to confirm what he has suspected all along – that he is not going to read the documents. Even were they printed in fourteen-point type, double-spaced, set in beautifully legible Times Roman or Garamond or Athelas, Skelgill would have found the two towering boxes of material a testing mountain – so the page before him penned in archaic quilled cursive script with elaborate swirls and loops (not to mention obsolete legal terms that would even defeat a lawyer) represents a precipitous literary scree in which his boots gain not an inch of traction. He slumps back in his chair and folds his arms, dark furrows lining his brow. If Fergal Mullarkey harbours any secretly malicious intent beneath his superficial helpfulness then he has succeeded – for the task he has casually inflicted is so overwhelming as to be almost suffocating, indeed Skelgill rises and strides to the window and raises the lower sash to admit fresh air, cold or not.

He marches back to the refreshments corner and makes himself another coffee. And now that his host has departed he attacks the biscuits with gusto, perhaps a small act of revenge, which he augments by using up all of the sugar. As he sits and slurps he must rue the absence of DS Jones – for if anyone could digest the material before him it is she. Indeed he casually finds her number on his mobile phone – but then he has second thoughts and rises again and begins to empty the boxes. Neatly, he lays out the documents in successive piles, ranging them around the table as though he has examined them in chronological sections. He looks at his phone once more and engages the camera app – but when he experimentally composes a photo he decides the exercise is futile. He wanders to the window and for a while he stands gazing out. Then he makes a small involuntary jolt and some purpose grips him: he slips the handset into a hip pocket, retrieves his gloves from the back of the chair, returns to the window, hauls the lower sash to its upper limit, and clambers out.

Thirty seconds later he is inside the 'locked' Boardroom. His hunch that it, too, is being painted proves correct. Here, also, the window catch has been removed. He scans about – at first sight it appears little different to the meeting room – perhaps a better class of table and chairs, but otherwise the same nondescript carpet and newly emulsioned walls. There is, however, a stack of about a dozen large framed photographs at one end of the table. The decorator has evidently removed them from the walls to do his job. Skelgill begins to work his way through the collection – group shots of members of staff – a historical record of the partners and their underlings, their names listed beneath, taken at intervals of roughly ten years. While the oldest pictures, dating from the early 1900s hold most intrinsic interest – brilliantined hairstyles, elaborate moustaches, starched collars and unintentionally hammed poses – it is to the more recent images that Skelgill gives his attention. He lays out the latest four in chronological order – and now he removes his gloves and takes snapshots with his mobile. When he has finished he spends some time poring over the originals. Then he replaces his gloves, re-stacks the frames, and climbs out onto the flat roof, shutting the window and returning to the meeting room whence he came. Having restored the sash to its closed position, he lays his phone upon the table and transmits a call, engaging the speaker when he hears the recipient pick up.

'Jones – where are you?'

'Oh, Guv – morning – er... in London, actually.'

'London?'

Skelgill sounds as indignant as if his subordinate had said New York or Rio de Janeiro or Shanghai.

'I travelled down yesterday afternoon – I went to see a show – with a college friend.'

It takes Skelgill a moment to collect his thoughts.

'What brought that on?'

DS Jones sounds a little guarded.

'The tickets came up – it was a spur-of-the-moment thing.'

Again Skelgill hesitates.

'When are you heading back?'

'I'm on the six o'clock express from Euston – it gets into Penrith at nine.'

'I'll pick you up.'

'Are you sure, Guv?'

'There's a couple of things I want to bounce off you.'

'Okay.'

There is ostensibly a note of reluctance in her voice – but perhaps Skelgill can sense there is something else – that she is building up to an inconvenient revelation. He remains silent, and his intuition proves correct.

'I might have some news by then, Guv.'

'What kind of news?'

'Well, er... about Brutus.'

'What about him?'

'He keeps texting me, Guv.'

'And?'

'I've agreed to meet him at lunchtime – just for a coffee.'

'Where?'

'It's *The Ritz*, Guv.' She blurts this out, as if doing so will diminish its impact. 'I thought I might learn something.'

'Aye, a lesson to regret.'

'But, Guv – I think he wants to talk to me.'

'That's not all he – '

As Skelgill checks himself DS Jones simultaneously interjects.

'Guv – I can handle it – don't worry – I'm a big girl, you know.'

'Jones – I'll see you at nine.'

Skelgill cuts off the call and stares at the handset. He leans over the table, his two hands resting on their heels. His expression is hard to fathom, but it could be assessed as a mixture of concern and irritation, with just a hint of jealousy. And perhaps there is a semblance of self-reproach for what he has said. He hauls on his jacket, and stuffs his gloves into the pockets. He takes his fur-lined trapper hat in both hands and gives it a shake, and then he holds it at arm's length and regards it pensively. The last time he wore it was on the ferry from Holyhead, when he clambered up on deck in the freezing night air to see the lights of Dublin.

19. RECONSTRUCTION – Monday 10am

'Tell Leyton what you told me last night.'

DS Jones looks apprehensively at Skelgill, and then at the newly arrived DS Leyton. They all three have travelled separately to Crummock Hall – to be admitted by the maid, Betty – and are now convened in Declan's study, still technically 'their' territory as a designated crime scene. DS Leyton is the last to arrive, bringing with him a black pilot's case from headquarters. He closes the door but remains standing against it; perhaps he detects a certain tension in the air.

DS Jones looks rather sombre, dressed all in black – leather jacket, ankle boots and stretch jeans and, unusually for her, a beret and scarf. The zipped waist-cut jacket emphasises her figure, and the fashionable ensemble gives her a continental look, her large dark eyes blinking soulfully behind hair pushed down by the beret. She is framed by one of the two arched windows to DS Leyton's right, standing rigidly with her fingertips pressed into the inaccessible front pockets of her jeans; directly ahead, across the room Skelgill half-sits against the edge of the desk, his arms folded.

'I spoke with Brutus yesterday – lunchtime.' She glances apprehensively at Skelgill, and then raises her shoulders to signify that her complicity was inadvertent. 'He got in touch with me.'

'Sounds interesting, girl.'

DS Leyton grins encouragingly – he must sense her predicament and that Skelgill's hackles are up. His response seems to relax her, and she takes a couple of paces towards him. Skelgill watches on censoriously.

'He told me about the family's decision – regarding Sir Sean O'More's will.'

DS Leyton makes an exclamation of suppressed anticipation.

'He says he and Cassandra want to sell Crummock Hall as soon as possible.'

'Cor blimey – I should've put a few nicker on that one.'

DS Jones responds with a wry smile, though she holds up a qualifying palm.

'But Martius and Perdita want to keep it – as a going concern – to appoint some kind of live-in estate manager.'

DS Leyton looks decidedly intrigued by this news. Though he knows little of Perdita, by living abroad she demonstrates scant interest in Cumbria – and in the case of Martius, certain financial indicators would lead one to suppose he too favoured a sale. DS Leyton counts off silently on the fingers of his free hand.

'We're missing Edgar.'

DS Jones nods eagerly.

'That's the thing – it's a stalemate – the split has effectively given him the casting vote – and apparently he won't reveal his hand. To quote Brutus, "That little runt Gerbil has got us over a barrel." Brutus doesn't know why he's holding out – but he says he's loving the power trip.'

DS Leyton rolls his eyes.

'Reckon he wants a bigger slice of the cake?'

Now Skelgill intervenes. 'What do you mean, Leyton?'

DS Leyton puts down the pilot's case and has a small battle with his somewhat ill fitting overcoat, which has managed to slip around sideways.

'Well, Guv – Edgar's due a fifth, right? – same as each of them. But if he wants to play them off – he can go to either side – say he'll throw in his lot with whoever comes up with the best offer. He's the accountant, after all, Guv – like you said.'

Skelgill's tone is sceptical. 'I can't see Martius standing for that. He's brassed off as it is – not inheriting the whole estate.'

DS Leyton shrugs.

'So, what happens if they can't strike a deal?'

'It would have to go to court, Leyton. Then it's anyone's guess – you know what judges can be like. They might not want to take that chance – never mind that it could last for years. I've spoken to Mullarkey – he'll be hassling them to come to a decision. If this place is mothballed the value starts to plummet.' Skelgill pushes off from the desk and jerks a thumb over his shoulder. 'Plus these books will deteriorate if they don't get them into proper storage.'

DS Leyton seems dissatisfied. He glances at DS Jones and then looks back at Skelgill.

'Why is Brutus telling us this? He might be a cocky little geezer, but he's not stupid. Reckon it's a double bluff?'

'In what way, Leyton?'

'Coming clean about his intentions – since we're likely to suspect anyone who wants the cash – stands to reason, Guv.'

Skelgill remains pensive.

'Does it?'

DS Leyton is nodding.

'Think about their movements – if the murder was 2 o'clock like you say, Guv. Brutus is nowhere to be seen until 2:30 – Cassandra claims she can't remember where she was – yet she's on the spot when Thwaites finds the body – and Edgar's handily placed up the staircase in his secret attic.'

Skelgill seems unconvinced – his expression is growing increasingly pessimistic.

'What about the others? Martius. Mullarkey. Thwaites. What about Perdita, for that matter?'

Now it is DS Leyton's turn to frown. He waves a hand approximately towards the windows.

'But, Guv – she was lost up the mountain.'

'Leyton, I can easily imagine how Perdita could have been here at 2 o'clock.'

Skelgill's countenance is grim – and his subordinates are startled, for surely this is a sizeable volte-face on the part of their boss. Of course, he may be playing devil's advocate for good purpose – but for the hell of it is just as likely. His frustration is plain; however he offers no further explanation and a silence prevails. Although there is apparently some background heating the room temperature is far from ideal, and none of them shows any inclination to shed their outdoor garments. After a minute, DS Leyton tries a more oblique tack.

'If only we could find that walking stick, Guv – old Declan's shillelagh.'

Skelgill glares at his sergeant.

'We're not going to find it, Leyton.'

'Why not, Guv? This snow's got to melt eventually.'

Skelgill digs his hands into his pockets and turns to stare at the hearth. In the grate there remains the large heap of cold grey wood ash.

'Because it went straight on the fire.'

DS Leyton glances sidelong at DS Jones, who gives a barely perceptible shake of the head to indicate this is also news to her.

'How do you know, Guv?'

Skelgill is still contemplating the fireplace.

'Remind me what it was made of.'

'Sandalwood, Guv – it's unusually dense?'

Skelgill looks like he is tempted to take up the theme of density. However, he refrains and tilts back his head.

'Unusually *scented*, Leyton.'

DS Leyton begins sniffing ostentatiously. In the background, DS Jones is beginning to nod.

'It's faded now.' Skelgill scowls impatiently. 'But you couldn't miss it at first.'

'My hooter's not what it used to be, Guv – plus I've had a stinker of a cold. The kids bring a new one home from school every Friday.' He shakes his head ruefully. 'Why didn't you say, Guv? I've had a couple of the lads up to their armpits in snow.'

Skelgill gives the semblance of a shrug.

'Why tell the culprit we've worked it out? Let them think we're daft country coppers, Leyton.'

This is a common and oft irrational excuse of Skelgill's, and one that in the present circumstances is unlikely to find favour with his subordinates – when they might reasonably infer it is *he* that is treating *them* as "daft country coppers". However, DS Leyton nods obligingly, and now he bends to pick up the black case, as if this notion has reminded him of their purpose in meeting this morning. He raises the bag one handed – it does not appear to be heavy – and pats it with the other. His tone of voice becomes decidedly optimistic.

'Well – at least we've got the rest of the stuff, Guv.'

Skelgill does not react immediately – but after a few seconds he nods rather reluctantly.

'Right – start laying it out.'

While his subordinates delve into the bag, Skelgill stalks across to the hearth and takes down Declan's tweed shooting-coat from its hook. He spreads it in a rough approximation of where Declan lay: head towards the desk, feet towards the clock. DS Leyton is more methodical: he refers to a folder of photographs, and carries the glass over towards the garden door and places it on its side – he stands back and checks the picture to confirm the accuracy of his handiwork. DS Jones has extracted Declan's logbook and pen from polythene bags and now positions them on the desk. Skelgill distributes the pendulum and brass winder key, again from memory.

That he has opted to stage this reconstruction – albeit of such minor proportions, and an exercise that could arguably be conducted from the comfort of his office using the extensive photographic record – might be regarded as a move of desperation. It could be surmised that 'the powers that be' see little or no progress on his part – that he has produced no systematic analysis of the information gathered: facts, hearsay, opinions and claims (many unsubstantiated); and thus he has not acted upon the evidence to date.

But this would be to underestimate Skelgill. That he harks back to his first few moments in Crummock Hall, when he felt that this room had its story to recount – whispering, unintelligible, piecemeal – tells that his inner thoughts (*gut feel*, to his critics) are inviting him to appreciate the narrative that has been progressively taking shape.

His subordinates perhaps sense something of this and they silently back away towards the windows. Skelgill stalks about the room – though with little regard to the 'clues' they have laid out. He looks more like a sergeant major inspecting his platoon's quarters with a mission to find fault. And in a sense that is precisely what he does. He stands facing Declan's antique partners' desk and glares at the arrangement of the journal and the fountain pen. Perhaps he is reminded of the parallel of Saturday evening, of Perdita's notebook and pen, when he replaced the lid – or perhaps it is a more obscure sense of discord – but either way he is prompted to pull out his mobile phone, and broodingly he thumbs through to the photograph he took of Declan's notebook on that first Sunday afternoon.

'The pen was on the left.'

'Oh – sorry, Guv.'

DS Jones starts – and swiftly moves to round the desk in order to correct her error. But Skelgill does not wait to see the adjustment – instead he strides over to pick up the brass winder key – and likewise the pendulum. He turns to DS Leyton, and hands him the two items together.

'Leyton – wind the clock.'

'Come again, Guv?'

'Wind the clock – with the key.'

DS Leyton looks a little bewildered.

'Won't it need the pendulum, Guv?'

'Just wind it, Leyton.'

Now Skelgill's tone is sharp – as if his sergeant fails to act quickly the moment will be lost. DS Leyton obeys without further dissent and rather awkwardly inserts the end of the key into the round hole on the tarnished clock face. It is just a simple square head bolt fitting and he makes half a dozen turns when Skelgill lunges from behind and wrenches him by the collar and roughly pulls him to the ground where Declan's jacket is laid.

'Whoaa! Steady on, Guv!'

'You're right-handed, Leyton.'

'Struth – I could have told you that, Guv – you didn't have to trip me up!'

DS Leyton flounders like a turtle that has been flipped over and is unable to right itself. But Skelgill exhibits no great sympathy – in fact, none at all. His attention is taken by the positions in which the key and the pendulum – jettisoned by DS

Leyton in his moment of panic – have come to rest: remarkably close to where they were first found.

'Declan was right-handed. He used his walking stick in church right-handed. His fishing rod was set up right-handed. Clearly, he wound the clock right-handed.'

DS Leyton is still dazed by his impromptu role as the fall guy in Skelgill's little charade.

'So what, Guv?'

Now Skelgill turns to face the desk. He points at the repositioned pen. DS Jones – behind the desk, rather frozen to the spot – stares at Skelgill for a few moments. But she is with him – and calmly she opens the logbook and pores over the most recently completed page.

'This is left-handed writing, Guv.'

Skelgill does not seem surprised, but DS Leyton – who has contrived to roll onto his stomach and is now heaving himself up – intervenes with a suitably voluble protest.

'Hold on – hold on – hold your horses – what are you saying?' He lumbers over beside Skelgill. DS Jones has now taken a seat, and is steadily examining successive pages.

'This is all written by a left-handed person.' She looks up into the faces of her colleagues: Skelgill keen-eyed, DS Leyton bemused. 'We studied it on the forensics course I attended in October. It's such a basic identifier – it's called the sarcasm stroke. When you cross a 't' you sweep the nib back towards your hand. Right-handers do it from right to left – left-handers the other way. It's easy to spot – as the pen lifts off the line becomes finer.'

DS Leyton is looking at his right hand – as though he wants to put this to the test; DS Jones watches Skelgill apprehensively. He is nodding grimly.

'Thwaites was left-handed.' And now both his subordinates look at him for confirmation. 'He told me – when we were looking at Declan's rod.'

A short silence ensues; DS Leyton is still striving to catch up.

'So what *are* we saying, Guv – that *Thwaites* wrote the bird book?'

Skelgill backs away and paces around – he comes to a halt in front of the clock.

'Why not, Leyton? He was here for donkey's years – since well before the date of the earliest entry. Look – it's a double desk – seats one person either side – get that chair.'

DS Leyton does as he is bid, and rolls the rosewood harpist's chair into position opposite DS Jones.

'Thwaites sat here?'

Skelgill nods.

'Aye – Declan sat where Jones is – all his books to hand behind him – dictated the notes to Thwaites.'

But now DS Jones looks uncomfortable.

'Guv – the logbook was here, on this side.' She indicates its position in front of her. 'And the pen.'

Skelgill is unmoved by this small inconvenience. He reaches for the journal – DS Jones still has it open at the most recent entry and slides it towards him. He reads Declan's final account – perhaps with fresh eyes, in the knowledge that this is the hand of Harold Thwaites. Then he returns the book to his colleague and wanders across to the nearest window and gazes out. The frozen backdrop is unchanging, but out of sight of his subordinates, something seems to bother him – it is a pained expression, like when he has set out to fish – his inner alarm squawks that he has forgotten something – yet he can't for the life of him think what it is – and knows he must depart and be disappointed later.

DS Leyton, meanwhile, has pulled a file of statements from the pilot bag, and has settled upon one particular page. He carries them across to Skelgill.

'Guv – these times you took, talking to Thwaites – and confirmed by me when I interviewed him later – we've got Thwaites saying he brought in Declan's lunch at 12.15. Declan was out bird-watching. Then Thwaites came back at 2.15 to collect the tray and found Declan dead.'

'Aye.'

Skelgill does not appear to be listening properly – but DS Jones has registered the significance of her colleague's observation – her eyes are wide. Skelgill continues to stare out of the window.

'Guv – it don't stack up.'

Skelgill now swings around.

'What?'

DS Leyton looks over his shoulder for assistance from DS Jones.

'What time does it say Declan got back?'

She consults the page.

'13.35 – twenty-five to two.'

'See what I mean, Guv?'

Skelgill is nodding slowly. Plainly, if Thwaites penned the log entry, he had to be in the study soon after Declan got back – and when he was still alive. Skelgill takes the papers from DS Leyton and glares at the column of timings. DS Leyton mirrors his superior and leans in with a suitably perplexed expression. But suddenly Skelgill jolts and points a finger across towards DS Jones.

'The waxwings!' His sergeants gaze at him in surprise – but he has remembered what he had 'forgotten'. 'The last entry doesn't mention the waxwings. Check the day before.'

DS Jones scans the journal with renewed purpose.

'You're right, Guv – here it is – Saturday: *"Waxwing 12 – constellation feeding on guelder rose to south of property."* Plus some other sightings.'

'A constellation of waxwings.' Skelgill nods with satisfaction. He holds out an explanatory palm, and now pontificates. 'Rare winter visitors – come in flocks and find a supply of berries – and stay until it's exhausted. There's no way Declan would have overlooked them on Sunday – and I saw them myself on Monday.'

DS Leyton looks puzzled.

'Maybe they went off for the day, Guv – there's no knowing what birds can get up to.'

Skelgill runs a hand through his hair and gazes off into the distance beyond the windows, as though there might be some clue to the significance of this omission. Or is it just an irrelevant anomaly? They are all three silent, and it is only when DS Jones makes a strange birdlike squeal – appropriately enough – that her male colleagues stare at her with alarm.

'Guv – listen to this.'

She has leafed back through the logbook and has pinched together a sheaf of pages such that she can see two entries simultaneously, from different dates. She quotes aloud.

"Barnacle Goose c. 20 – small skein N from Buttermere. Raven 8 – unkindness W from Grasmoor End, high to Mellbreak. Fieldfare c. 30 – mutation taking haws at Lanthwaite Beck. Brambling 13 – charm amongst beech mast in copse below Cinderdale Crag."

Skelgill frowns.

'Aye, I've just read that.'

'Except –' And now she pauses – it would seem for dramatic effect, were not for the genuine light of discovery in her eyes. 'Except, Guv – *you haven't*. It's an entry from December last year – the same date. It's been copied verbatim.'

DS Leyton strikes up.

'Cor blimey, girl – what made you check that?'

DS Jones shakes her head.

'I don't know – I suppose it was because there were no waxwings.' She grins a little self-consciously at Skelgill.

Skelgill looks from one to the other of his colleagues. Perhaps for each of them – he included – a penny is beginning to drop. Skelgill stalks back to the clock. The front is still open and now he pokes experimentally at the big hand with a forefinger. It is on a ratchet and moves only clockwise. He winds it twice round until it reads 2 o'clock. Then he does it ten times more, returning it to 12 o'clock. Now he stoops to retrieve the pendulum and hooks it into place. He gives it a gentle tap and it begins to swing – and then almost immediately the clock starts to chime. Quite likely they each count to twelve, and only when the last echoes have subsided does Skelgill turn to face his colleagues. His features are grim – anguished, even – like a

fisherman who has waited patiently for many hours – only to reel in and find his bait has gone.
'It's back to the drawing board.'

20. REFLECTIONS – Wednesday 9pm

The metaphorical 'drawing board' for most investigating officers would comprise a lengthy session surrounded by all the evidence, poring over statements and reports, meticulous note-taking and the compiling of flow charts, lists and tables. Skelgill is sorting out his fishing tackle.

He has swept unfinished DIY projects from his garage workbench, hauled in a stack of storage crates from the back of his car, and spread before him their contents. From the unruly assortment of tins and reels and bags and cases, he has selected three containers that the angler will recognise as fly boxes. The trout fishing season closed ten weeks ago, and there is an end-of-term task that is long overdue: the overhaul of his extensive collection of artificial flies.

Deprived of the possibility actually to fish – the unrelenting freeze precluding all methods available in the neighbourhood – it could be that he regards something akin to angling as the next best thing. That is, an activity that demands a certain degree of concentration, and yet which is also sufficiently methodical and repetitive in its nature to allow his mind – if it should wish – to drift. Assuming, of course, that he has some conscious intent for the latter to occur. It is equally probable that, simply 'fed up', frustrated with his job, and there being no decent fishing programmes on TV this evening (or lively company in the bar of his local hostelry), he has resorted to some other suitable distraction.

Earlier in the day Skelgill was obliged to submit a report summarising the case to date. Compiled by DS Leyton, proof-checked by DS Jones – cursorily edited and signed off by Skelgill – it was no more than a one-page summary stating the salient details. Much to Skelgill's chagrin this had then been circulated to other officers of his rank. While not an unprecedented procedure – positioned by the Chief as for the purposes of keeping her senior team informed – it was far from regular. Skelgill naturally interpreted the act as a personal slight – and a broadcasting of his failure thus far to make any substantive progress. This was compounded by the fact that among 'officers of his rank' is included DI Alec Smart. And the snide Mancunian had wasted no time in appearing gleefully at Skelgill's door to tell him how it was.

"Plain as day, Cock. Your butler murdered his master and then topped himself – made it look like an accident."

DI Smart had only lingered a moment to savour Skelgill's apparent humiliation in front of his team. He had shown them a clean pair of heels – no doubt to be the first to put this theory to their superior – a quick, neat solution; a feather in his cap and bragging rights over Skelgill. Skelgill had been obliged to quell the faint rumblings of a mutiny among his crew – for DS Leyton had the naïve temerity to ask, "What if he's right, Guv?" – requiring a thunderous broadside from Skelgill, but one sorely lacking a logical counter argument.

Reflecting now, Skelgill is forced to concede that an outsider looking at the case would quite likely conclude that there is one outstanding candidate for the murder of Declan Thomas O'More – his long-serving butler, Harold Thwaites, as DI Smart postulates. And this is based on the broad facts alone – for Skelgill's expurgated report was free of such intriguing nuances as Declan's ghost-written journal, interference with the clock, or the likely combusted shillelagh. Indeed, when this extra layer of detail is admitted – that Thwaites had seemingly concocted an entirely fictitious sequence of events in relation to Declan on the day of his death – the case against the old retainer becomes even more convincing. Why else would he do this, other than to create an alibi for himself?

That Thwaites might suddenly have feared for his livelihood – with Declan inheriting charge of Crummock Hall for the foreseeable future – is a viable motive. Now that Sir Sean, Declan and Thwaites are all dead, there is no way of exploring what new dynamic Thwaites might have anticipated. Perhaps he was not only long-serving but also long-suffering, and some remark or threat from Declan – casually uttered whilst he was winding the clock, his weekly habit of a Sunday noon – prompted Thwaites to pick up the walking stick and unleash decades of pent-up frustration. The straw that broke the camel's back. And then – and this is by no means implausible (indeed, probably less so than the faking of the log entry and the contriving of the alibi) – overcome by the gravity of what he had done – he took his own life – but in such a way as to make his death appear accidental, perhaps to minimise the shame he had brought upon the family. It fits the facts.

All well and good. But it doesn't fit the feelings.

Since Skelgill has moved amongst the actors in this rather grotesque production – a peripatetic extra – his perspective is not that of the impartial investigator looking from the outside in. He is working from inside out. And he works not with facts, but with feelings. That is not to say he ignores the facts – certainly he absorbs them, blandly, neutrally, not knowing whether they are true facts, mistakes or lies, filing them somewhere, all equal in his estimation – but he judges them against how he feels about any possible conclusions. And the possible conclusion that Thwaites murdered Declan does not have resonance. In Thwaites he did not detect the soul of a murderer. (And there may be facts as yet unrecognised by his consciousness that will back this up.) Thwaites was badly affected by the death of his master, but not in a way that suggested guilt or remorse. Moreover, there is a tide of suspicion that laps about the other players – they are too little forthcoming, they have subtly closed ranks, there is too much at stake for him to feel at ease with DI Smart's glib explanation.

However, in his logical deliberations – and discussions with his two sergeants – the new facts have certainly undermined his feelings. The revelation that, after all, 12 o'clock and not 2 p.m. was the likely time of Declan's murder – that Dr Herdwick's obstinacy was likely vindicated – came as a "curved ball from left field" (as he put it to himself, doubling up on the metaphor with belt and braces). Indeed it has shaken the foundations of a tentative belief he has been building about the case – and reminded him of the dangerous temptation offered by 'facts'. He has been rocked.

*

Skelgill likes to start the trout season with three fly boxes. The first is small enough to fit into a pocket of his jacket or gilet; it will be empty. The second, also pocket-sized, will typically contain about a tenth of his collection. The third, the largest by far, houses all the rest, and slides about in the stern of the boat.

Box number two contains all those flies on which he caught fish in the previous year. As the season progresses, 'successful' flies gradually migrate to box one – mainly from box two, but also some from box three, as they are speculatively tried, and prove their worth as 'catchers'.

One clever aspect of this system is that as box one gradually fills, it becomes a chronological record, a kind of three dimensional *logbook* of successful patterns as the months roll by. Some are predictable. Typically there will be a hawthorn in late April (mimicking the hairy black St Mark's fly so voraciously gobbled by trout), mayflies in – yes – May, and a daddy longlegs in June. Such a sequence provides Skelgill with a handy reminder of what he might next dangle as the calendar advances.

A non-fisher might ask, so what is the job to be done? Surely this year's box two is ready to go as soon as the season is over? It is simply last year's box one, last season's 'catchers'. But not so. Unlike Skelgill's home-made pike lures, wrought from indestructible household objects such as paintbrush handles and pool cues, and fitted with terrifying treble hooks, an artificial fly is a delicate thing, almost as ephemeral as the creature it mimics. Fashioned from fur and feathers, intricately wound and tied, delicately glued and varnished, it is rare for a successful fly to emerge unscathed from the fishy jaws of victory.

Thus Skelgill's task in preparing for the new season is to replace battle-scarred flies – for he has reinforcements aplenty. When he ties flies he makes a dozen at a time, and these are mostly confined to their barracks, box three, until called upon. But frugal by nature – de rigueur for a man bred in these parts – where possible he resuscitates those chewed and slime-encrusted flies that respond to a little soaking in soapy water, draining on a sheet of newspaper, and a blast of the hairdryer while gripped in pliers – a kind of field hospital for wounded fishing tackle.

It is a fiddly task, though Skelgill's calloused palms and rough-skinned fingers are deceptively dexterous – and seated at his bench he works assiduously, content despite the chill (he has an old and somewhat ineffectual paraffin heater going, and wears two moth-eaten fleecy tops, and there is the homely hiss of a gas lamp that hangs above him). And it must be a contemplative experience; a little trip down the memory lane of last year's success stories on lake or river, of endlessly sunny days (a funny thing, the memory), of tricky fights with unexpectedly big fish, and the outwitting of these canny wild creatures with a tiny assembly of natural materials – formed and presented by his hand alone.

And there is another, intrinsic, pleasure in fly fishing tackle. For this is a sport that has occupied the best hunting brains down the ages – witness Izaak Walton's *The Compleat Angler*, published in 1653. Much blood and sweat and tears have been spilled in the perfecting of the traditional patterns that have proved their worth, to be passed through generations, from father to son, angler to angler. Each fly boasts its own social history, and a flavour of this often captured in its name – the whole body of work a wonderfully evocative nomenclature that fires the imagination and fills the novice fisher with the confidence that they stand on the shoulders of giants.

As Skelgill journeys mindfully through his season past, the flies that served him well likewise captivate him. Thus far he has admired *Royal Coachman* (invented by John Haily, New York City, 1878), *Lunn's Particular* (developed by River Test keeper William Lunn, Hampshire, England, 1917) and *Peter Ross* (no hiding of his light under a bushel for the eponymous 19th century Perthshire shopkeeper).

And of course there is *Greenwell's Glory*. That Skelgill now ponders unduly long over this rather innocuous dry fly might cause the onlooker to wonder why. Perhaps he had some particular success – it mimics the Pond Olive, a common variety of mayfly, a staple of trout therefore – or maybe he is debating whether to replace his slightly ragged catchers with new stock. But there is something more profound in his expression. Though he pores over the fly, his eyes unmoving, unblinking, his focus does not fall on the bench before him. It drills back in time – though not so far back as Canon William Greenwell in 1854 – but to a generation ago, when the Reverend's brainchild featured in another narrative. This fly was witness to 'The Accident.' Aye – the rod that was rigged ready to go early that morning – that fateful morning – when the foolhardy Edward Regulus rowed his beautiful young wife Shauna O'More across Crummock Water – was tied with Greenwell's Glory. It was Declan's fly of choice. And where the old split cane cork-handled rod survived, the boat and its occupants did not. And Declan should have been in that boat.

21. THE HANDBOOK – Friday, midnight

If it's Friday there must have been a funeral.

For now, however, the Vale of Lorton sleeps beneath its blanket of snow. The little church of St James, Buttermere has once more served a solemn congregation. Harold Thwaites has been laid to rest. The wake has passed, a subdued affair dulled by yawning platitudes and stifled by lip service. The company, weary of travel and the repetitive strain of melancholy psalms, has retired as one to bed. Majestic in the southern heavens, Orion the Hunter shifts imperceptibly westwards. A grey tomb amidst black pines, Crummock Hall lies in shadow.

And then a flicker of light illuminates a window of Declan's study.

It would seem to be the beam of a torch, and to emanate from within. Exactly how this might be the case is a small mystery in itself. While the crime scene has been officially released – and notified to the family through their solicitor – the study has been left locked (albeit the lock-stoppers removed) and the keys retained in the possession of the police. The explanation provided seems eminently sensible: given that the contents are valuable the family would presumably wish them secured. It is Skelgill's intention to repatriate the keys in the morn – an excuse perchance casually to insinuate himself among the occupants once more. Failing that, there is always the possibility of a cooked breakfast.

The flashlight appears to play around the room, crossing the two arched windows and the porthole of the external door a couple of times, before settling internally – indeed, its movement ceases, as though it has been placed in a static position; only a faint glow now radiates. A curious watcher – were there to be such a person improbably loitering (or stationed) outside, defying the sub-zero conditions – might creep with care over crunchy snow to peer cautiously in. And there would be something to see. The door to the corridor ajar, diffuse light filtering from beyond. The torch resting upon the desk, angled across a book such that its beam illuminates the shelves beyond. And a hooded figure – wearing what could be a charcoal dressing gown – standing on the top rung of the library step. He or she – being of uncertain gender – takes down one book at a time, flicks through it, replaces it, and moves on to the next. That the room is shrouded in gloom does not seem to be an impediment – certainly reading does not appear to be their object. More likely it is looking for a bookmark – or a photograph – or a flower that has been pressed – although the inspection is perhaps even too cursory for that.

For someone concealed inside the room – equally improbable, of course – it is the sounds that narrate the events. There is the initial scrape of a key in the lock. The library step dragged across the floor. The breathing – certainly heightened – of the newcomer; perhaps anxiety, but also perhaps the effort of balancing upon the curved step and continually reaching up; some of the tomes must weigh several pounds. And all the while in the background the steady tick of Declan's clock – for Skelgill left it running. Indeed now it strikes twice – though this is midnight; he did not trouble to correct the time, and it was 10 a.m. when he set the hands to twelve. The putative book thief is unperturbed by this discrepancy – and works on methodically – and even seems unconcerned when the study door is pushed wider, and a slender form clad only in skimpy nightwear appears cautiously in the opening.

'Who's in there?'

'Ah, Perdita.'

'Oh – it's you.'

'Come inside.'

'But what *are* you doing?'

There is a sinister chuckle. The shadowy figure descends the library step and moves across to pick up some object from the desk; it glints as it crosses the beam of the torch.

'Let's say I couldn't sleep – and decided to find some bedtime reading.'

'But – the study was locked – by the police?'

'Ah – yes – spare keys are always expedient. Come in – close the door.'

Perdita does as she is bid – though she seems uncharacteristically apprehensive; she leaves the latch unfastened, and steps a few paces to her right in front of the clock, away from the incumbent.

'I thought you were a second intruder.'

'Who says there was a first? You must know the police suspect one of us.'

'Someone has to guard our property.'

'That is rather valiant of you – did you wake any of the others?'

'I –' Whatever Perdita is about to say, her slight hesitation gives away the truthful answer – and indeed she replies obliquely. 'I came down to the drawing room – to get a nightcap – I couldn't sleep, either.'

In the murk the hooded figure reaches for the torch, and plays it illustratively upon the shelves before shining the beam directly into Perdita's face. Her pupils constrict like those of a trespassing feline that has triggered a security light.

'You know these are intended for you.'

It is a question but the tenor sounds almost accusing.

'The books?'

'Declan made a will.' Now the tone is scathing. 'A month ago – witnessed by our esteemed Sir Sean and the trusty Thwaites.'

'I find that hard to believe of Great Uncle Declan – after his last words to me.'

'It is hidden – in the boathouse.'

'The boathouse?'

'I'll drive you there – we'll use the garden door – nobody will hear us. Go ahead – it is unlocked.'

Perdita's eyes are narrowed and her full lips register alarm. She does not move.

'But – I can't go outside dressed like this.'

'But I think you can.'

And the object picked from the desk is now raised into the beam and extended at arm's length. It is a wartime revolver

– recognisable as one kept in a display cabinet in the main hallway with its live cartridges ranged alongside.

'I – I don't understand –'

'You will Perdita – oh, little lost one.'

The voice is now harsh and menacing, and the gun is jerked to indicate the order.

'The garden door – open it.'

But this command seems to have magical properties – for the garden door swings open – and there silhouetted against the moonlit snowscape is the stocky figure of Detective Sergeant Leyton.

'Police – drop the weapon.'

And now with hardly a delay the hall door follows suit – and braced for action stands Detective Sergeant Jones.

'Do as you're told – then no one gets hurt.'

Perdita glances anxiously from side to side – though she must be largely blinded, for both the gun and the torch remain trained upon her. And neither does their bearer move, though the voice becomes more strained.

'You will notice this is a six-shooter.'

'Lower the gun – you won't get away with it.'

'Really?'

There is a quiver conveyed through the torch beam – perhaps a stiffening of the adjacent wrist as a precursor to firing. It is at moments like this when it seems ludicrous that the British police are not routinely armed. But then again, who needs firearms when you have Skelgill concealed in the log coffer. Behind the would-be shooter – and invisible to the dazzled Perdita – the freshly oiled lid of the coffin-like mule chest silently opens. In one swift movement Skelgill rises, raises a branch of convenient cricket bat proportions and brings it down with malevolent force to break the wrist and send the revolver spinning across the room. The torch falls, too; its bulb shatters. In the darkness, Leyton and Jones pounce.

*

'What were you looking for?'

No answer. Either Fergal Mullarkey adheres to the clichéd lawyer's maxim, "no comment" – advice that his firm must timelessly have dispensed – or he is in shock of the injury inflicted by Skelgill. His good wrist is unceremoniously handcuffed to a wooden spindle of Declan's sturdy chair. Skelgill turns to Perdita – she is shivering, though she is wrapped in his oversized fleece top.

'What do you reckon?'

'I have really no idea, Inspector. I only thank God that you guessed all this.'

Skelgill frowns. That he guessed? She does have no idea. He thrusts his hands onto his hips and regards the towering library. Whatever Fergal Mullarkey sought he had a long night's labour ahead of him. He had examined barely a hundred books – when there must be a good four or five thousand ranged wall-to-wall, floor to ceiling. That he refuses to speak suggests it is something of import. Skelgill glances again at their captive – then he addresses DS Leyton.

'I'll wake the others. Ask them.' He makes for the door – then he hesitates. 'Jones – you'd better come – you take Cassandra.' He notices that Perdita sways and has to correct her balance. 'I reckon you need that nightcap. Go to the drawing room. Chuck some wood on the fire – get comfortable. We'll send the rest along.'

Skelgill exits with DS Jones and they make their way through the darkened halls and corridors, switching on lights as they go. In the entrance hall they climb the main staircase, and split at the top, for the male and female chambers are segregated on either side of the central atrium. Skelgill wakes Martius first – and is impressed by his swift uptake of the situation – though he can cast no light on Mullarkey's quest. Skelgill decides to leave him to rouse Brutus – and heads for Edgar's room. He knocks, perhaps rather forcefully, and announces himself – though he waits a decent two or three seconds – and hears some scrabbling within. When he enters a table lamp is on and Edgar sits up blinking on the far side of the bed, the blankets raised to his chest. His expression hovers somewhere between alarm and dismay. Skelgill is about to speak when a noise behind his right shoulder disturbs him. He turns and instinctively pulls open the door of a wardrobe. Crouching inside, clutching at a pillow to preserve his modesty is a cringing Toby Vellum. At this moment DS Jones – who has finished with Cassandra and sent her downstairs (needing little encouragement for a stiffener) – appears in the doorway.

'All okay, Guv?'

She cannot see at what he stares with such disquiet. For perhaps five seconds he does not reply. Then he shuts the wardrobe door and stalks away – pushing past DS Jones and heading for the stairs.

'Hunky-dory.'

He strides through the house at a speed that obliges DS Jones to skip to keep up.

'Cassandra doesn't have any idea, Guv.'

Skelgill speaks out of side of mouth.

'I don't reckon any of them will – but I know who might help us.'

As they are about to pass the drawing room Skelgill indicates to DS Jones that she should remain and intercept the family as they arrive.

'Keep them all here for the time being.'

DS Jones nods her understanding. Skelgill continues briskly to the study, where the solitary DS Leyton stands sentry just inside the door. His sergeant seems relieved that he has returned. Skelgill glances briefly at Fergal Mullarkey and then spends a few moments contemplating the bookshelves once more. He takes out his phone and rests it on the desk and digs in another pocket for his wallet. From this he extracts a rather bent business card, which he places beside the handset. Squinting in the poor light, and with the mobile set to loudspeaker mode, he taps out the number. He growls with discontent as it strives to transmit.

'One bar – come on.'

In the hush of the room the ring tone seems indecently loud – then it is answered.

'Oh – Inspector.'

The voice is tremulous. Toby Vellum. He sounds like he anticipates a reprimand.

'If Declan had to chose a book – the most important – which would it be?'

'Oh – er – well –' This inquiry momentarily wrong-foots Toby Vellum – but his confidence begins to return as the realisation dawns that perhaps he is not to be pilloried after all. 'Well – I should say – Declan being such a dedicated bird-watcher – it would be *The Handbook*.'

'The handbook?'

'Yes, Inspector – some call it *The Witherby*. Witherby, Jourdain, Ticehurst & Tucker – *The Handbook of British Birds*, 1938 – first edition that is. Many authorities say it has never been bettered.'

'What does it look like?'

'It's a five-volume set. It has a beige dustwrapper with plain black text on the spine. About nine inches high.'

'If you could only choose one?'

'Well – I suppose Volume 5 has the index. It holds the key.'

'Thanks.'

Skelgill pokes at the phone and cuts off the call. He looks at DS Leyton and points to the opposite corner.

'You start at that end – I'll use these steps and do the top four shelves. Witherby, right?'

'Roger, Guv.'

Purposefully – and thus wholly oblivious to the demonic expression that has possessed the features of Fergal Mullarkey – the pair set about their task, Skelgill upright, imperious and hawklike; DS Leyton, crouched, painstakingly tracing an index finger along the spines of the old books. Silence descends, but for the metronomic beat of the clock, and the sporadic grunts of DS Leyton he progressively bends and squats – when suddenly there is a strident rending of wood – and Fergal Mullarkey makes a break for freedom! Declan's antique chair is not as robust as it looks – and with a violent jerk he wrenches the spindle from its mortises and vaults across the desk, explosively scattering the accessories stacked upon it – the lamp, the telephone, the field glasses and a small assortment of books. He gains the floor on the other side and in a swift movement stoops to grab up one particular volume and lurches for the door, slamming it shut behind him.

It takes precious seconds for the detectives to react – by the time they have the door open Fergal Mullarkey has fled – but there is an obvious route of escape to the front of the house – and Skelgill chances it. He rounds into the hallway outside the drawing room to be confronted by the sight of DS Jones – she lies crumpled – however she begins to lift her head. He straddles her torso and by the armpits heaves her into a sitting position.

'Guv – what happened?' She is plainly groggy – and now DS Leyton lumbers along to make an undignified landing at her side. 'Someone whacked me from behind.'

Skelgill pats DS Leyton on the shoulder.

'Make sure she's okay.'

Without more ado he is gone. A dozen seconds later he reaches the entrance hall to find the front door wide open – from the darkness beyond there comes the sound of an engine turning over. He races out – a car is threatening to leave its parking space, though the wheels spin hopelessly upon the packed snow. But just when it seems the fugitive will be thwarted the tyres find some grip and the vehicle begins to rumble away. Skelgill sprints and catches a door handle – but Fergal Mullarkey twitches the steering wheel and Skelgill is left flailing. In desperation he makes a last-ditch lunge for the roof bars – and with a herculean effort swings himself onto the trunk. The car picks up speed – swerving frantically in an effort literally to shake off Skelgill. His teeth are bared, his hair trailing in the bitter wind, his knuckles like ivory as he grips for all he is worth.

Fergal Mullarkey's driving is badly hampered by his injury – he steers one-handed and cannot operate the manual shift; the engine screams out for a higher gear. He has no headlights on and is hardly familiar with the winding route – and rounding a sharp curve he is unprepared for the t-junction. Too late, he brakes. The motor slews out of control, spins across the lane and demolishes a five-barred gate that marks the continuation of the track down to the boathouse. The sudden deceleration throws Skelgill into the field – and now the conditions are a blessing, for a soft drift cushions his fall, albeit he is temporarily buried. Righting himself, spitting snow and blinking away ice crystals, he sees the driver's door is open – the interior light on – and the cockpit empty. But in the angled rays of the moon a line of fresh prints leads away – Fergal Mullarkey is heading for the lake.

The going underfoot is not easy – knee-deep snow with a collapsing crust – and neither hiker nor tractor has been this way to beat a path – nor is the erratic trail of fleeing footprints one upon which Skelgill may capitalise. And perhaps he is more stunned by the impact than he would like to admit. The scene beneath the moon is surreal in itself – a world in dreamlike duotone, in negative; the winter sky a great canopy of midnight blue, the snow-covered fells an undulating swathe of spectral grey. Skelgill stares at the ridge of Mellbreak; it rises steadily from north to south, a lung-busting run he has completed on countless occasions. He tells himself this is no more difficult. The track dips into a black copse of dense pines – and now from his left the *'twit'* of a tawny owl is answered on his right by the *'to-woo'* of its mate – and Skelgill finds himself raising a palm as if to acknowledge their coded advice.

The boathouse is in shadow, where the wood overhangs the shore. It is a simple affair, really little more than a shed that is open at both ends. The human tracks disappear into the darkness within, and Skelgill becomes more cautious as he approaches. He realises that the building is badly neglected, there are planks askew and the roof is in need of repair – but, of course, Sir Sean prohibited all boating after 'The Accident'. The place has been abandoned for a generation. He hesitates at the entrance, stretching wide his eyes and scanning from side to side to make the best of his peripheral vision. He can't be certain that during his flight through the corridors Fergal Mullarkey did not grab some other weapon – a cutlass or dagger from the wall. He steps inside. As his sight adjusts to the greater gloom he sees there is a deck on the left that extends as a pontoon beyond. The ice has encroached within, despite the shelter, although the first yard from the bank is unfrozen.

And now suddenly this water begins to swell – Skelgill immediately understands why – Fergal Mullarkey is on the ice – pressure waves will be radiating from beneath his feet to find their outlet wherever there is clear water at the shore. Skelgill stalks along the landing stage – and, sure enough, some dozen yards away and moving steadily further is a hunched figure, monk-like, still wearing the long dark gown, the hood again raised, his forearms cradled about his chest.

'Stop – you'll never make it!'

Does Fergal Mullarkey think he can reach the opposite bank? Does he not realise the ice sheet is incomplete? That it becomes thinner with every step he takes? But he pays no heed to Skelgill's warning – other than the unexpected proximity of his pursuer shocks him into renewed vigour – he begins to run – but instantly the ice responds to the extra downforce with creaking protests – and he has taken but three loping strides before it yields to his weight.

What Skelgill witnesses now occurs in slow motion – there is a resounding crack that pierces the still night air and echoes from the wooded bank behind him – and a great slab of ice, perhaps three inches thick, tilts like a surfboard – Fergal Mullarkey the improbable rider, suspended in mid-air – until gravity prevails – and he drops. He submerges entirely, but only for a second, and comes back up gasping with the shock of the icy water. In one hand he still grips the book – and now he lunges for the ice shelf, elbows first, and thrusts his forearms onto the glistening surface – but his weight simply breaks off a new section and he goes under once more. Then he is back up – less buoyantly – trying again – but to no avail.

Skelgill turns and dashes to the boatshed. There is nothing so much as an old rotted ring or rope. Instead he begins tearing at a loose plank. He bends his back and with a splintering squeal it comes away and now ferociously he rips free its neighbour – more easily since he can get proper purchase. He returns halfway along the boardwalk, to a point where the frozen surface is some three feet below. He tosses the planks onto the ice and removes his jacket. He strains to check the exact location of Fergal Mullarkey – it is a chilling sight as the choking lawyer raises his good arm and holds aloft the book he has so coveted – and slides beneath the black water in a grotesque parody of the Lady of the Lake, and Excalibur.

And then an irresistible force hits Skelgill from behind and flattens him into the snow.

'No way, Guv – we ain't losing you!'

A breathless DS Leyton has taken him down with a thumping rugby tackle – perhaps enjoying some small and justifiable revenge for the incident with the clock. A second later DS Jones descends upon Skelgill's legs. He curses and writhes but their combined weight is too much for him – and perhaps there is some relief in their thwarting of his rescue instinct.

DS Jones cries out through gritted teeth.

'Guv you can't! You know you can't! You'd be diving in pitch dark – the cold shock would kill you!'

Skelgill does know this. He utters a few token protests – but he gives up the struggle and his colleagues release their grip. DS Leyton rises and offers a helping hand. DS Jones retrieves her superior's jacket and presses it upon him. Then slowly, together, they tread carefully to the end of the landing stage. The spot where Fergal Mullarkey went down is marked by broken chunks of ice that lie upon the frozen surface. In their midst is a smooth patch of clear black water, where there floats the pale dustcover of a book.

'That'll be Volume 5.'

*

The Regulus-O'Mores – or as they each might prefer to be called, Martius Regulus, Cassandra Goodchild, Owain Jagger,

Edgar Regulus-O'More and Rowena Devlin – along with a rather self-conscious looking Tobias Vellum have strayed from the drawing room: upon their return the detectives find the group convened in the study of the late Declan Thomas O'More. But for Vellum – who is fully dressed in his fashion of the middle-aged gentleman – they all sport stylish nightwear of haut couture. There is a strained chatter – which subsides as the police enter – and Martius has his shotgun, of which he is duly (and not unwillingly) relieved.

'Just for our protection, you understand, Inspector – we had no idea whether Mullarkey was likely to give you the slip and come back looking for us.'

Skelgill's expression is severe.

'He won't be giving anyone the slip.'

For the time being, however, Skelgill is no more forthcoming, and the family can only speculate upon Fergal Mullarkey's fate – for all they know he is in custody and speeding to jail in a black maria.

'I swear I've heard the blighter prowling about before – at night.' This is Martius again. 'His room abuts onto mine.'

'I've *seen* him.' Now all eyes turn to Cassandra. She is holding a rocks glass, and she reclines in the harpist's chair. Her legs are crossed and unconcernedly she exposes a generous stretch of naked thigh beneath her silk gown. She smiles coyly at Skelgill and tilts the glass back and forth – it seems to be a signal that she has observed Mullarkey during a nocturnal visit to the drinks trolley. 'Prowling – either he or a ghost.'

Skelgill is visibly discomfited by her somewhat brazen manner.

'We'll be needing new statements from you all – in light of what we now know.'

'I take it the matter is closed, Inspector?' Martius's tone is insistent. 'The murder?'

'I shouldn't say closed, sir – more like blown wide open.' Now Skelgill folds his arms, lines crease his brow. 'We may be talking four murders.'

A small ripple of indeterminate excitement (or it could be shock) permeates the group; glances of anxiety and expectancy are exchanged – but no one now seems prepared to speak. Perdita still wears Skelgill's fleecy over her pyjamas – it almost reaches down to the lace-trimmed hems of her satiny shorts – and as she steps forward there is a peculiar sense that she has acquired some privileged position – de facto spokesperson – by virtue of this conquest of his garment. Her strawberry blonde mane is dishevelled, and her dark oval eyes underscored by matching crescents – but there is vitality about her sylphlike form, and she rises up on her tiptoes and spreads her arms appealingly.

'But what on earth was he looking for?'

'Something hidden in a book. We plan to recover it.'

Though his words are intended to convey a command of the situation – and he avoids mention of the small matter of the lake – his tone cannot conceal a distinctly pessimistic note. The effect is another hiatus – however, there comes a nervous cough, the kind of *'ahem'* that politely requests permission to speak. It is Toby Vellum. He has been standing beside the desk, his hand upon a small stack of books that he has evidently gathered up and restored to its place, perhaps the bookseller in him unable to bear them strewn so uncaringly about the floor.

'Er – Inspector – The Handbook.' Lightly he touches the set – incomplete, of course – four volumes (of five) with familiar beige dustcovers.

DS Leyton suddenly interjects.

'Fancy that, Guv – there was Mullarkey and us searching the shelves – and they were on the desk all along.'

Skelgill glares sharply at his sergeant, like a schoolmaster rebuking a garrulous pupil. DS Leyton grins somewhat sheepishly. Skelgill turns back to Toby Vellum.

'What about The Handbook?'

'Er – well, Inspector.' He raps a knuckle on the top copy. 'This is the 1945 edition – reprint, strictly speaking – Vellum & Co supplied it to Declan a couple of years ago. He wanted what he called a 'workaday' set – to save his precious first edition from wear and tear.'

Though Skelgill's features remain implacable, a small fire burns in his eyes.

'Where is it?'

'Just over here, Inspector – I'll show you – Volume 5, wasn't it?'

Toby Vellum seems to know exactly where to look – in the centre of the bookshelves, directly behind Declan's damaged chair, at a convenient waist height. He slips around the furniture and extracts the book, and obediently carries it back to Skelgill. As he holds it out two-handed he gives it a little shake, as though there is something wrong with the weight – or perhaps the balance – his features register alarm, and he meets Skelgill's gaze with a small nod of affirmation.

Skelgill opens the volume – and immediately it is plain that this is no ordinary book – a central section has been hollowed out to form a cavity in which nestles a black velvet drawstring bag. There is a collective intake of breath. Skelgill extracts the pouch and calmly passes the book to DS Jones at his side. Brutus is quick to move in – he places a hand on DS Jones's shoulder and cranes to get a better look – and now the whole company crowds around voyeuristically as Skelgill unfastens the ties and tips out the contents. It is a single object, about the size of a walnut, and almost as great a contrast as there can be to his calloused palm – an immense diamond that sparkles even in the inadequate light of the study.

'Cor blimey, Guv – that puts the *Koh-i-Noor* in the shade.'

In the stunned silence that ensues Martius clears his throat.

'The *Koh-i-Noor* is valued at over a billion dollars.'

And now Perdita finds her voice again.

'And all who own it are said to be cursed.'

22. DRAWING CONCLUSIONS – Saturday 3pm

'Aye – aye – that's much appreciated, Jim – tell your pal thanks very much. When I'm back in Dublin the black stuff's on me. I'll look forward to the email.' Skelgill now listens into the earpiece of the antique telephone (for this morning changed atmospheric conditions have precluded any mobile signal whatsoever from reaching Crummock Hall). 'Aye – well the offer of a day on Bass Lake's always open – just say the word – if this thaw's permanent we could be in business next weekend – that double-figure pike's just waiting for you.'

Skelgill ends the call to retired professor Jim Hartley and stalks across to the windows of the drawing room. The familiar view of Grasmoor is obscured by cloud, in fact nothing is visible beyond the conifers at thirty yards, and even they are hazy silhouettes against uniform grey; a fine drizzle drenches the vale – though it is yet to make any impression on the deep snow, now a uniform wash that merges seamlessly into the mist. He ponders for a few moments, and tilts his head – an evaluative gesture, indicative of some considerable surprise. He returns to the sofas beside the fire and takes his seat opposite DS Leyton and DS Jones; his female colleague reaches to top up his tea, and they both watch him expectantly. However, Skelgill bides his time – and when he does respond, it is to resume the conversation they were having prior to the call being put through.

'Whoever moved the clock back wanted to be sure we thought the time of death was 12 noon not 2 p.m. Why?' Now he jabs an accusing index finger towards the outdoors, and the question is rhetorical. 'Because if it were 2 then Perdita was out there – out of the frame. And why would you want Perdita *in* the frame? Because she'd had a blazing row with Declan – that morning – by her own admission – she even told us the time – between 11:40 and 11:50.' He looks at DS Jones for confirmation and she nods obligingly. 'So who knew that?'

And now he does wait for a response. DS Leyton is first to supply what might be considered rather an obvious answer.

'Well – Mullarkey, Guv. We only had his word for his whereabouts before lunch. He could have been eavesdropping.'

'Aye – Mullarkey.' However Skelgill regards DS Leyton somewhat distractedly – for it is not the solution he seeks. 'Aye – he moved the clock back, alright – it suited him best that way – but that's not the point, Leyton. You have to look at this the other way around – I'm talking about Thwaites. We know from the statements of the family and the other staff that he was helping in the kitchen and setting out the buffet between 11:45 and 12:15. But he was in his butler's pantry beforehand – likely as not he overheard the argument.'

Now Skelgill stands up. He takes a small turn about the room, as though relaxing on a sofa and such deliberative cogitation are not easy bedfellows.

'So Thwaites knows Perdita has just visited Declan – that they argued – and at 12:15 he takes in Declan's lunch. He finds him dead. Naturally he assumes it's Perdita that's killed him.'

Skelgill pauses to check the reaction of his sergeants. DS Leyton is looking a little bemused. DS Jones is listening acutely.

'So what did he do? Did he raise the alarm? No – the exact opposite – he covered it up. He copied an authentic logbook entry from a year before, as if it were his regular dictation – he invented times that had Declan bird-watching between 11:55 and 13:55 – and he wound the clock forward to make it seem the attack took place at 2 p.m. – when Perdita was a couple of thousand foot up Grasmoor. It wasn't himself he was creating the alibi for – it was her.'

Now DS Leyton's features have become troubled.

'But, Guv – you said yourself – you could think of how she could have been here?'

DS Leyton's apprehension reflects a belief that his superior had made this remark more out of defiance than from some reasoned basis – and he knows Skelgill will not take kindly to being reminded of the fact. But Skelgill does indeed have a theory. He produces a wry smile and makes a scoffing sound.

'I can't help it Leyton – when something seems impossible it's like a red rag to a bull. If Perdita had wanted to give herself an alibi – by pretending to be lost in a blizzard – sure, she did a good job of it. But she owns snow boots and a jacket with sewn-in avalanche reflectors. She was some kind of ski champion at university. And she knows her way about the fells. She made that distress call from near the summit at 1:45 – all she had to do was switch off her phone and jump on a pair of skis. She could have been at the boundary wall of Crummock Hall in six minutes.'

DS Leyton exhales extravagantly.

'Flippin' heck, Guv – you kept quiet about that one.'

Skelgill contorts his features in mock relief.

'Probably just as well, Leyton.'

Now DS Leyton chuckles.

'Don't want to confuse us daft country coppers, eh, Guv?'

Skelgill reacts with uncharacteristic humility – he comes back to the sofa and gestures apologetically with two hands.

'It was confusing enough, Leyton. We've been asking ourselves why did someone kill Declan; when the real question was why did Thwaites cover it up? In fact – why did he cover it up believing it was Perdita?'

'I think I might know.'

This is DS Jones, who has risen unobtrusively and wandered across to the grand piano where the photographs are displayed. Skelgill watches her with interest. DS Leyton swivels round. She returns with the photograph of Edward Regulus and Shauna O'More that they had examined on their first visit.

'This is a bit of a long shot, Guv.'

But Skelgill is nodding grimly – it seems she may have found the target. She lays the picture on the coffee table so they can all see it. Then she twice taps the glass with a polished nail, indicating the tragic couple.

'These are her parents.' She glances at Skelgill. 'It's not entirely clear from the quality of this image – though it would be easy enough to verify – but it looks to me like they're both blue-eyed.'

DS Leyton appears perplexed. But Skelgill is nodding almost imperceptibly.

'So are Martius, and Cassandra, and Brutus, and Edgar.'

DS Leyton now stares at each of his colleagues in turn – he might almost be checking their eye colour, as some sort of cross-reference for what DS Jones is about to say. She continues.

'It used to be thought impossible for blue-eyed parents to have a brown-eyed child. It's actually not – however it is exceptionally rare. And Perdita has brown eyes.'

And now Skelgill chips in.

'She's also left-handed. And my guess is Thwaites was a redhead when he was younger.'

DS Leyton's brow furrows as the rather shocking implication sinks in – and not least that, while DS Jones has perhaps just worked this out, Skelgill has obviously suspected for some time.

'Cor blimey, Guv – what are you saying – that Thwaites was her father?'

Curiously Skelgill begins to shake his head.

'I reckon what matters, Leyton – is that he *thought* he might have been.' Skelgill now grimaces and combs the fingers of both hands through his hair; it is a gesture that seems designed to assuage the notion; that it has been preying uncomfortably upon his mind. 'Another one of my daft-copper ideas – I picked up on some local hearsay – I figured that Thwaites could be the illegitimate son of 'Mr Padraig' as he called him. That would have made him younger half-brother to Sean and Declan – reason to suspect him for Declan's murder – since he could make a claim on the estate. But I got that completely wrong – his father was a Yank – an airman who was stationed hereabouts in the war.' Now Skelgill sinks back into the sofa and clasps his hands over his midriff. 'Thing is – when I began to suggest it to him he became really unnerved – but it never occurred to me that he thought I was going to ask him about Perdita.'

DS Leyton leans forwards, his expression full of doubt.

'But that would mean him and – well – Shauna – you know, Guv?' He lowers his gaze as though he is embarrassed to be any more explicit in present company.

Skelgill chuckles at his sergeant's prudishness.

'These things happen, Leyton.'

'But the age gap, Guv?'

Now Skelgill folds his arms rather defensively. He flashes a glance at DS Jones.

'Aye – but do the sums, Leyton. You've met Thwaites as an old bloke – Perdita's now thirty-three. Wind it back – he would have been in his early forties – and Shauna in her thirties.'

'That's no big deal, Guv.'

This is DS Jones who interposes. Skelgill regards her pensively for a moment – though he continues with his exposition.

'We also know that Shauna often came here alone – just her and the kids. Edward Regulus largely stayed away. There was talk of tension between them. She even went to Dublin to have the baby – what was that all about? And then Perdita – she told me that Thwaites always paid her special attention – she could never understand why.'

DS Jones is listening keenly, her eyes narrowed.

'Think Perdita has any idea, Guv?'

Skelgill shakes his head. Then he throws out his hands.

'Look – whether it's true or not makes no odds – but if Thwaites believed it were, then it explains his behaviour.'

'Be easy enough to find out, Guv – DNA tests.'

This is DS Leyton – and perhaps he has not detected Skelgill's reticence about the matter. Now Skelgill shrugs rather dismissively. It seems his policy is one of letting sleeping dogs lie, for he declines to be sidetracked by this rather intriguing facet of the mystery.

'I considered that the drowning – 'The Accident' – was the result of some fight between Edward Regulus and Shauna

O'More. Perhaps even that he lured her out on the lake with malicious intent. But now I don't think so.'

'Why not, Guv?'

'Because it was meant for Declan. The boat was sabotaged – by Mullarkey.'

Though it can only be conjecture, on this point Skelgill seems adamant. He jerks his head in the direction of the piano. Then he rises again and like DS Jones has just done, collects a photograph and returns.

'There's more to these pictures than the family. I asked Mullarkey to help me identify his uncle – the lawyer who was his predecessor on the O'Mores' account. I sent him a shot of this – according to Thwaites it was taken around the time of 'The Accident'. He never got back to me – claimed he'd not received the text. When I went to their offices in Dublin I found some staff photographs from about the same era. The lawyers' names were listed on a caption.' Now Skelgill places a finger carefully upon the glass, beneath the face of one of the young men grouped about the Land Rover with Edward Regulus, and rotates the frame so that his colleagues may see. 'It wasn't just his uncle coming to Crummock Hall back then – so was Mullarkey. Yet he told me he had no involvement while his uncle was their representative – that he didn't even know Edward Regulus and Shauna O'More. This is him.'

DS Leyton is captivated.

'So it is, Guv! You can recognise him, once you know what you're looking for.'

Skelgill returns the photograph to its approximate place on the grand piano. He remains for a few moments to gaze out of the window. When he turns his features are troubled.

'My one regret is that I alerted him – made him think that we were on to him. And Thwaites was still alive then.'

His sergeants simultaneously protest; Skelgill seems surprised that they rally so vehemently to his side. DS Leyton jabs a forefinger in his direction.

'Guv – there's no way you could have known – like you say – you weren't even suspecting him at that point.'

'Leyton I was suspecting everyone.'

Skelgill grins – rather sheepishly, it must be said – and DS Jones seems eager to focus upon a point that will restore his dignity.

'The sinking of the boat, Guv – how could he have brought that about?'

'Simple enough. Bore half a dozen holes just a touch above the waterline. Plug them with bread paste – or boilies like carp anglers use. Lick of varnish for disguise – and that would give temporary waterproofing. Remember what I told you about the draught? As soon as someone gets aboard, the boat sinks lower in the water. The patched holes are now below the waterline. Give it half an hour and the bread will dissolve. Bingo.'

DS Leyton's heavy features are disconcerted, his dark brows compressed.

'So he tried to murder Declan all that time ago – to get at the diamond.'

Skelgill inhales – as though there is much yet to tell, and that he wrestles with a suitable opening line.

'Leyton – I'll explain in a minute what the Prof just told me – he's got a colleague in Dublin who's a historian with a legal interest. Mullarkey's firm have been lawyers to the O'Mores since the 1600s. Happen Mullarkey didn't know exactly what Declan had inherited – but I'm pretty sure he'd studied the archives and discovered there was something seriously valuable.'

'So he hatched the plot to sink the boat.'

'Aye – and it went spectacularly wrong. He killed Edward and Shauna. Just think about it – all hell's let loose, it's all over the media – and Declan suspects he was targeted. Remember – how he went bird-spotting – maybe it wasn't that he didn't care, but that he was spooked. And he wouldn't have known who was after him. Thereafter – he kept up his guard. He became more of a recluse. His study was either occupied or locked – or watched by Thwaites from his butler's pantry. Meanwhile Mullarkey only had limited excuses to be over here.

He had to play a long game. At some point he got access to the keys – took a plasticine impression and had copies made.

'Come to the present day. Sir Sean is dying. Declan decides he'd better make a will. He consults Mullarkey – maybe he writes to him or phones. He tells him he's thinking of bequeathing the books to one of his great nephews or nieces. Mullarkey reads between the lines – he must realise that the diamond is hidden – concealed inside one of the books. It might be obvious – but it's effective when you've got so many. Folk must have wondered how come Sir Sean inherited the estate and Declan got nothing but an allowance – especially since they were twins – but maybe he didn't get such a bad deal.'

Now DS Jones comments.

'It makes you think that no one else in the family knew about the diamond.'

'I reckon we can be confident that Perdita didn't. Declan may not even have planned to tell her immediately – happen not until he was on his death bed.' Skelgill places his hands on his head and intertwines his fingers. 'What we do know is he called for Mullarkey – Saturday, the day before his murder. But Mullarkey realises we'll hear about this meeting, so when interviewed he gives us a distorted version of it. He says Declan told him he intended to draft a will and give him to him – but that he never did. In fact, Declan had already done it – as we overheard Mullarkey tell Perdita. It wasn't a formal document, but it was properly witnessed by Sir Sean and Thwaites – good enough to be legally binding. Perdita was to inherit the books. My guess is that the wording would cover the diamond – "all my worldly goods" – that kind of thing.'

DS Leyton is looking increasingly perplexed – some point has been brewing that plainly confounds him.

'But why Perdita, Guv?'

Skelgill drops his hands and pats his thighs absently.

'She might have offended Declan by calling him a dinosaur – but the family tradition meant a lot to him. And then compare her to the rest of them. She's made the most of her Irish heritage. She's a writer – she loves books. And she's the only one not driven by money. He summons her on the Sunday morning after Sir Sean's funeral – but they're both of them bloody-minded and end up having a row. Instead of buttering him up, she stands her ground – she probably goes up in his estimation. Mullarkey must have got wind of the meeting – he creeps along and eavesdrops – and hides on the little spiral staircase when she storms out. Then he goes in to see Declan – maybe on pretence of discussing some legal point. He knows it's just a matter of time before Declan tells Perdita about the will – he takes his chance and whacks Declan – chucks the stick on the fire – steals the document – and slips along to lunch as though nothing has happened. Now he's got some breathing space – Declan appears to die intestate – and he can probably get the books moved to Dublin.'

DS Leyton has been patiently holding up a hand – for permission to speak. Now that Skelgill pauses, he pitches in with some gusto.

'But Thwaites – he must have known about the will!'

Skelgill seems not to perceive his sergeant's intervention as an obstacle to his logic.

'Aye – exactly – and given what we've just said about him and Perdita, all the more reason that he wouldn't tell us. What stronger motive could she have to bump off Declan than that she was his heir? Plus Thwaites would have no inkling he was in mortal danger from Mullarkey – not while he thought Perdita was the murderer.'

DS Leyton remains troubled.

'But, Guv – what I'm saying – Mullarkey *knew* that Thwaites knew there was a will – so he had to die – it wasn't because you rattled Mullarkey's cage with that stuff about the photograph.'

Skelgill is pensive for a moment. He evidently does not want to seem too eager to accept this explanation – but DS Leyton has a supplementary question.

'Do you think Thwaites noticed the clock had been changed for a second time – back to 12 – when I took him to check over the study? That would have had him worried, Guv.'

Skelgill is nodding slowly.

'Quite likely – except he wouldn't have known when it happened – he might have thought it was when he 'discovered' Declan's body and they all came running. He was too busy play-acting to notice – so it could have been any one of them as far as he was concerned.'

'Think it was Mullarkey that wiped that glass, Guv – that had no prints on it?'

Skelgill produces a wry grin.

'Leyton, here's my idea about the glass. Thwaites comes into the study at 12.15 with Declan's lunch – sees his master laid out on the floor – he slams the tray down on the desk and the glass of water rolls off.'

'But why no prints, Guv?'

'Because that was one of his duties – he polished the glassware and he always wore those white butler's gloves.'

'Cor blimey, that's some red herring, Guv.'

Skelgill's mood continues to loosen, and he makes a further admission.

'Never mind red herring, Leyton – I thought it was deliberate, too – it could have been a quick way to disguise droplets of snow melt – off someone's boots who'd come in through the garden door. Part of my daft skiing theory.'

His sergeants respond with smiles – but the ring of the telephone interrupts this theme – it is an old-fashioned single trill like in the early American movies. DS Jones glances at Skelgill – he gestures to her to go ahead. His gaze follows her movements as she walks across to the bureau where the handset is located. She picks up the base by its stem, lifting it to her lips, and raises the wired earpiece accordingly. Then she turns to face her colleagues. They hear just one side of the dialogue.

'DS Jones.'

'Oh, hi – good, thanks – you?'

'Good.'

'Already?'

'Ah – no – we can't get a data signal – it's this fog.'

'Okay – just give me the top line.'

And now she listens for a minute, punctuating the silence with nods and the occasional "Aha" and "Right". Finally she thanks the caller – it is evident that it is one of her DCs, and they have related to her some information. She signs off and returns the old Bakelite telephone to its place.

'Wow.' She exhales and seems to take a couple of deep breaths as she returns to her seat. Her colleagues look on expectantly. 'That was the station, Guv – there's a preliminary report from Forensics on the examination of Mullarkey's bedroom here at Crummock Hall. They found a balled up strip of packing tape at the back of his fire. He must have intended to burn it – but it rolled down behind the grate, and just melted superficially. It's got Mullarkey's prints on it – and on the sticky side, traces of varnish and wood fibre that exactly match the bottom of Thwaites' bedroom door, and the floorboards below it.'

Skelgill is nodding – he looks like this is a confirmation rather than a revelation.

'So that's how he did it. He blocked the chimney during the day – then taped up the door after Thwaites had gone to bed. Must have gone back for the tape in the early hours, and switched it for the door-stopper on the inside – to make it look like an accident caused by Thwaites trying to keep himself warm.'

DS Jones has more to add.

'We think the nest material came from the chimney in the attic room that Edgar was using as an office. There were similar remnants of twigs and straw in the hearth.'

'Aye – he had a fan heater, remember? Probably because they couldn't get a fire to draw properly in there.'

The team becomes introspective for a few moments. Though they have solved the crime it is a source of dismay that they were unable to prevent what is almost certainly the murder of Thwaites. However it is some consolation that they intervened when they did – Fergal Mullarkey had more than enough evil intent – and bullets – to bring an entire dynasty to its end on Friday night. Who knows what staged internecine killings he had planned for the five siblings. Might the police have arrived to discover four of them shot as they slept, and a fifth – their 'killer' – having apparently committed suicide down at the lake?

Now DS Leyton breaks the silence.

'Once he thought he was in the clear, Guv – over Declan and Thwaites – why do you reckon Mullarkey didn't just sit tight – maybe even wait until the books were transferred to Dublin?'

Skelgill shrugs and looks hopefully for tea – but DS Jones indicates there is none left.

'I suppose there was always the chance of the family digging their heels in – it would have made it more difficult for him if the collection was kept here. Plus there's other things that must have rattled him – like I said, the photo – and then me rocking up unannounced in Dublin. I reckon he spotted me on the ferry – and kept quiet about it. There was something odd about him that niggled me. And Toby Vellum – don't forget. He appears out of the blue – and not only is he an old chum of Edgar's – but also his firm is Declan's long-standing supplier of books. Mullarkey puts two and two together and makes five – he's probably thinking that Vellum and Edgar are in cahoots – that they know something about the diamond and are preparing to act.'

Again they each consider this explanation – and it is DS Jones that makes a supplementary observation.

'I also believe, Guv – that Fergal Mullarkey was not a sane person – this obsession must have been eating at him for decades – I think by the end of it his mind was running riot.'

Skelgill nods.

'Aye – you're not wrong there, Jones. Greed got the better of him and he showed his hand.'

Skelgill's phraseology does not go unnoticed by his colleagues – for, thus far, they have not directly asked him to what extent he suspected it would be Fergal Mullarkey that fell foul of their stakeout. Or was it was just an optimistic shot in the dark? After all, the group was back together for Thwaites' funeral, and the time was ripe for the guilty party to make some move. So now DS Leyton seizes his chance – in a tactfully oblique fashion.

'I must say, Guv – Mullarkey was the last person I expected – he had me convinced he was totally above board.'

Skelgill grins generously.

'The lake, Leyton, the lake. And good old Greenwell's Glory. I had this powerful feeling that Declan was the target of the drowning – 'The Accident' – and if that was right, then this crime wasn't about the family clearing Declan out of the way to speed up the inheritance of Crummock Hall – or even for some perverse revenge – it was about Declan, and his will. And there was all this background noise about the books – even Mullarkey overdid it – pressing me, telling me that the family wanted them put in safekeeping. And that Declan's murdered so soon after it emerges he intends to bequeath the collection to one of his great nephews or nieces. If 'The Accident' and the books were connected – then the family couldn't be in the frame.'

DS Leyton is nodding.

'They were just a bunch of kids, Guv.'

'And there was something that Thwaites mentioned to me – a throwaway remark. He said Declan would scold the maid when she was dusting the shelves – and he'd complain to Thwaites – he'd say, "All my wealth is in my books". It was a kind double bluff – he meant it. Literally.'

DS Jones cannot suppress a giggle – she gives him credit for his apposite choice of adverb – and follows up with a more tangential inquiry.

'And what you learned in Dublin, Guv?'

There is a suggestion of ingenuousness in her tone – albeit that Skelgill has not been particularly forthcoming about his unofficial expedition across the Irish Sea.

'Not everything I learned in Dublin would have kept me on the right track.'

His reaction is a little prickly – and she folds her hands upon her lap. She seems unprepared for this and does not have a ready reply. But now his expression softens, and his tone becomes almost teasing.

'Just like you discovered in London, I don't doubt.'

Now DS Jones's cheeks seem to take on a faint flush – and Skelgill continues in his conciliatory manner.

'What we can't know when we get handed a case – is that it's not one jigsaw but three or four jigsaws all mixed up in the same box, with no picture on the front – but now we've got the pieces we want – we can bin the rest and move on.'

Though his graphic analogy is somewhat facile, it seems his point is insightful – at least as far as DS Jones is concerned – for she relaxes, and nods, and smiles with some relief.

'It's been an eye-opener, Guv – but not my kind of scene.'

DS Leyton is not entirely on their wavelength – but nonetheless he chips in with what he thinks is an appropriate contribution.

'It's another world, eh, Guv – the rich and famous.'

Skelgill abruptly rises. This catches his subordinates unawares. There is a strange light in his eyes, perhaps of anticipation. He grabs his jacket from the back of the sofa, and pulls on his fur-lined trapper hat, rather askew.

'On which note we need to pay a little visit to the Gilhooleys.'

His colleagues are perplexed.

'The Gilhooleys?'

'Aye – they might have just won the lottery, Leyton.'

'Come again, Guv?'

Skelgill makes a telephone with his thumb and little finger.

'Professor Jim Hartley?' (DS Leyton nods his understanding: that Skelgill refers to the call a few minutes earlier.) 'His Irish pal has unearthed an interesting story. The Gilhooley family was originally in partnership with the O'Mores – we're talking centuries back – to the time of the Triangular Trade. Seems they had a big bust-up over some valuable 'asset' obtained by dubious means from an African trader. There was legal action and the Gilhooleys came off second best – the whereabouts of the 'asset' couldn't be established. The costs were punishing and they ended up being bankrupted. The O'Mores took some sympathy in victory – looks like that's when they granted the Gilhooleys their tenancy. But now – if the 'asset' has turned up – there's a chance that the historical claim can be revived.' He grins at DS Jones. 'The Gilhooleys might not be as batty as we thought – or as poor.'

Skelgill consults his wristwatch.

'Come on – we've just got time before the Taj opens.' (This suggestion meets with suspicious glances.) 'Don't worry – it's on me.'

DS Leyton chuckles.

'That's what holding a billion-dollar diamond does to you, Guv – it's scrambled your brains.'

'I've got no brains to scramble, Leyton – and, anyway, it's better than that – I'm on a promise from Perdita.'

Skelgill's thoughts appear momentarily distant – and DS Jones looks a little alarmed. But he gives a shake of the head, and grins self-effacingly.

'She's offered me the set of first edition *Wainwrights* from Declan's library – I just have to find the will in Mullarkey's office.'

DS Jones stretches her lithe form up onto her tiptoes, and then slowly sweeps the fingers of both hands through her hair.

'Maybe you'd benefit from some back-up this time, Guv?'

Skelgill is regarding her with interest.

'Don't worry, Jones – I never make the same mistake twice.'

'In which case, Guv – that hat's got to go.'

***

Printed in Great Britain
by Amazon